The Second Wife

ACCOLADES FOR THE SECOND WIFE

Amazon 2016 Kindle Book Awards WINNER

The McGrath House Independent Book Awards 2016 WINNER

Maggie Award for Excellence FINALIST

B.R.A.G. Medallion HONOREE

"This book goes to dark places but the healing interactions between all the people who love Alisha are achingly tender and the heart of the story." ~NPR

"Paul places the violence in direct contrast to Alisha's Indian family, who have taken David deeply into their hearts, and who serve as his strength while he copes with her disappearance." ~Sonali Dev, *Award Winning Author*

"The Second Wife is one of those rare novels that will lurk in the back of your mind for weeks. With stunning precision, Kishan Paul throws the reader into a world of clandestine organizations and brutal politics. The gripping characters wrench your heart and make you cringe with fear. A rollercoaster of suspense and emotion not to be missed." ~Aubrey Wynne, *Bestselling and Award Winning Author*

“I cannot think of another book I’ve read this year that moved me, made me gasp or still make me full of emotions days after reading it. So thank you Kishan Paul, this book was my favorite and will be one I will re-read often to feel the feels and emotions again.” ~Guilty Pleasures Book Review

Book 1 of The Second Wife Series

Kishan Paul

Kishan Paul Publishing

Dedication
Acknowledgments
Read The Second Wife
Excerpt to The Widow's Keeper, Book 2 of The Second Wife Series
Information about Human Trafficking
Kish's Collective
Newsletter
Titles by Kishan Paul
About the Author

The Second Wife: Book 1 of The Second Wife Series

ISBN-13: 978-0-9985294-3-1
Edited by Tera Cuskaden Norris and The Editing Hall
Cover by Original Syn
Formatting by Anessa Books

To Steph...
A beautiful woman with a quick wit.
It was not cancer that defined her, but her strength and that big beautiful smile.

ACKNOWLEDGMENT

Writing The Second Wife was one of the hardest projects I've ever undertaken. This story ignited a variety of emotions within me. So much of that work was spent with me locked away from family and friends. It took an army of people to make this happen, and I couldn't have done it without their encouragement and support. I am constantly humbled by the love my army showers upon me.

To my husband: Having a writer for a wife wasn't something you signed up for, yet you never once complained. You've always said you hated reading books, but not only did you read The Second Wife, you gushed about it. That means the world to me. Thank you for your constant love, your infinite confidence, and unrelenting faith in me.

To my children: For being the wonderful, beautiful young woman and man that you are. I can't even begin to describe how proud I am of you both. You two will always be my greatest accomplishment.

To my parents and siblings (both the biological and the ones gifted to me by marriage) and three beautiful nieces: I'm very blessed to call you family. For stepping in and taking care of things so I can write, even if that meant jumping in a plane and flying halfway around the world. For your excitement and for celebrating my journey into a world I never ever considered possible.

To my friends Jay, Ash, Sandy, Lij, Leni, Been and Bind and little cuz Renee: For cheering me on and for putting up with my questions about book covers and trailers, things you know nothing about. For beta reading The Second Wife. For dreaming about Ally and Dave and forever being too traumatized to walk alone in a dark parking lot. But most of all, for just being there. Jay and Ash, a special thank you to both for reading all one million five hundred thirty two versions of this story and loving each one and pushing me to keep writing.

To those of you on Scribophile who have read The Second Wife: I am grateful for your time, your advice, and your honesty. You were the first unbiased group to read this story, and it was your encouragement and support that pushed me to finish.

To the ladies of Coffee Talk Writers, past and present: I admire you, respect you, and am so glad you blessed my life.

To my street team, Kish's Collective: You ladies are freaking amazing. Thank you for believing in me and for talking nonsense and putting this stupid smile on my face on a daily basis.

To the authors I've met along the way, who have given me advice, given me a chance, and invested your time in a nobody. I admire you and am humbled by your generosity.

I was fortunate to have two editors help me with The Second Wife. To my editor, Tera Cuskaden, for tearing this story apart then picking me up and helping me weave it back together again. Your attention for detail and your critical eye was exactly what I needed.

To Chris Hall: Not only for doing a final read through and giving the story its final polish but also for being a wonderful friend and not letting me put this story in a box in the attic under the elliptical . I'm glad to have met you so early on and that you've stuck around.

To my cover artist, Syneca Featherstone (Original Syn): Capturing the essence of the story in one image is hard, and yet you did it beautifully and made it look easy. Thank you for putting up with my crazy.

And last but not least, to my fans: The fact that you read my books blows me away. I am humbled by your support and well wishes. You are truly the reason I do what I do.

If you want to live, you must let go of the past...

Twenty-eight-year-old psychologist, Alisha Dimarchi, is abducted by an obsessed client and imprisoned in his Pakistani compound for over two years. Forced to change her name and live as his second wife, her life is filled with trauma and heartbreak. Thrust into a world of violence and oppression, Alicia must fight not only to keep herself alive but to protect the lives of the people she now considers family. At night, she retreats into her memories of the only man she has ever loved—a man she believes no longer loves her.

Thirty-two-year-old handsome surgeon, David Dimarchi, has spent the last two years mourning the disappearance of his wife. After a painful and isolated existence, he begins the process of healing. It is then that he is visited by a stranger, who informs him that his wife is very much alive and needs his help. In a desperate attempt to save her, David enlists the help of a Delta Force Operative. Together they find themselves in the center of more than just a rescue mission. Will he be able to reach her in time, and if he does, will she still want him?

CHAPTER ONE

Kidnapped

March Twenty-third, Philadelphia

The slow drip of a leaky faucet disrupted Ally's otherwise quiet slumber.

"Ally." The distant sound of David's voice soothed her, enveloping her in a warm blanket of safety.

A smile tugged at her lips. Soon he'd crawl into bed and wrap his limbs around hers, cocooning her with his love.

Instead of the heat she anticipated, something coarse scraped against her cheek. When she tried to swat it away, her arms refused to comply.

"*Baby, wake up.*" Her husband's echoed tone became louder, rougher. "*You need to wake up.*"

The urgency in it made her eyelids flutter, pulling her further away from the dark claws of sleep.

Like a silent movie, foggy images of a dimly lit parking lot invaded her dreams. A woman, tall and lean, walked the deserted space alone. With each clip of her heels against the paved road, the haze cleared a little more. Ally's heart raced when the woman's features came into view. Long, curly black hair, dark brown eyes, tanned complexion.

It was her.

Two sets of hands emerged from the shadows, dragging her into the woods. The taller of the two men covered the woman's mouth, muting her screams as she wrestled to break free, until the other one slammed a brick into the base of her skull, plunging her into darkness.

This must be a dream.

Rays of light pierced the darkness as Ally's heavy eyelids fought to open. When she shifted, instead of soft sateen, her cheek scraped against a cold, hard surface.

"Alisha? Can you hear me?" This voice wasn't David's. It sounded thick, heavy with accent, and oddly familiar. So familiar, she shivered.

Again, her mind transported her to another scene. This time, she found herself in her office at the counseling center. Seated across from her in his trademark black three-piece suit was her client, Mohammed. Thick, ebony brows sat over a pair of probing, dark eyes. As usual, his black beard was neatly trimmed and thick hair slicked back.

He nodded, not even challenging her recommendation that he work with another therapist. She shifted in her seat as she blamed her decision on scheduling issues, omitting the part that he scared the hell out of her. The man never did anything inappropriate. What really frightened her was how he stared and the possessive way he said her name.

"Alisha. Love, wake up."

Like right now.

Please, God, be a dream.

"David?" Her whisper came out muffled.

Rough hands brushed her cheeks as they lifted her head. The movement sent jolts of fire rippling from the wound in the back of her neck down her spine. It jerked her awake.

When her eyelids shot open, instead of the soft, sea-green eyes she prayed to see, the pair of widely set dark brown ones she dreaded fixed on her. Between the orbs sat a crooked nose, too large for the man's round head. His bearded face stretched, flashing a yellowed smile.

She screamed but the sound came out muffled, making her yell louder. With each cry, the tape across her face strained and split the tender skin beneath. The metallic taste of blood seeped onto her tongue.

Mohammed swiped a tear off her cheek and pressed his lips on her nose. "Shhh. You're safe. Everything will be okay."

The stench of alcohol and cigarettes mixed with sweat filled her nostrils. Her stomach turned, and she tried to pull away but couldn't. Her hands were tied behind her, and her feet were bound together.

He rested his forehead against hers and blew his soured breath in her face. "I was worried you wouldn't wake up. You are okay, aren't you?"

A trickle of sweat dripped down her neck. Alone. Restrained and at his mercy. She needed to get away. Ally nodded as she collected her thoughts.

He grinned. "That's my good girl."

His hands moved from her face to her neck and finally rested on her shoulders. Carefully, he propped her up, leaning her against the wall before caressing the back of her neck. "I'm sorry about your head. They were told not to harm you. It never should have happened..."

While he explained how the kidnappers had failed, she scanned the space for an escape. Other than large containers stacked against a metal wall, the room was empty. A warehouse, maybe?

Somewhere in the shadows, the two men who abducted her probably stood guard. If she could get away from Mohammed, maybe she could sneak out before the others noticed.

With unsteady fingers, she felt for an edge to the tape binding her wrists.

"...but they will be dealt with. Their actions were unacceptable."

The sound of scraping metal filled the space, silencing him but making her heart pound faster against her chest. As rubber soles squeaked, Mohammad's attention turned to the visitor, and Ally worked harder at finding a seam.

Tall, in a dark shirt and jeans, one of the kidnappers from her dream appeared. A contorted smile stretched across his face as he spoke to Mohammed in a language she didn't understand.

A nauseating burn built deep inside her stomach, filling her chest and streaming from her eyes. Dealing with Mohammed was challenge enough, but now having two men, the chances for survival had plummeted.

Mohammed rubbed her arm and hugged her tight as he glared at the kidnapper. "I promise you, he will never hurt you again," he growled.

The man froze in his tracks. The look of shock on his face turned to fear when Mohammed rose to his feet. Still in a three-piece suit, he approached the abductor, his voice low and angry, conversing in a foreign tongue. Soon his black dress shoe slammed into the man's thigh.

Ally pushed herself into action while Mohammed yelled and pounded his foot into the attacker.

Run. She had to run.

Keeping her palms flat on the ground, she raised her hips, threading her legs through the restrained wrists. With her hands in front, she searched for an edge to the thick tape wrapped around her ankles.

An explosion rang through the warehouse, piercing her eardrums. Ally closed her eyes, covered her head with her arms, and curled in a ball, bracing herself for more.

A heavy weight thudded nearby. With every gasp of air she took, the smell of smoke and gunpowder burned her nose and throat. When she opened her eyes and lifted her head, it was to gaze at the kidnapper's lifeless body.

Ally's muffled sobs filled the silence, making it hard to breathe.

Mohammed squatted beside her and dropped his gun a few feet away. He planted a hand on her thigh and squeezed while he tried to catch his breath.

His grip tightened when she shrunk away from his touch.

"Problem solved. You are now safe," he wheezed. "Like you said in our sessions, sometimes people in our lives disappoint us. It is *how* we deal with the disappointment that matters." He smiled and waved at the dead man. "Obviously, I dealt with this one very effectively, and I assure you it will *never* happen again."

CHAPTER TWO

AN HOUR WITH TOM

TWENTY-FIVE MONTHS, THREE WEEKS, AND TWO DAYS AFTER ALLY'S DISAPPEARANCE

Dave released a breath as he mindlessly flipped through a sports magazine. It was almost eight in the morning. His tired ass should be home in bed right now, not sitting in the waiting room of a counseling center. But since he kept walking into the kitchen and finding his wife, here he was. It wouldn't be so bad, except for the fact that she wasn't really there, and hadn't been for over two years. His grip on the glossy paper tightened.

The vision was always the same. Seated at the breakfast table, Ally flips through one of her psych magazines. Her head propped on one elbow, a curtain of black hair caresses the soft skin of her arm. When she notices him, her chin tilts up and their eyes lock. Soon those kissable, perfect corners form at the edges of her lips when she smiles, taking his breath away each time.

And then things get all sorts of fucked up. Her mouth moves but no sounds come out. Typically, that was when reality hit.

She was gone and he was losing his mind.

Each time, it was a punch to his gut, knocking every ounce of air out of him.

God, I miss her.

Her voice.

Her touch.

Everything.

No matter how hard he tried to block the memories, she haunted him. And this was why he and his messed-up head were at the counseling center.

Dave leaned against the sofa and sucked in a breath. His mind raced at all the possible topics that might come up during the session. None of which were ones he wanted to discuss.

Like the dreams he kept having about her. Some of them so intense he'd jump out of bed covered in sweat, terrified Ally needed him. Then there were the others. The erotic ones where he woke up hard and hungry for her.

What would the good doctor do with that screwed up piece of information? Shouldn't those dreams—those aches—be gone by now? The sad reality was he didn't know if he really wanted them to be.

And what about the real reason he closed his eyes when he and Kate had sex? The heat of shame burned his face.

I don't need to pay someone to tell me I'm a piece of shit.

His magazine slid to the table, and the leather couch creaked when he rose, heading for the door.

"David?"

Damn.

With the doorknob partially turned, he froze and for a moment considered pretending his name was Peter or Paul—anybody else. Instead, he released the knob and faced his fear.

A gray-haired gentleman with a warm smile and gentle eyes stood across the room. He was shorter than Dave, but at Dave's six-foot-three, most people were.

"I'm Tom." He approached, hand extended.

"Hi, Tom."

He waved to the other side of the door. "Come in."

With a nod, Dave followed him into a back office.

The walls were painted pale blue and the room furnished with a leather sofa facing a matching armchair, very similar to the way Ally's once looked. The resemblance was comforting.

Dave sat in the armchair and wondered if the therapist was analyzing him for what seat he picked. As if reading his thoughts, Tom smiled and positioned himself on the sofa. "So, David, what brings you here today?"

"You were referred to me."

Tom shot him a curious glance. "Who can I thank for the referral?"

"Alisha Dimarchi."

As Tom mouthed her name, Dave sucked in a nervous breath. "You might have heard of her. She was a psychologist here in the city. She disappeared a couple years ago."

He nodded. "Yes, I remember."

"She had a list of therapists she referred to and your name was on the top."

"I see. You have the same last name. How are you related?"

She was my life.

"She was my wife."

Concern flashed across Tom's face, lowering Dave's guard an inch.

"I'm sorry for your loss. How long has it been?"

Twenty-five months, three weeks and two days.

"Over two years. Do you remember her?"

"I had the pleasure of sitting in on some of her supervision groups. Dr. Dimarchi was an excellent therapist." The old man fixed his gaze on Dave. "I can't imagine how painful that must have been for you."

The concern etched all over his face caused a familiar burn at the back of Dave's eyes. He focused on the stash of bottled water and tissue on the end table.

Fuck. A simple statement and I'm already eyeing the Kleenex.

"Is that why you're here, David?"

An image of Kate—blonde, blue-eyed, and so different from his wife—popped into his mind. An impulsive firecracker, she was four inches shorter and three years younger than his Ally.

"No. Kate asked me to come."

"Kate?"

"My girlfriend. We've been together about six months. She says there are things I need to work through, unresolved stuff from my past that's affecting our relationship."

"I see." He pulled out a thick packet of papers from his file. "I assume she's the one who filled out your online forms."

A smile crept across Dave's face. "You don't seem surprised."

Tom chuckled. "Most of my clients answer the questions in first person." He shifted through the forms." Let's see... She put your reason for counseling as 'to work on *his* current relationship and unresolved grief issues'. Here."

Dave took the stack, immediately dropping it to the floor beside him.

"So, do you need counseling?"

No. He leaned forward, rested his elbows on his knees, and provided the appropriate answer. "I do."

"Then tell me what brings *you* in to counseling?"

"I need to get over losing my wife and focus on my future. On Kate. She's part of my life now and I need her."

"You need her?"

He shrugged. "She's been good for me."

"I see. Do you mind if we focus on Alisha today?"

Dave leaned back and squeezed the armrest. *Might as well get it over with.* "What do you want to know?"

"As much as you're comfortable sharing. This is your session."

After a couple gulps of air, he started at the beginning. "I met her in Denver, my senior year of college."

The onslaught of memories transported him to a smoky room filled with couples dancing and making out as strobe lights flashed and music blared. He and his roommates were downing shots when Ally and her friends walked in the door.

The blue dress she wore molded to every one of her curves and where it stopped, long legs took over. His fingers had itched to trace her slender, tanned neck up to her perfectly oval face. When her enormous brown eyes, outlined by the thickest, longest lashes known to man fell on him, he dropped his drink.

"David?"

Tom's voice pulled him out of this trance. Embarrassed, Dave cleared his throat and focused on the man seated across from him.

"You were about to tell me how you two met?"

"Sorry. We met at a frat party. It was her freshman year and my senior year. It took a lot of chasing and persuading, but I got the girl." A proud smile tugged at his lips.

"We dated for a year, and then I went to St. Louis for medical school. She stayed in Denver. Three months after classes started, I proposed. By the end of her second year, we were married and she'd transferred to St. Louis U."

Images of a breathtakingly beautiful Ally in white, walking down the aisle, intensified the ache in his chest. "My heart went zero to sixty in a split second when she entered the sanctuary. I remember thinking, 'How the hell did you get so lucky?'"

"How old were you when you married?"

"Young. I was twenty-four. She was twenty. Too young."

"Do you regret it?"

"Not for a second." Dave shifted in his seat as he considered omitting the next part. At this point, what difference did it make? "Four years in, our marriage fell apart. I wasn't around much. When I was, I didn't have time for her, and it got worse when I started residency. She got tired of waiting and left me."

"How did that impact you?"

He shrugged, unsure of how to answer. Of course there was an impact, but it didn't compare to losing her two years ago. Of the two, he'd go back to when she walked out in a heartbeat. Yeah, she left, but he knew she was alive and safe.

"It was hard. She moved to Philadelphia with her sister and said she wasn't coming home."

Tom gave him an encouraging nod.

Dave took a breath. "So I went into individual counseling to fix myself, my marriage."

"Did counseling help your marriage?"

"Saved it, actually. I applied and got into a Surgical Fellowship program here in Philly, and we made it work." His voice trailed off. "Things were perfect until she disappeared two years ago."

Dave's throat tightened at the thought of when everything in his life went to hell. He grabbed a bottle of water from the end table and took a gulp. "Before Kate came along, it was a lonely life. One I don't want to live anymore. She's my world now, and I'm here to work out my issues with her before it falls apart too."

Tom nodded and leaned in. "Sometimes to fix our present, we need to work on our past."

Ally used to say crap like that to me all the time.

"My past is painful. It changed me. It's not something I know how to work on."

And hurts like hell.

"Well, from what you've told me, therapy worked before because you actively sought it. First and foremost, you need to decide if this therapeutic relationship is something you want for you, not Kate."

Did he want counseling? No. But if he didn't come, Kate had threatened to walk. The last thing he wanted was to be alone again.

He eyed the therapist. There was something calming about Tom. Kinda reminded him of his dad. Funny. After working hard to forget Ally and their life together, in a few short minutes, this stranger had forced those doors open. If she were here, she would be clapping her hands like a stupid seal right now. "I'm willing to give it a try."

"Do you feel comfortable sharing what happened?"

No.

He took another swig of water. "She disappeared two years ago. No one's heard or seen her since."

"How have you survived her disappearance?"

Dave fiddled with the lid of the bottle and focused on the paisley area rug. "It's been hard. Really hard." His voice sounded hoarse, even to his own ears.

It had been a while since he'd talked about the disappearance and opening Pandora's box hurt like hell. Yet for some reason, he found himself prying the lid, wanting to let the demons out.

"She was beautiful, and God, I loved her. She used to tell me to take her off the pedestal. That I'd wake up one day and be disappointed. After eight years of marriage, I still had it bad for her. How many husbands can say that?"

Tom nodded, encouragingly.

"I was so proud she was mine. She was amazing in every way...as a wife, a friend—smart, funny, the whole package, There was nowhere on earth I'd rather be than with her."

He blinked back the emotion and fast-forwarded to the morning two years ago. "She disappeared on March twenty-third. I got home to an empty apartment about four thirty that morning after being on call. At first I thought she'd left me again, but that didn't make any sense. So, I made some phone calls then drove to her office. Her Lexus, purse, and keys—even her shoes—were in the parking lot. But no Ally."

As many times as the story had been shared, he should be able to recite it automatically, but today was different. His voice cracked, and the waterworks he thought were over tried to push to the surface. Dave slammed his eyes shut and pushed the words through. "I called the police. The rest is history."

"How have you held up through this?"

Dave rubbed the wetness away and continued, "No words. I keep thinking if I'd been home that night this wouldn't have happened."

"Do you believe you could have prevented it?"

"No, probably not. But I let her down. Didn't protect her."

He accepted the Kleenex Tom handed him and wiped his face dry. His head lowered and voice soft, he recounted his hell. "They investigated her clients. Everyone had an alibi. People came in and out of the house for weeks. The media plastered information everywhere. Calls poured in about bodies, and each time I wished I was dead. I couldn't sleep. Eat. Breathe. My life was gone. Two years later, here we are, no news, no leads, nothing. She vanished from the world."

Emotion sat heavy on his chest, choking him and making it impossible to speak. After an eternity of silence, Tom's firm hand gripped his.

"I can't imagine how hard that must have been for you."

Still is.

Dave nodded and cleared his throat. "The first year, I did everything I could. Kept in touch with the police, FBI, private investigators, psychics...everything. I yelled, threatened, bribed, but no one could find her. How can someone just disappear? Finally, her parents sat me down, told me to stop doing this to myself, and go to work. So I did."

The hard part finally over, he stretched and checked the time on his cell.

Only twelve minutes left.

"Were you angry?"

He laughed. "Still am. But I have to move on for my own sanity. I was out of money and needed to do something more productive with my life. Now, work is my distraction. Except even there, I can't get her out of my mind. She's always right there at the edge of my thoughts. The only time I don't think about her is when I'm in surgery."

"Tell me how Kate fits into that."

With the conversation away from Ally, Dave let out a breath. "Kate's a nurse at my hospital. She's twenty-five and funny as hell. She walked up one day and asked me out."

"Do you think you love her?"

He shrugged. "I could. She loves me and wants to tell people we're together. Even talks about moving in. But I can't. I'm not ready."

"Which part are you not ready for?"

"Any of it."

"Why?"

The leather chair cracked when Dave shifted in his seat. Tom wanted answers to things he had never allowed himself to say out loud. This was uncharted territory, yet here he was swimming for shore.

"I'm ninety percent sure she's dead." He hesitated about speaking the rest but shook his head and took a sip. The doctor might as well know just how fucked up his client was. "There's that ten percent. What if I move out of our apartment or get a new number, and one day she escapes from whatever hell she's in and comes for me?"

"So you want to keep everything the same in case Alisha returns?"

He cringed at how bad that sounded. "And I like our home. If I'm not working, that's where I am. It's unrealistic, I know. But I can't shake the fantasy. I haven't told Kate and don't plan to. She'd run. I don't want that. I need her."

"And if Alisha came home, what would you do?"

Dave closed his eyes, imagining the same scene he'd envisioned for over two years. The warmth, the smell, the peace of her in his arms. "I'd hold her and never let her go."

"And Kate?"

Instantly the warmth drained, chilling him. "I'd have to hurt Kate. But it won't happen, and these are all hypotheticals. The reality is Ally's dead. She's my past."

"Can you give Kate a future while holding on to the hope that Alisha might come back?"

A valid point—one for which Dave had no response. He grinned. “I guess that’s why she sent me to you, Doc.”

After scheduling another appointment, Dave sat in his car in the parking lot. What if she did come home? The crater her disappearance left in his chest throbbed.

He pulled out the owner’s manual from the glove compartment and flipped through the pages until he found her.

A smiling Ally stared back and his eyes watered. Sometimes, after long shifts at the hospital, this was how he found his solace.

How the hell am I supposed to get over you?

CHAPTER THREE

IMPRISONED

TWO WEEKS POST KIDNAPPING

Ally floated in a sea of warm, soothing blue. There was no fear. No pain. Silence and peace blanketed her world. Until...the heavy rhythmic pressure on her chest began. It tugged at her. With every push, it pulled her from the calm.

Don't make me...

Before the thought completed, a force ripped her away from her dream, sending her flying back to reality.

As the hazy fog in her head thinned, blurred yellow lights burned her eyes. She opened them slowly, allowing her vision to adjust.

When she looked down, it was to find a spectacled man straddling her hips and pushing down on her chest. Emotions too dulled for her to react, Ally observed as he pushed again and again on her chest. When his gaze locked with hers, he froze for a second before looking at the ceiling and muttering something she couldn't understand.

The stranger climbed off her and leaned over her face. "Alisha, can you hear me?" He lifted each eyelid, peering into them. "My name is Nasif. Do you remember me?"

Her tongue resisted her attempts to speak. Instead, she shook her head.

A rhythmic beeping echoed from somewhere in the room.

From deep inside her brain, a voice whispered she was in danger. That she needed to get away. Ally tried to listen, but her body refused to move. On her second attempt, she rose a couple of inches before Nasif pushed her down.

"Rest. Your heart stopped, and I need to make sure you are stable."

Maybe it was his thick accent or the fact that her brain was in a drugged fog, but none of what he said made sense.

Beside the bed was a metal pole on which hung an IV bag filled with liquid. Nasif switched out the sack for a smaller one.

No. The silent protest floated in her head.

She tried yanking the line out, but her arm was too heavy to reach the spot on her hand.

"Where," her voice croaked. After clearing her parched throat, Ally tried again. "Where am I?"

"Quiet." He fitted an oxygen mask over her face.

Ignoring his command, Ally managed to prop herself on her elbows, but as soon as she did, the room spun like an out of control carousel.

"Stay down," Nasif repeated and stuck a syringe into the IV.

She fell onto the pillow. The fog thickened, returning her to the peaceful world of blue.

~

Every muscle felt like lead and her tongue a big wad of cotton. The room and her stomach spun faster and faster.

A lizard crept across the ceiling, stopping directly overhead. Ally focused on it while she worked on long, slow breaths. Finally, the circling ebbed.

Silence.

The beeps and machines had disappeared, and she remembered the parking lot, Mohammed, the dead kidnapper, everything. She needed to get away. Just didn't know how.

Nasif lay curled up on a straw mat on the floor, watching her. When she shifted to get off the bed, he made his way to her side. Wordlessly, he placed a hand on her back, another on her arm, and helped her sit. She stared in awe at the spots where his skin touched hers.

Why can't I feel him?

She should be scared, should be trying to get away. Although her brain was clear, it was slow, and her limbs acted as if they weren't her own.

"You have been asleep a long time. Your body needs to adjust," Nasif said as if reading her thoughts. He turned her so her ankles hung over the bed. "Straighten your legs."

"I'm trying," she grunted, willing them to move.

"Try harder," he ordered.

She concentrated, imagining them stretching. Finally, they complied.

"Good, now move your toes." After several attempts, they wiggled. Limbs tingled as memory returned to muscles. Once the movements were more controlled, Nasif wrapped an arm around her waist and lifted Ally to her feet.

As her body buckled under its own weight, he caught her and pulled her onto the bed. He lifted her legs to the mattress, adjusting the sheet over her body.

"Where am I?"

He turned to rummage through a brown backpack. "Pakistan. We brought you here two weeks ago."

Two weeks? She shook her head. How could that much time have passed without her knowledge?

Nasif pulled out a stethoscope from the bag. "I have been giving you medicine throughout the journey. You've been in and out of sleep. Do you remember?" His voice was gentle, almost kind.

"No."

"Take a deep breath," he ordered.

As soon as the cold metal of the instrument pressed against her back, goose bumps pebbled the area. When he tried to put it down the front of her white gown, she pushed it away.

"Do I need to restrain you?"

This time she didn't fight his touch.

"Good. Now deep breath, please."

She sucked in a breath and looked him over. Short and thin, he wore a loose-fitting, long-sleeved shirt that fell to his knees, with matching white pants. What few strands of hair he had were black and lay flat over an otherwise bald head. There was a kindness in the man's hazel eyes.

"Good. Now exhale."

The thought that she could easily overtake him floated through her brain. But that would require the ability to walk without falling. Obviously, she wasn't capable yet.

"Your heart and lungs sound normal."

"How did I get here?"

He removed the stethoscope and reached into his bag a second time. "We can do many things."

She racked her brain trying to remember but couldn't. It seemed like everything went black at the warehouse.

Nasif turned her wrist and pressed a finger against the vein. "The medicine can sometimes make the heart stop, like yours did. Fortunately, it didn't happen until we were home, and by the grace of Allah, I was able to bring you back. "

A chill ripped through her. "You were there?"

He nodded. "By the time I got there, you had fainted. Probably due to shock." Nasif popped a thermometer in her mouth. "Sayeed, or Mohammed as you know him, would have been very angry if you died."

Images of her former client and the dead man on the warehouse floor sent another spasm of fear through her. "Why did he do this to me?" she mumbled, balancing the glass tube under her tongue.

He shook his head and checked her blood pressure. "He says he loves you. Believes you are destined to be his wife."

Nasif pulled out the thermometer and frowned. "No more sitting. Your blood pressure is low, and you have a slight temperature. Let's get you on your back."

He positioned her on the bed, covering her with a sheet.

"I need your help," she whispered seconds before the fog pulled her under.

~

The smell of onions and garlic permeated the room. Ally's mouth watered and stomach growled. A smile tugged at her lips.

Wonder what masterpiece he's creating today?

David didn't cook often, but when he did, it was always good.

Seconds after the thought, the sounds of a man singing in a foreign tongue floated to her ears. With the song came the memories of the kidnapping, Pakistan, and Nasif.

Trying to be as still as possible, Ally peered through cracked eyelids. She was lying on her side, covered up to her neck by a blanket, and facing a wall.

Thank God.

As discreet as possible, she went through a quick body check. Her toes and fingers wiggled, thighs and arm muscles flexed. Everything moved on the first attempt. *Good.*

If he didn't have a gun—and she hadn't seen him carrying one—chances were good that she could take him down. But then what? What about Mohammed and the other kidnapper?

"I know you're awake."

She sucked in a breath as the tapping of Nasif's shoes against the floor grew closer. Her brain reeled with ideas. None of which were plausible. There had to be a way.

I could outrun them.

When he squeezed her shoulder, she flinched. "I want to go home."

"In time, you will see this as your home," he said from behind her.

Ally's eyes brimmed. "That will never happen."

"How are you feeling?"

Her body heated at how easily he blew off her response. She pulled herself up and glared at him through her tears. "I've been taken away from my home and locked up. Some crazy man thinks I'm supposed to be his wife. You're telling me this is my home. How do you think I should feel?"

Guilt flashed across his face, and when he leaned in, Ally inched away.

Had she gone too far?

Nasif put out his palms. "I won't hurt you."

A tear spilled down her cheek. "But *he* will, and you're going to let him."

He averted his eyes and pulled the covers to the foot of the bed. "We'll discuss that later. Let's see if you can walk."

Her heart pounded against her ribs as she moved to the edge of the bed. How could she get away if she couldn't walk? She placed her feet on the floor and held her breath. The walls didn't move, and to her relief, her legs carried her weight without buckling.

When he offered her his hand, her body screamed to wave it away. She eyed the frail arm for a moment before accepting the palm. It would take more than the use of her legs to get out of here alive.

She looked down at her white cotton gown and ran her fingers through her hair, which fell over her shoulder in a long braid. Who had dressed her? Bathed her?

Ally raised her brows at him. He smiled back, his face flushed, and guided her toward his straw mat.

The windowless prison was sparsely furnished with a twin bed, chair, and a mat on the floor. With its unpainted walls, black marble floors, and the faint, wet smell of mold, it seemed unfinished, as if the owner had never gotten around to putting the final touches on the space. Two intricately carved doors hung on adjacent walls, out of place in the concrete room. The one in the far corner was open and led to a bathroom, the other was closed and probably was the only escape from this hell.

Nasif seated her on the mat and placed a bowl of clear yellow broth in her hands. The spicy aroma filled her senses and her stomach rumbled.

Ally stared at the bowl. "How do I know it's not drugged?"

He laughed. "You are safe. It is not tainted. See?" He swallowed a spoonful. "It is lentil soup, nothing more." He then dipped the spoon into the bowl and lifted it to her lips. His brows rose from beneath his glasses as he waited for her to make a decision.

Nasif had an air of gentleness around him and, from the way he cared for her, was probably a doctor. Thus far, he seemed to feel bad about her situation. But was it genuine or an act? There were so many questions running through her brain, all of which he held answers to.

She opened her mouth and accepted the food.

He prepared another serving, waiting for her to finish the first. Instead, she put the bowl down and grabbed a banana from the tray.

"Does my family know where I am?"

When he didn't answer, she stopped peeling and stared at him.

After he put the spoon down, he shook his head. "*This* is your family now."

As soon as he spoke the words, her hands shook. Ally returned to peeling the banana, trying to calm her trembling frame. "Will I ever see my husband or my family again?

"It is best you not think of them anymore."

A tear slipped down her cheek. His answers were not the ones she'd expected. When he tried to feed her, she turned away. "What's going to happen to me when Mohammed shows up?" The question was whispered, but from the way he sucked in a breath, he obviously heard every word.

"Sayeed. His name is Sayeed." He waved at the fruit in her hand. "Eat and I will talk."

Food was the last thing on her mind, but she bit into the banana while he filled their cups with tea.

"Your name is no longer Alisha. It is now Sara Irfani. You are the wife of Sayeed Irfani."

She paused mid-swallow as his words echoed through her head. Moisture pooled in her eyes, and her chest seemed to be filled with lead. Ally forced air into her lungs. Any chance of escape required she keep it together.

Nasif sipped his drink and waited for her to collect herself before continuing. "You had a court marriage a few weeks ago. The papers have been completed and signed. It is done."

Her body chilled at the implication of his words. It was becoming harder to breathe through the building panic. "I didn't sign anything."

He shrugged. "It was done for you."

Simple. Absolute. Final. Grabbing his hands, she begged. "Please, don't let him do this. Help me get away."

He pulled away and refused to meet her stare. "If you want to live, you will have to let go of such ideas."

The old man stuffed a hand in his pocket, pulled out a handkerchief, and passed it to her. "You must understand, Sayeed is a dangerous man. If someone betrays or does not appreciate him, like you saw in America..."

A shiver ripped through her.

"But he is only bad to people like that. If you are good to him, he will take care of you."

His words sunk in, choking her. Nasif patted her shoulder. "Take slow, deep breaths and you will be okay."

He sat quietly and waited until she calmed before continuing. "Don't worry, I will be taking care of you for the next two weeks until Sayeed returns. Now, no more questions. Eat your food. I need to go after this."

She stared at the spoonful of soup he positioned in front of her mouth. "Where are you going?"

"Home. But you are safe and I will be back in the morning." Nasif put the untouched serving back in the bowl and grabbed her hand, leading her back to bed.

"Go to sleep. I promise to return by the time you wake."

Sleep was the last thing she had in mind. After the door closed, Ally waited a few minutes, listening to his footsteps fade before creeping from her bed. Her pulse raced against her ears as she searched under the bed, behind the toilet—every inch of space. The walls were solid, and the floor was seamless marble. No secret passages.

She eyed the locked door. The only escape. Already aware of the answer, she turned the knob anyway. It jiggled but refused to turn. When she tugged harder, a male voice heavy with an accent yelled out, "No!"

Ally jumped at the sound. There was no way out.

Leaning against the wall, she slid to the floor, allowing hopelessness to push to the surface. David and her family were out there searching, and they'd never give up trying to find her. But if she was locked away on the other side of the world, what were the chances?

An image of her husband flashed in her head. Brown hair, eyes mixed with green, blue and a touch of gold, and that smile. Her chest tightened. It was one he reserved only for her. David had a way of looking at her that made her feel like there was nothing in this world she couldn't do. But the sad reality was, he was wrong. A sobbing, crumpled mess, she finally fell asleep huddled in a ball against the door.

At some point, she woke up and crawled into bed. Tears finally spent, she stared at the ceiling. Somehow, she'd make it home. She just needed to think.

The idea of fighting Nasif popped in her head again. She looked over at the locked door. And then what? Could she take on the man on the other side too? Probably not.

Which only left her two choices. Either resign herself that it was hopeless and end it all now, or follow her gut that somehow Nasif could be won over.

She wiped the moisture from her cheeks. Killing herself wasn't an option. She couldn't do that to David or her family. The old man said Sayeed would be gone for two weeks. A lot could happen in fourteen days. She wasn't ready to give up.

Not yet.

CHAPTER FOUR

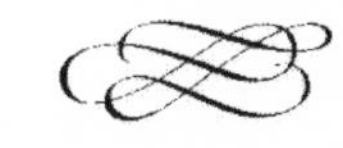

THE RING

TWENTY-SIX MONTHS AFTER ALLY'S DISAPPEARANCE

Soft fingers traced a path along Dave's inner thigh. He kept his eyes shut and let himself get lost in the caress. With each brush of her digits, his dick lengthened. Soon, a naked breast pressed against his bare chest, followed by a leg tucking between his two. As her hand inched higher up his thigh, his back arched, and he moaned in anticipation.

Instead of giving him what he wanted, she continued to trail the same path over and over. Painfully slow. Centimeters from where he needed her.

When he couldn't wait any longer, he caught her wrist and guided it to the ache she inspired. She laughed at his impatience and feathered his neck with kisses, while her experienced hand combed the patch of hair that crowned his hunger.

Damn that woman.

Lost in her, he grabbed fistfuls of sheet and shuddered. All his senses danced under her assault, and each time she grazed his erection, his breath caught—waiting, hoping.

She was going to kill him.

He lifted his hips, begging for more, and finally she gave him exactly what he wanted. Like a sculptor and he her clay, she molded and kneaded, sending him higher and higher, intensifying his need for release.

"Fuck. Ally. Don't. Stop."

But stop she did. Then jerked her hand away. The warmth of her body quickly followed, leaving him cold and panting.

Was she teasing him?

Finally, the bed shifted when her naked body left it.

What the…

Dave's eyelids flew open and he bolted up. Instead of raven hair and golden skin, his eyes rested on a sexy porcelain ass and long, golden curls right before the bathroom door shut, blocking his view.

Fuck.

"Kate, wait." Dave jumped out of bed and rushed after her. He turned the locked knob and tapped his knuckles against the dark wood. "Honey, I'm sorry. Please open the door."

Silence.

"Kate, please talk to me."

A loud banging on the front door made a complicated situation even worse. He checked the clock beside the bed. Five fifteen.

Who the fuck?

The pounding got louder. He looked between the bathroom and the hallway leading to the living room, contemplating his next move. "Kate, I'm sorry about what happened. Give me a chance to fix it."

It sounded like someone was using a sledgehammer outside his apartment.

"Baby, I need to get that before they wake up the fucking complex."

Throwing on some pants, he sprinted to the door and peered through the peephole. A metal thermos floated into view.

"Good morning, big brother. I come bearing chai."

Shit.

He leaned against the door in near panic as he tried to figure out what to do. These two worlds weren't supposed to collide. Not yet.

"I saw your lovely eyeball through the peephole, dummy. Don't pretend you're not there. Open the door."

Can this day get any worse?

Kate entered the living room with her duffel bag hung over her shoulder.

Yup.

Everything about her screamed *sexy* and *touch me*, from the way her jean-clad hips moved to the teal-blue shirt that clung to her in all the right ways, and how her hair bounced with each step.

The woman, who up until ten minutes ago was naked in his bed, now avoided his gaze, shoved him out of the way, and unlocked the bolts.

When she opened the door, his heart about stopped. Dave sent up a silent prayer while the two women sized each other up. The only thing they had in common was their height, both around five-five. Where Kate's hair was long and blonde, Reya's was short and black. Beautiful blue eyes fixed on dark brown ones. Reya crossed her arms and raised her perfectly arched brows.

Keep your mouth shut, Reya. For once, just keep it...

"Well, good morning. You must be David's bed buddy."

...shut.

"Damn it, Rey..."

Kate put a hand on his shoulder, quieting him. "It's okay, Dave." She offered Reya a smile and her hand, "Good morning. I'm Kate, the bed buddy."

Between him calling out another woman's name, and Reya's reminder that he hadn't told anyone she existed, there was no question in his mind that Kate was pissed.

Ignoring the extended greeting, and in her typical intimidate-and-control manner, Reya leaned in and kissed Kate's cheek. "I'm Reya. His *wife's* sister."

Dave closed his eyes as his face heated. Maybe he could buy Kate jewelry.

As if reading his mind, Kate smiled her beautiful whites and hugged his sister-in-law. "I'm so sorry. I can't imagine how hard it must have been to lose your sister like that."

Something with diamonds.

He fought the urge to laugh at the wide-eyed, open-mouthed expression Reya shot him. Releasing the woman, Kate turned to him, placed her hand on his chest, and planted a kiss on his mouth.

"You owe me lunch today," Kate said, her piercing gaze

informing him their morning was far from forgotten. She was right. He did owe her lunch—and a lot more.

Dave wrapped his arms around her and tugged her close, hoping it would send a message to Reya to back off.

"Is one okay? I should be done with surgery by then."

Another kiss, this one long and lingering—his reward. "That would be perfect." With a smile and a wave at Reya, she left.

Reya closed the door behind Kate and walked to the kitchen, thermos in hand. "I was worried she might raise her leg and pee on you while she was at it."

"That's enough, Reya."

She rummaged through his cabinets, pulling out a saucepan and the supplies to make tea. "What? I'm just sayin'."

"Be nice. She's important."

"Important enough to forget your family? I mean a call or a text saying 'Hey, I'm alive' every few months would be nice. Don't you think?" The hurt in her words made the sting worse than usual. He didn't respond. What was he supposed to say to that?

She waved a steel mortar and pestle in the air. "Fine, don't answer. Just go put on a shirt and I'll start the tea."

Instead, he sat on the barstool facing the kitchen and watched her grind cardamom seeds. "You show up at five on a Saturday morning, offering chai you don't have, and order me around? I'm staying shirtless. Why exactly are you here, anyway?"

She rested her elbows on the counter and leaned in. "Eh, then don't. You're right, this is your place. You can do whatever you want."

He held his breath for the "but" that would come right about...

"But you really should consider going to the gym every now and then."

Reya waved the pestle at his chest. "Those peach nipples would be a lot sexier over tightly formed pecks instead of your flat, pale-white flesh. You should go tanning with Parker, by the way. Should I call him so he can come over?"

"Jesus, Rey. Make the damn tea. I'll put on a shirt." Halfway to the bedroom, a chuckle escaped his lips.

~

Nipples and pale skin chastely covered, Dave entered the living room and paused as the scent of spices and sweet cream filled his nostrils. His chest tightened. It used to be the first thing he smelled when he woke up, a part of his morning routine with Ally. Shaking off the pull of sadness, he approached Reya.

In a black hoodie and matching pants, her back was to him. She sat on a barstool at the kitchen counter with two steaming cups of chai in front of her.

Ally used to say Reya was the beauty and their big brother, Nik, was the brains of the Sharma family. Dave's chest squeezed. He hadn't told her enough how she was both—beautiful and smart. So many things he never said...

"You staring at my butt, Big Dave?" Reya asked while messing with her cell phone.

He shook his head and positioned himself on the seat beside her. "I'm trying to figure out why you have sparkling words stretched across it."

She chuckled while her fingers flew across the tiny keyboard.

"Who are you texting?"

"Parker."

Dave took a sip and savored his drink before fishing further. "You didn't answer my question. Why are you here?"

She nodded, put her phone down, and played with the rim of her cup. "As you pointed out, I lied. The thermos *was* empty. You've avoided me so much lately that I knew it would only piss me off more if I went to the trouble of making you chai and you didn't open the door."

Ignoring the *you suck* voice in his brain, Dave pushed on. "What's going on, Rey?"

She stared at the mug as if it were some sort of magic orb about to give away prized information. "Last night, Parker asked me to marry him."

The sadness in her voice seemed out of place, considering the topic.

"And that's a bad thing?"

"No, it's a good thing. You're the first person I've told." Eyes filled with tears, she rested her cheek on his shoulder.

"Hey, what happened?"

"Di's not here." Three whispered words and everything was clear. "I picked up the phone to call her. Then remembered I couldn't. She was supposed to be the first to know."

He squeezed her close, fighting his own emotions.

"He didn't even buy me a ring..." She whimpered. "Because I'm picky. Said we'd go together. If she had been here..."

Dave finished the sentence. "She would have figured it out and gone ring shopping with him ahead of time."

Her head bobbed up and down. "I can't get married. She's supposed to be my maid of honor."

"Except she's not here." Dave's voice cracked. "And we both know, she'd want you to move on without her."

"That's the problem. I don't know how."

Finally, someone put into words how he'd felt all this time. Dave gazed at his palms and searched for the right response. "I'm trying to figure that out too, Rey. It's what she'd want. For us to learn how to be happy again."

She wiped the wetness trickling from his eye before returning her cheek to his shoulder. "Big Dave, I can't lose you too. Don't make me do this alone. Please."

He wrapped an arm around her shoulder and nodded.

~

Sprinting to the staff elevators, Dave hit the Up button. He eyed the door to the stairs a few feet away, considering the option when the bell dinged and the electronic doors slid open. An elderly couple slowly exited the space. After waiting not so patiently for them to leave, he entered and pressed Eight.

Kate had ignored his texts all morning and he deserved it. Other women would have left a long time ago for much less. It was time for him to get his head out of his ass and do the right thing. It was time for her to meet the families.

But first, he needed to find Phil and beg him to cover the next couple of hours. That was the only chance he had of getting to the restaurant by one. As soon as the doors opened, he scrambled to the right.

Both sides of the hall were lined with medical offices and testing centers. The carpeted floors, beige textured walls, even the non-antiseptic smell were all staged by management to make the area appear different than the patient rooms below. He weaved through visitors and made his way to Phil's door. It was locked and the blinds closed.

Shit.

He texted Phil while turning the corner toward his own office. As he hit Send, he slammed into someone. The victim was an older Middle Eastern man, short and bald with thick, black-rimmed glasses. The man sat on the floor, staring up at him.

Dave extended his hand and helped the guy up. “I’m sorry. I wasn’t looking where I was going.”

In a brown suit at least one size too big, the old man grinned as if he’d just heard a great joke.

“Are you okay?”

“David. You’re Dr. David Dimarchi.” His accent was thick.

“Yes, I am. Can I help you?”

He looked around the hall and leaned in closer. “I need to speak with you alone, David.”

Dave focused on the man, trying to figure out how they knew each other.

Former patient? *Maybe.* Considering he was a general surgeon at the hospital, he didn’t spend a lot of time looking at their faces. Or it could be a family member of a patient wanting to say thank you. Perks of the job. It didn’t really matter. He needed to get out of here if there was any chance of meeting Kate on time.

Dave’s cell phone dinged, and Phil’s text agreeing to cover him flashed across the screen. He looked over at the stranger.

Perfect. Now, how do I get rid of you?

The man looked around again and walked closer, forcing Dave to step back.

Shit. Psych patient. “I’m afraid I don’t have time right now. Would you like to schedule an appointment?” He widened the distance between him and the stranger.

The man reached out his hand. When Dave extended his own, he turned Dave’s palm up and dropped a shiny object onto it.

Everything froze the instant the diamond-encrusted band touched his skin. When he brought it closer, his breath caught in his lungs.

“Please, I need to talk to you. Alone,” the man said in a hushed voice as he surveyed the hall for the hundredth time.

Dave closed his fingers around the precious piece of his past and unlocked the door, hoping to God that he was about to regain his future.

CHAPTER FIVE

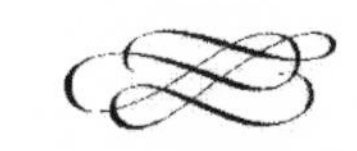

SARA'S RANSOM

TWENTY-FIVE DAYS POST KIDNAPPING

Ally's lungs were cement blocks, heavy in her chest. Unable to breathe, she lay curled in a ball on the floor, gasping for air, drenched in sweat.

Waiting.

The panic attacks had started after Nasif's first night away and progressively worsened each day. She wanted to pretend it was because he wasn't there to distract her. But she knew better.

Sayeed would be here soon.

The gnawing voice in the back of her head wouldn't stop reminding her of the hell his arrival would bring. As the day grew closer, the voice became louder, urging her to do something. But there was only so much she could do locked away in a concrete box.

Unable to shut out the images or find a way to escape, hopelessness would again to choke her, triggering another panic attack. Funny thing was, those episodes she spent struggling for air gave her a little hope. Maybe this one will kill me. Something she knew better than to believe. After all, she'd spent her career teaching clients that panic attacks were typically non-life-threatening.

While this morning's episode subsided, she stayed on the floor slick with perspiration, staring at the ceiling.

He said Sayeed would be here in fourteen days.

Ally crawled beside the bed and dug under the mattress until her fingers wrapped around a thin, wooden pencil. After dragging the frame away from the wall, she slid between the headboard and concrete and sat on the floor. She added another tally mark to the twelve already there. Praying she'd counted wrong, she tapped the back of the eraser against each line and counted again. The end result was the same, Nasif had left thirteen times already. Her pencil slipped out of her shaky fingers and fell to the floor.

One more day.

Images of Sayeed violating her flooded Ally's thoughts. Her chest tightened and her body chilled. Time was running out. Her breathing became labored, and a cool sweat beaded across her lip.

"No." She covered her ears and shook it all away. *Whatever happens, I will survive. Rape will not kill me.*

The days of crying...fantasizing needed to end. Now. Those dreams of being rescued, of home and her family waiting for her return, none of them would help her escape this hell. She would have to do this on her own.

Ally closed her eyes, remembering what David used to tell her. "There's nothing you can't do." Maybe if she said it enough times, she might trust it?

After repositioning the bed, she hid the pencil under the mattress and snatched the brown bag of clothes Nasif had left for her. She sifted through it, grabbing the brown cotton long-sleeve dress he called an *abaya* and a matching scarf before heading for the shower. This was her last chance of convincing the old man.

By the time Nasif appeared with a tray of breakfast, she was dressed, composed, and seated on the mat. He nodded approvingly but didn't say a word. Not even a hello.

Fortunately, the long sleeves of the abaya hid her shaky hands. She hadn't had the courage to directly ask him for help, and now she had no choice but to beg.

After placing the food on the floor, he sat across from her and served them both. A manila envelope lay in his lap. She pretended not to notice and fought the urge to ask—her irrational way of maintaining control of the situation.

They spent the meal in silence. Food was the last thing on her mind, so Ally sipped her tea, eyeing him from over her cup. He kept shifting, seemed nervous. Her gut screamed something was wrong. But at this point, what could be worse than the things he'd already shared?

After they ate, he put the dishes back on the tray before finally sliding the envelope to her feet. "Sayeed asked me to give this to you."

When she stared at him to continue, he rose and walked to the other side of the room.

Her stomach twisted and her hands shook as she ripped open the seal. From inside, she pulled out a picture of a man seated on a park bench. Alone.

It took only a moment for recognition to hit, but when it did, it was a punch to her gut. A gasp escaped her as tears welled. Terror tightened her chest, and the morning's tea inched up her throat. She swallowed it down and focused on the image.

His cheeks had hollowed, and his thick brown hair was tousled. Shadows formed deep rings under his eyes. But there were no injuries or signs of fear. David stared blankly, lost in thought.

Her mind filled with questions. Each one intensifying the dread in her gut.

Where was he?

Did they have him too?

She scanned the background, recognizing the bench and trees behind him. It was part of the trail she jogged every morning. A whispered moan escaped her lips.

He was waiting for her.

Ally clenched his picture against her chest and cried. No matter what happened to her, the thought of David safe at home kept her going. If they had him locked away, hurt him in any way...

She glared at Nasif. He kept his head down and fiddled with his fingers while he leaned against the wall.

"Where is he?" she hissed.

He didn't respond. She hurried to him and grabbed his wrist.

"How. Did. You. Get. This. Picture?"

"He's home safe for now, but Sayeed wants you to be aware he is being watched."

Ally's stomach dropped. She grabbed hold of the wall as her knees weakened. "Safe for now? What do you mean?"

"Look carefully."

She stared at the image.

"Behind him, do you see anyone else?"

In the distance stood a man with dark features and a thin frame. She shuddered. *The second kidnapper*.

He was out of David's line of sight and stared at the camera.

"Do you remember him?"

Unable to speak, she nodded.

"If you try to escape or do anything Sayeed disapproves of, that man will kill your husband."

Ally's lungs turned to ice and the blood drained from her veins, chilling her soul. The room moved while Nasif's words played in her head. At first it was a slow turn, but soon it spun out of control. Nasif grabbed her when her legs buckled.

"Don't touch me." She jerked out of his grasp and sunk to her knees. "This is your fault. You did this."

She needed to control herself, to rein in her sobs, but she couldn't. All this time, she had kept her emotions in check in front of Nasif. Showed just enough tears to try and gain his pity without making him consider her weak. Shared about her home and asked about his all to build a connection, a potential bond with the only man who could help. But now everything was different.

She wheezed for air while her throat squeezed shut. Soon, she found herself curled in a ball, clutching David's picture as she suffered the worst panic attack yet. After a long time, her muscles eased and breathing returned. And unfortunately, she was still alive.

When Nasif touched her shoulder, she didn't shove him away. Instead, she shook her head in defeat. "I have nothing. You and Sayeed took it all away."

Nasif pulled her up and sat her on the bed. "Look at me, Sara."

Instead, she stared at her husband. He looked so good in blue. She remembered buying him that shirt a lifetime ago.

"If you stay here and listen, *he* will remain unharmed."

"Say his name," she whispered. Strange, wasn't it? There she was accepting the fact that her life was over and willing to pay the final price, and all she wanted at that moment was for Nasif to just acknowledge her husband existed.

After a brief pause, he continued, "I hear *David* is searching for you."

A tear slipped down her cheek onto the picture. "Is that why you're doing this to him?" Ally asked as she wiped the moisture off the paper.

He sat beside her and dabbed her face with his handkerchief. "I didn't do any of this. Sayeed is a powerful man who always gets what he wants." He tilted her chin, forcing their eyes to lock. "He will kill to make that happen."

Her stomach twisted as her breakfast refused to be ignored any longer. She swallowed the rising bile and rushed to the bathroom. Before shutting the door, she met Nasif's concerned gaze. "Please leave. I need some time alone. To think."

After being hunched over the toilet for an eternity, Ally finally crawled into bed and stared at David. By changing the stakes, Sayeed had won. There was no way she'd fight him now.

By the time Nasif returned, David's picture was tucked under her pillow. She lay staring at the ceiling, refusing to acknowledge his arrival.

He sat beside her. "Sara, you have every reason to believe I am a bad person. But I need you to understand, sometimes good people must do bad things." He paused for a response. But she had none to give.

"My wife, Hasna, is dying of cervical cancer. When she was diagnosed, I had to make a choice between my family and my morals."

Had this been any other time in Ally's life, the pain in his voice would have stirred an ache in her heart. But this wasn't any other time, and she had nothing to offer to him or anyone else. She had nothing.

"I could not stand by and let her suffer. Not if there was something I could do to help. So, I agreed to work for Sayeed. In return, he covers all medical expenses and sends her to the best hospitals. One day, I know, I will answer to Allah for my choices. I am at peace with this because I deserve to be punished."

His voice brimmed with guilt and she believed him. Every word. But it didn't change what he'd done. He'd helped bring her into this hell, and no matter his reasons, what he'd done was unforgivable.

"You can't blame other people for your actions, Nasif."

The otherwise quiet room filled with his bitter laugh. "You are very right on that. I have not slept since the day I met you. Every time I close my eyes, I see you. You were so scared. Your body was shaking when I found you. I wanted to help. I even told Sayeed that I wouldn't drug you and take you away. That it was wrong. He gave me a choice—either follow his instructions, or no more help for Hasna." He let out a long, sad breath. "This has been the hardest thing I have ever done."

"I'll never get out of here, will I?"

Nasif squeezed her arm. "No one ever has. Once you are in Sayeed's pocket, you are always there."

"Why do you make him sound so potent? He's just one man."

"A man, yes. But one who sells weapons to some powerful organizations and doesn't care what suffering results from it, as long as he gets paid."

She rubbed her temples to ease the throbbing pain in her head.

"Religion, pride in his country, his people—those mean nothing. In his mind, he is God, and he enjoys wielding his power and hurting others."

The mattress shifted when he rose, but she didn't bother to look up.

"It is a drug. I have watched him torture and kill for no reason whatsoever. It gives him joy. If he smells fear or hatred in someone he uses it to destroy them."

A cool cloth was placed against her forehead, instantly easing the pain.

"He is a predator, Sara, in the truest sense. One I have learned to survive. This is the part I am teaching you. Show no emotion: no fear, no anger. It's the reason I am still alive. He respects me and believes I will be honest with him. In return, he takes care of my family—Hasna—and reminds me he can kill me at any moment."

"It makes sense that Sayeed keeps you. You are his doctor, and he knows you need him so you will be loyal. But what's my purpose? He can have any woman he wants."

Nasif laughed and pressed gentle fingers over the pressure points around her eyes and forehead. "When he went to the States, it was to find funding and new suppliers. He saw you at some convention and immediately knew you were created for him. Whatever you said to him in your appointments made him admire you. He says you make him think.

"What did he say?" He paused for a moment before continuing his massage. "Yes, he said you help him see a different way to achieve his goals. And you will need to keep doing this for him. Counsel him the way you did in America."

When Ally shook her head, he moved close. "Make him believe you provide a valuable service. Never show him your fear. To survive you must act strong."

"I can't. Everything's different. Back then, I wasn't caged and my husband's life wasn't threatened."

"You can and will. You are stronger than you realize. But there is another reason he wanted you." He hesitated.

She sat up and handed him the wet handkerchief. "What could be worse than what you've already shared?"

The old man rubbed the back of his head and stared at the floor. "You are not his only wife. He has another, Alyah. But he thinks her to be barren and is convinced you are destined to give him a son."

Ally inched away from Nasif as the nausea returned. The other wife didn't seem important compared to the other part. Even the rapes she had begun to mentally prepare for, but carrying his child?

"You know why he named you Sara?"

She shook her head.

"It's after the Prophet Ibrahim's wife." Nasif laughed. "Sara is believed to have cured a tyrant of his disease. See, Sayeed knows he's a monster, and like that Sara, he is hoping you will be his cure by providing him with an heir."

She clenched her fists in disgust.

"But the two things Sayeed fails to realize are that *Sara* was the cause of the tyrant's illness in the first place and that she herself was barren." Nasif leaned over and patted her leg. "Don't worry, you will not be able to conceive either. I gave you a shot and in three months, I will give you another. Our secret," he said proudly. "If he finds out, he will kill us both. But this world can't handle another Sayeed."

Overwhelmed, Ally raised her hand to silence him.

So many things filled her head, she focused on the only option she had left. "Nasif, I have no choice but to play this game. I am grateful for the things you've done, but I need you to do one more thing, please."

His brows narrowed.

"I need medicine," she whispered. "Something that can kill. Quickly."

She drew a breath and squeezed his arm when he shook his head. "If I was your child, would you allow this to happen?"

He rubbed his forehead and let out a ragged sigh.

"You had no choice but to put your family first, and I may have done the same thing in your position. I promise you, I won't show any fear and be strong for as long as I can. But if it doesn't work, or it becomes unbearable..."

She didn't need to finish. Didn't bother to say if the drug would be for her or Sayeed. Her message had the intended effect. He averted his gaze but didn't quiet her. Ally leaned closer. "You said yourself he was a predator who tortures others."

He patted her back and climbed off the bed. "I'll see what I can do. Now, you must get some rest. Sayeed arrives in the morning."

Before she could say anything more, Nasif picked up his belongings and left for the night.

~

Sleep didn't come for Ally. Her mind raced with images of what Sayeed might do to her. She gave up trying to block them out and paced the room as scene after horrific scene played in her brain.

When the panic attacks would start up, she'd sit on the bed and cling to David's picture. It made her feel less alone. She had to trust there was an escape. Just needed to stay alert and wait for the chance. It was what could happen during the waiting that terrified her.

~

Morning came too quickly. Bathed and composed, she sat on the bed, waiting for the devil to make his appearance. When his voice echoed down the hall, Ally's gut twisted. She wrapped her hands together and squeezed to hide the tremors rocking them. Keys jiggled and the door opened. Her gaze fixed on the specks of gold in the marble as shoes tapped against the floor. Black patent leather came into view.

As a tray of food slid onto the bed, Nasif's advice from the day before drifted through her head. *Look strong. Show no fear.*

She rose and stared into dark, frigid eyes. Her throat tightened. He wore his usual three-piece suit, this time gray. When his gaze roamed over her body, she fought the urge to turn away. His bearded face stretched into a smile of approval, and he waved in her direction. "You look good, Sara. The abaya suits you."

Sayeed moved in, wrapped his arms around her waist, and pulled her to him. Her heart raced as she tried not to fight his touch. But when his lips inched closer to hers, her disgust overpowered her. She planted her hands on his chest and pushed.

He chuckled, tightening his grip and crushing her to him. As his laugh vibrated against her chest, his arousal dug into her groin. The harder she fought, the tighter he clung.

A figure in the background caught her eye. Nasif Out of Sayeed's sight, he put his palm up, mouthing for her to stop. Every cell in her body screamed to fight, to push away, and run. But she knew Nasif was right; that would only make things worse. After a slight nod, Ally closed her eyes and stayed frozen as Sayeed's lips brushed against her cheek.

"I'm a big man, Sara. You will not be disappointed," he whispered. The smell of cigarettes and Scotch overwhelmed her. Fists clenched, she fought the repulsion while he nipped at her lip. "Tonight you will see how happy I am that you are my wife." His beard scraped her skin when he pressed his lips against hers. Her body shook and tears streamed her cheeks.

After an eternity, Sayeed loosened his hold and rested his forehead against hers.

Swallowing her fear, she forced the words out. "I don't want to be your wife."

The heat of his breath hit her face when he laughed. "With destiny, there are no choices, love."

Eyes closed, she steadied her voice. "This is not my destiny. You took something that wasn't yours."

He grabbed her chin and squeezed, sending currents of pain through her jaw. "Look at me."

When she did, he smiled and rubbed the wetness off her cheek with his thumb. "You are mine and that is all that matters." He released his grip and walked out the open door.

CHAPTER SIX

The Stranger

Twenty-six months after Ally's disappearance

With the office door firmly shut and locked, Dave threaded Ally's wedding ring onto his pinky as far as it would go. Rows of diamonds wrapped around the band and pointed to a large square solitaire, surrounded by more of the stones. This was her favorite piece of jewelry. It had never left her hand, until now.

The rustling of plastic and metal drew his attention away from the ring and focused it squarely on the man wandering his room. The space was set up like a basic office. Two armchairs faced a heavy mahogany desk. His favorite leather chair sat tucked under the table. A large glass wall of windows behind the desk provided a killer view of downtown Philadelphia when open. The blinds slammed shut as the old man closed the last of them.

Dave's muscles were tight, ready to act as he watched the stranger's every move. When the man finally turned to face him, Dave approached and thrust the ring in his spectacled face. "How did you get this?"

Though at least a foot shorter, the little fuck stared up impassively. Dave raised his brows, waiting for the man to answer. Instead, the stranger reached out and touched the band. When the wrinkled finger brushed his own, a shudder ran down his spine.

Have those hands touched her? Hurt her?

He pulled his arm away.

"I have wanted to meet you and give that to you for a long time."

Dave's body heated and he clenched his teeth as impatience brewed. He grabbed a fistful of the man's shirt and shoved him against the blinds. "How did you get the ring?"

Instead of answering, the man closed his eyes and sucked in a breath.

He leaned in. "Maybe you didn't hear me, I said..."

"Yes, I heard what you said. But as long as you stand over me like an angry bull, I can't answer you. Give me some space, and you will get the information you need."

The little son-of-a-bitch. A part of Dave screamed to throw him out the window, that he was somehow responsible for her disappearance and maybe even her death. But he ignored the voice. After all these years, he needed answers. No matter how bad they were. He released his grip and backed away.

"Thank you. May I?" Without a pause, the man walked around him and sat at his desk, in *his* leather chair.

Dave filled his lungs and tried to rein in the anger and confusion. Positioning himself in the armchair between the man and the door, he leaned forward and, in a more controlled voice, tried again. "Where. Is. My. Wife?"

"In Pakistan."

Twisting her ring, Dave digested what the man said. Two years of searching and she was in... "Pakistan?"

Although the word sounded odd coming out of his mouth, the deeper meaning of it wrapped around his neck and squeezed. "She's alive."

A smile stretched across the stranger's face and he leaned in. "Yes, very much alive."

Alive.

Emotion burned the back of his eyes as the assurance he'd hungered for replayed in his brain.

The old man grabbed the framed picture of Ally taken on their honeymoon from the corner of Dave's desk and stared at it. "She is one of a kind, your Alisha."

The anger that ebbed seconds ago, reemerged. Dave leaned over and grabbed the man's wrist. "Who the hell are you to tell me about my wife? What have you done to her?"

"I am a friend who wants to help. And I have a lot to tell you, just not much time, so please listen to what I have to say."

Dave stared into the old man's eyes, trying to unlock the secrets in his head but found nothing. "How do I know if I can trust you? That you didn't kill her and bring me the ring?"

"You don't. But I have not, and would never hurt her." He pulled the picture from Dave's hand and pointed to her image.

Ally's head was tilted slightly as she smiled at the camera. His voice cracked. "In the time I have been with her, she has never looked like this. There is nothing I want more than to put *that* smile on her face."

The stranger glanced at the hand still wrapped around his wrist, as if waiting for Dave's next move. Letting go of the man, he leaned back in his chair and waited. If the guy tried to run, there was no doubt he could take him. Break his legs, neck whatever it took.

"Thank you." He set down the frame. "As far as proof..." He pulled out a Blackberry from his suit pocket. After an eternity of fiddling, he handed it over.

The phone, still warm from his touch, felt dirty in Dave's palm. He pushed the thought away and focused on the little screen. A bag of bricks had just been shoved into Dave's chest, pushing what little air he had left out of his lungs, while his heart tried to pole vault out of the way.

The picture was small and grainy but clear enough. The woman who stared out had enormous, chocolate-brown eyes. Although her hair was covered by a dark scarf, her face was visible. It was longer than he remembered, and cheekbones more prominent. It didn't matter; he would recognize her anywhere.

Ally.

Questions ran through his head faster than he could comprehend. "How did you get this?"

When the man didn't answer, Dave glanced at him before going back to the phone.

"I took them about four weeks back."

He messed with the buttons in an attempt to text himself the image. The device popped up an error message each time. The perceptive little bastard waved his hand toward the Blackberry.

"You won't be able to do that. The phone is not connected to a network. Scroll through them. There are more."

And there were. Image after heart-aching image of Ally. Like a man stumbling on an oasis after wandering the desert, Dave's thirst for her was unquenchable. She looked the same in each: the tilt of her face, a smile that didn't meet her eyes, the dullness in her gaze. Every muscle in his body clenched. The pain written all over her stabbed at his core.

"What's wrong with her?" Dave's words came out choked.

"Her life has been difficult. She will not be able to take much more."

He wiped away the bead of sweat that settled on his forehead and tried to contain the fear snaking up his spine. "I'm listening."

"There is a man named Sayeed Irfani. He sells weapons to terrorist organizations. Three years back, he was able to get a visa and come to America. While he was here, he made some very rich and powerful friends and met your wife."

The stranger reached into his jacket pocket, took out a memory stick, and placed it on the desk. "Everything you need is in here: the address, his contacts, everything. But be careful whom you trust with this. There are many in your government and mine whose pockets are padded by Sayeed. If you want your wife, Sayeed must die."

"Who are you?"

He shook his head "It's best you don't know my name. Just that I am a friend of your Alisha's."

Something about the way he said her name sounded off. "What do you mean, *your* Alisha?"

"Where I come from, her name is Sara Irfani, Sayeed's second wife."

Dave sucked in some air, squeezing the ring. "She married him?"

"No, he married her. There's a difference." He rose from the chair and pushed it under the table. "I must go before anyone notices I'm missing. She is a good girl, and she does not deserve this."

The stranger walked over and stood so close that Dave saw his own stunned reflection in the man's glasses. "Be careful. You are being watched and have been from the beginning. And remember, you must kill Sayeed. Otherwise, even if you are successful at bringing your wife home, he will come after her."

With a pat on Dave's shoulder, he walked to the door. Sayeed, illegal weapons, government officials. The information whirled in his head. "Wait. You can't say all that and just leave. How will I find her?"

He jutted his chin toward the desk. "It is on the memory stick."

Dave rushed to his side. "How do I find you?"

"I have done all I can. The rest is up to you. But please, hurry," the man added before walking out the door.

He grabbed the drive and stared at the small metal object as his brain replayed everything the stranger shared. She's alive. In danger but alive. Who could he trust?

CHAPTER SEVEN

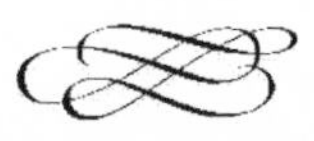

FIRST NIGHT

TWENTY SIX DAYS POST KIDNAPPING

As soon as Sayeed left the room, Ally's shoulders slouched. She sat on the bed before her knees gave way. Her face was drenched with perspiration and tears, and she wiped the wetness onto her sleeve and worked on steadying herself.

So much had happened and even more would follow, but for now, she was safe. As she stared at the still-open door and considered the option of walking out of it, Nasif and two men entered. Ally gripped the mattress and assessed the new visitors.

Large machine guns hung over each of their shoulders and fully stocked ammunition belts hung around their hips. After entering, one stood guard on either side of the threshold, overcrowding her small prison.

Nasif leaned against the wall and spoke quietly to the smaller man. Although the shorter of the two guards, the man was still well over six feet in height. Catching her eye, Nasif rested his hand on the guard's shoulder. "Sara, this is Amir."

Amir nodded. He looked young, late teens or early twenties, with a serious face and enormous hazel eyes. His thick, black mustache didn't fit his youthful features and the oversized jeans and short-sleeve shirt he wore made him look like a child playing dress-up. If not for the gun and belt, she'd not have even considered him a threat.

"And over there is Kadeen." Nasif waved toward the giant of a man standing a few feet away. Like Amir, he too wore faded jeans and a tee. Kadeen's brows rose and his dark eyes narrowed when her gaze locked with his. The scar across his cheek, the tight line his mouth made, all of it sent a shiver down her spine. Everything about him screamed danger.

Nasif gestured to the open door. "Come, let me give you a tour of your new home."

Sucking in a breath, Ally clenched the sides of her abaya and exited the prison for the first time.

At the threshold, she hesitated. There was a good chance that whatever lurked out there would be worse than being holed up in the room. She scanned the area. The hallway stretched in both directions. Its walls were painted a golden orange, which made the bits of gold in the black marble sparkle. Dark wooden doors of varying sizes, all closed, lined the way. Aside from the metal chair and small wooden table across from her room, the corridor was empty.

When Nasif disappeared to the right, Ally followed, fully aware Amir and his gun were close behind. There didn't appear to be locks on the rooms she passed. Her fingers itched to test her theory. She craned her neck behind the young guard and was relieved to see the older one was not accompanying them. Her eyes locked with the man shadowing her. When he tipped his head, encouraging her to keep moving, she nodded and shifted her focus back to Nasif.

Images of Amir pointing his weapon at the back of her head and firing made her pulse accelerate. She tightened her grasp on her skirt and shook the fears away. One of these rooms would lead her out of this hell, but now was not the time to figure out which.

By the time she caught up with Nasif, he stood in front of a closed room. Through the thick, dark wood, she heard the clatter of pots and the voices of women. When Ally reached his side, he tipped his chin toward the entrance. "This is the kitchen. You will be spending a lot of time in here with the others."

The smell of aromatics filled her sinuses as soon as he opened the door. Peering over his shoulder, she took in the oversized room. A long, black marble countertop matched the floor and wrapped around the space. On it were two portable stoves, pots, utensils, and food being prepped. Rows of shelves filled with glass containers lined the walls.

The voices grew silent and five sets of eyes fixed on Ally. Four of the women wore *salwar kameez*—long tunics that fell to their knees—with matching pants. Unlike Ally, their heads were uncovered. She sucked in a breath and searched their faces. Would at least one of them help her?

The fifth, a petite woman dressed in a light blue dress, *hijab*, and abaya approached. Her complexion was creamy white—a perfect canvas for her sea green eyes, a touch paler than David's.

"Sara, let me introduce you to Alyah, Sayeed's first wife." Nasif gestured toward her.

Alyah ignored the greeting and spoke to Nasif in Urdu. Her voice was high and inflamed and her hands animated while she spoke.

The other women returned to their duties, two of which grabbed knives and cut produce. Ally's gaze lingered on the blades before resting on the girl in the middle of the room. She was frail, small and stood frozen, staring at the floor. Dressed in a dull brown salwar kameez too big for her thin frame, her hands lay folded in front of her. The only hint of her nervousness was the way her thumbs rubbed against each other.

Alyah's high-pitched voice drew Ally's attention from the child and squarely on Sayeed's first wife, who currently glared at her while she ranted at Nasif.

"Reema." Nasif gestured to the girl. Wordlessly, she followed them out of the room. Alyah waved her hands as if in defeat and returned to kitchen duties while still muttering under her breath.

He shut the door to the kitchen and the four of them moved down the hall. "Ignore Alyah," Nasif advised. "We all do."

Five more rooms lined this side of the corridor. A couple of the doors were slightly ajar. She stared into the gloomy spaces as she walked past, hoping for clues, but found only darkness. The old man stopped in front of the fourth room and unlocked it.

The only one with a deadbolt. There was no doubt it was her room. She swallowed her fear. When he opened the door, the overwhelming fragrance of roses and jasmine choked her. As soon as he turned on the light, Ally's stomach dropped.

Strings of white flowers draped across the ceiling, converging near the center where they fell to the floor and created a canopy around the bed. Red petals blanketed the white linen on the mattress. Unlit candles placed strategically throughout, waited to be set ablaze.

A chill of horror shot through her veins, making her body tremble. The reality that this would be where Sayeed would rape her slapped the breath out of her. She stepped back, shaking her head. "I can't. Please don't do this to me." Ally turned and ran, only to slam into the hard-bodied Amir. Nasif cupped her elbow, tugging her inside.

Her vision blurred. She reached out, bracing herself for the fall.

Nasif's grip tightened, steadying her. "Sara, you will survive."

The same thing he'd said for weeks. What he failed to acknowledge was that she didn't want to survive. Nor did she want to be strong. When Nasif guided her to the bed, she pulled away.

A mix of terror and anger coursed through her veins. "No. I won't sit on this bed. I don't want to do anything on there." She ran to the door, only to have her passage blocked again. Emotionless, Amir gazed down at her, his gun cradled in his arms. They stared at her; no one said a word. The only sound was her heart racing and the loud gasps of air she sucked in. With nowhere to run, she backed away until her frame hit the wall and slid to the floor. Ally hugged her knees to her chest, and like a child, she rocked as she cried.

This couldn't be happening. Why were they allowing him to do this?

"Sara," Nasif squatted in front of her. "I have done all I can. There is nothing more I can do."

"How can so many people be rendered helpless by one man?" she whispered through her tears.

He opened his mouth as if to respond, and then shut it. "Reema," he called. The girl crouched beside him. "Sara, this is Reema. She will help you get ready. Reema is a mute so she'll keep all your secrets. I trust her completely. She has a wonderful soul."

Ally continued rocking.

"Amir will be outside the door." He patted her head before rising and walking away.

Her chest tightened as she listened to his footsteps. "Nasif." When he turned, she stared at the man who was abandoning her. After all these weeks, he had made his choice: her life wasn't valuable enough to save. Teeth clenched, she choked through her hatred. "Sleep well tonight, my friend."

Guilt flashed across his face. "I will pray for you."

When he turned and left the room, Amir followed. The sound of the metal hitting wood filled the silence as they locked the door.

She hugged her knees to her chest as terror rocked her body.

A small hand squeezed her shoulder. Ally looked up into the face of the child crouched in front her. Her cheeks were hollow and eyes inset, both indications of malnourishment. Was she a prisoner like the rest of them? Whose life had Sayeed threatened or taken to keep her there?

The girl flashed a shy smile before turning and disappearing into the room's bathroom. Ally scanned the space for a window or some sort of escape but found none.

Reema returned with a paper bag. The child sat cross-legged in front of her and dug through the sack, producing a manicure set. Silently, she began to work on Ally's toes.

~

Hours passed. Under Reema's care, Ally's unwanted hair was removed, nails filed and buffed, and her curls pinned carefully in a bun.

The blue silk outfit Reema dressed her in was encrusted with diamonds. Its tight, sleeveless bodice covered her chest like a second skin, all the way to her navel, where the fabric stopped. Ally pulled on the top in a futile attempt to cover her stomach while Reema zipped the floor-length skirt, which sat just below her waist, accentuating her hips.

With no one to talk to and time running out, Ally closed her eyes and pleaded with the only one she could. God.

How am I supposed to survive?

Hot tears streamed her cheeks for the thousandth time.

"Didi, don't cry." The whispered voice startled her. She scanned the room for the source. Reya was only one person in this world that called her Didi. One of the many rules their Indian parents enforced on them at an early age: respect your older brother and sister. And even then she'd shorten it to Di.

She stared at Reema. The girl's back was to Ally as she lit candles.

Could it be? No, she's mute.

Wiping the tears away, Ally realized she was on the brink of psychosis.

Reema stood back to inspect her. Diamonds dangled from Ally's ears, neck, and arms. The room glowed from the candles she lit. After she wrapped a long, matching scarf around Ally's head, she wiped a stray tear off Ally's cheek. Their gazes locked for a moment, and she knew the fear she saw in the girl's eye was for her. After a nod, the child picked up her things and knocked on the door. Amir opened it and allowed her to leave.

Ally stared in the mirror, numb and alone.

Seconds later, keys jingled and the lock slid open. Rooted to the floor, she watched his reflection through the mirror on the wall. He had replaced his suit for casual gray pants with a loose, long-sleeved shirt that hung to his knees. His dark hair was slicked back and when their eyes met through the glass, his bearded face stretched into a smile of approval.

He closed the door and approached her. There was nowhere to run. The escape she tried so hard to find never materialized. Her heart pulsed in her ears. She gripped the sides of her jewel-lined skirt.

When Sayeed's fingers wrapped around her bare waist, goose bumps erupted across her skin. He pulled her to his hips, the heat of his breath burning her shoulder in the process. The mixture of alcohol and talcum powder repulsed her.

"I have waited a long time for you, Sara."

His lips and tongue found their way to her neck, creating a wet path to her ear. Ally swallowed the revulsion as new tears heated her face. Biting her ear, Sayeed pulled her head back to rest on his shoulder and looked down her bodice. When her labored breathing made her breasts more pronounced, he groaned his approval.

He ground his hips against her, stabbing his hardness into her back. Ally's mind raced but there was nothing she could say or do. He palmed her stomach with one hand and squeezed her breast with the other. She tried to step away, only to be held tighter. Rough lips scraped her cheek. "Mmm, even your tears are delicious."

He positioned his leg between hers while his hand moved downward. She stopped his descent and pressed his palm against her hips. "Sayeed, I'm not ready."

He pulled it from her grasp and traced along her cheek with

his nose. "It's not your choice, love."

She squirmed out of his hands and turned to face him. A smile crept across his face.

"Please, Sayeed, don't do this." With each retreating step, he followed until her back pressed against the wall.

He stopped inches from her face and drew a deep breath, a look of pleasure on his face. "Say that again."

Moisture pooled her eyes. Her voice quivered when she whispered, "Please."

His hips slammed into her stomach as he pulled her hands over her head. "You are my wife, Sara, and tonight we will consummate our marriage." She turned when his lips approached. He pressed them against her neck.

Clasping her wrists in one hand, he grabbed her head and twisted it up to face him. When his lips scraped against hers, Ally sealed her mouth shut and swallowed the sobs erupting within. Sayeed released her face, grabbing her hair. When he jerked on the bun, a thousand pins shot through her scalp. She squeaked out in pain. He slammed his mouth over hers. His fingers held her chin in place while he explored.

Unable to move, she clamped on his tongue. Sayeed's fingers jumped to her throat and squeezed until she gasped for air and released her hold.

Again he cupped her chin and forced her to face him. He rested his forehead on hers. "Did you enjoy the photo I sent you?"

A shudder ripped through her.

"Are you sure you want to have this fight?"

Drawing a gulp of air, she pushed the fear into her gut, cleansed herself of emotions, and shook her head.

"Good. You are mine, and no matter how much you fight, tonight I will have you." His tongue traced her sealed lips. "I have wanted you since that first day in your office. So many nights I dreamed of you." Sayeed ran his fingers down her shoulder. They lingered on her chest, grasping and squeezing. "Touching you."

She shut her eyes, forcing herself to stay still.

He leaned in and pried her lips open with his. When she granted him access, his tongue snaked its way inside, exploring her. She didn't return the kiss, but didn't fight it either.

Sayeed stepped back and studied her. When he released her

hands, they fell to her sides like dead weight. "Take off your clothes."

Her chest squeezed and limbs refused to comply. He pulled her from the wall, twisted her around, and fidgeted with the zipper of her blouse. Soon the fabric dropped to the floor. He stepped closer, his hands exploring her breasts.

Fists clenched, she tried to drift away to another place. A happier one. But she couldn't focus on anything else.

"Take off your skirt."

Painfully slow, she unzipped the fabric. As the silk crumbled to the floor, so did any hope she had. Naked, unprepared, and powerless to stop the assault, the pain of a hundred daggers pierced her being.

Sayeed turned her to face him. "Look at what you do to me." Undressed as well, he held his arousal in his hand. Large and thick, his uncircumcised penis poked out from under his heavy stomach, pulsing as he stroked it. Ally turned away, trying to block the sight.

"Get in bed."

But she couldn't. Her legs stayed planted to the floor until he dragged her across the room and threw her atop the mattress. When she scooted back, he grabbed her leg and climbed on. He rested the full weight of his body against hers, pressing every ounce of oxygen out of her lungs.

Parting her legs, he crashed into her. The blow of pain was immediate and all-consuming, pushing out a sharp cry from her lungs. He placed one hand around her throat as he worked.

With each thrust, ideas of escape floated away and were replaced by much stronger ones: hatred and a deep hunger for revenge.

He slammed harder and faster. She managed not to cry out again, and imagined the pain he inflicted as the agony he would experience when she grabbed one of those knives from the kitchen. She envisioned slicing him over and over, each cut more lethal, more painful than the last. When the pain of his assault became too much, Ally clutched the petal-covered sheets and closed her eyes.

CHAPTER EIGHT

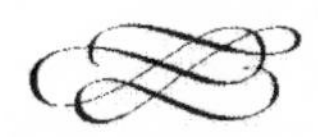

A PERSON OF INTEREST

TWENTY-SIX MONTHS AFTER ALLY'S DISAPPEARANCE

Why is my office so damn far from the hospital elevators?

Heart pounding, Dave weaved through the individuals walking up and down the hall while he fought the urge to run.

And why the hell are so many people here on a Saturday?

Between making arrangements to have his patients covered for the rest of the week and texting an apology cancellation to Kate, he had already wasted precious time he should have been using to find Ally. A mixture of anger, fear, and excitement had played havoc inside him since the morning's unexpected visitor.

The flash drive dug against his big toe with each step. At the time, the sock seemed the safest place to store it. It was that or his underwear. Now, he wasn't so sure. His fingers brushed against the two cell phones in his shirt pocket as he pulled out his personal one. He scrolled to the text he sent to Reya and made sure he'd hit Send. *Need you and Nik to meet me ASAP.*

Wait, what if my phone's tapped?

When he reached the elevators, Jerry McIntosh was leaning against the wall, smiling at him. He was the current Director of Surgery at Philadelphia County and a retired special ops medic. The man was a badass and Dave's good friend. Specks of gray peppered his dark hair. Creases across his forehead and the corners of his eyes added to the movie-star quality that made him a magnet for every woman in the hospital.

"Dave, just the man I was looking for."

Jerry had a way of reading people, knew when they were full of shit. Dave pressed the down arrow and focused on the display above the doors. "Sorry, now is not a good time." Rocking on his heels, he waited for the elevator to arrive.

11...10...

"It's going to have to be. We need to talk."

He pretended to check his watch and avoided his boss's gaze. "I'm late for an appointment. Phil's covering for me. Call him. I'm sure he can handle whatever it is."

9...

Instead, Jerry grabbed his elbow, pulling Dave away. "'Fraid he can't. And your appointment will have to wait. Come with me."

The electric doors slid open and the urgency of the past few minutes turned to sheer terror. Dave tried to tug his arm out of the death vice. "Jerry, I have to go. I wouldn't do this if I had a choice."

"Understood, and neither would I." The man tightened his grip and pushed him down the same hall Dave had dashed through minutes ago. Jerry dragged him into his office, shut, and locked the door.

Arms crossed, the man leaned against the door, blocking Dave's escape. He raised his brow and looked over at him.

"Jer, please, you don't understand."

"Why was Nasif Abassi in your office?"

"Who?"

"The man you just talked to. Why was he there?"

The old stranger's words of caution rang in Dave's ears. Was Jerry one of the bad guys? Fists balled, heat flooded him. "He wanted medical advice. That's it. Are we done?"

"Nope, just starting. You might as well have a seat."

When he kept his feet securely planted on the floor and shook his head, Jerry continued. "His wife died this morning. Unless you were telling him how to resurrect her, I'm not buying it. So, let's try this again. Why was he in your office?"

Dave's muscles tightened, his senses on high alert. Hands on his hips, he glared at the man. "You've been spying on me?"

"You? No. Him? Yes." Jerry pinched his forehead. "Look, I'm going to take a chance and trust you, and I'm praying I don't regret this. I do some work for the CIA. They are of the opinion thatthe old man's involved with some questionable characters and asked me to keep them in the loop about his comings and goings. I've been in charge of Nasif and his wife's care for over two years, and to be honest, I kinda like the guy. Granted, I don't know what he does when he's not in the hospital, but he loved his wife and has always been respectful and kind to the staff. When the agency called me about you a little while ago, imagine my surprise. So I told them the truth, I know you and you're one of the few people I trust completely."

Rubbing the nape of his neck, Dave paced the room and tried to process the information. Who the hell could he trust?

Jerry leaned forward. "You're dripping with sweat and look like you're having a fucking seizure. Whatever Nasif said scared the shit out of you. What the fuck happened in there?"

When he didn't respond, Jerry's face darkened. He jabbed his finger into Dave's chest. "In the three years we've known each other, I've never screwed with you, have I? When you needed a fellowship position at County, who created it for you? After Ally disappeared and you locked yourself away, who dragged your pathetic ass into the hospital?"

Their eyes locked.

"That's right, me. I've always gone to bat because I trust and respect you. Hopefully, you feel the same way."

Everything Jerry said was true. There had been very few constants in Dave's life. But in the past few years, his boss had become one of them. He'd sat in this very office with the man and cried his eyes out. It never changed the way Jerry treated him.

Dave paced the room as the pros and cons of telling Jerry whizzed through his head. His stomach twisted at the weight of the decision. As if understanding his dilemma, the guy grabbed his arm, stopping him in his tracks. "Something's obviously wrong. Let me help you."

After sucking in a breath, he nodded and decided to take the chance. "Ally's alive and the old man knows where she is."

Jerry's hand dropped and his eyes widened. "What?"

Dave pulled out Nasif's Blackberry from his shirt pocket.

"Here. Scroll through the pictures." Seating himself in the armchair, Dave rested his face in his hands and waited.

He had to trust someone. It was the only way he'd find her. With his special ops background, if there was anyone who would know what to do, it would be Jerry. Acid crawled up his stomach, burning everything in its path along the way. On the other hand, if he was wrong, Ally might die.

The soft clicking of the Blackberry's buttons echoed through the office. "Holy shit," Jerry whispered.

"Exactly. I've never met him before. He was outside my office when I got there. I had no clue what his name was until you said it just now. She's in Pakistan and some asshole named Sayeed has her there against her will." As he spoke the words, excited energy replaced his fear.

Dave shot to his feet and reached for the phone. "I gotta go. Ally's out there, alive. I need to bring her home."

Still rooted in the same spot, Jerry moved the cell out of Dave's reach and shot out his hand to stop him. "Let's say, for the sake of argument, he's telling you the truth. How do you plan on doing that?"

Dave sucked in a breath and ran his fingers through his sweaty hair. "That's what I need to figure out."

When he reached for the phone a second time, Jerry dodged his hand again and tipped his chin at the chair. "Take a seat."

The seed of doubt that plagued Dave about trusting the guy in the first place had just became a full blown forest of trees. He lunged for the device again only to find himself face down on the couch, grasping air. Dave rose to his feet, his teeth clenched. "Give me the damn phone, Jer."

His boss crossed his arms, and his brows rose so high they got lost in his hairline. "I will. Just sit your ass down first and let me think. I'm going to help you."

Nothing made any sense. Up until half an hour ago, he thought he'd never see Ally again. Now everything had changed, and he didn't know what the hell to do. After a few minutes of their staring competition, Dave finally shook his head in defeat. Heart in his throat, he did as his boss ordered.

Jerry positioned himself on the coffee table in front of him, phone still firm in his grip. "Listen. You have no idea what you've just gotten yourself into. If she really is alive, the CIA are the only ones who know enough about the situation to get her home."

"I can't. He said Sayeed has powerful friends all over the country and to be careful who I trust. No police, no government, I gotta figure this out on my own."

A knock at the door sent Dave jumping. Jerry pushed him down and glared. "It's the CIA. They called me. I didn't call them. This is beyond your scope. Do you understand?"

The person outside knocked again. Jerry looked over his shoulder at the door and back at Dave. "*If* she really is alive, you could get her killed. You need help and Eddie's one of the good guys. If you want her, he can make it happen. Trust me on this."

Dave closed his eyes and rested his head on the back of the couch.

Trust me.

Famous last words.

While Jerry opened the door, Dave prayed he'd made the right decision.

"Dr. MacIntosh."

"Morning, Eddie. Come in."

Dave sized him up. With his black hair cut short and dark eyes, he looked very Middle Eastern. *Maybe he could take me to Pakistan.* And he was built as if he'd walked out of a men's fitness magazine. *Probably kick some serious ass.*

When Eddie scanned the room, his gaze fell squarely on Dave. He seemed intense, like someone who didn't waste his time laughing or cracking a smile often. Intimidating. *That could be a good thing too.* Even the way he dressed in all gray from his long-sleeved shirt to his dark slacks, sent a *don't fuck with me* message. All of which would help find Ally, unless he was one of the people Sayeed was bribing, and then Dave was the one fucked.

Eddie flashed a smile and reached out his hand. "Dr. Dimarchi. I'm Eddie Ghani. I'm with the CIA."

Dave stood and accepted the outstretched palm. The man pulled out a white piece of paper from his pocket. "My card."

He took the card and, incapable of reading, stared at the letters. In the past few minutes, a thin bead of perspiration had developed across his forehead and now dripped down his temples. Dave swiped at the moisture and stuffed the paper and his fists into his pants pockets.

"Dr. Dimarchi, I'd like to sit and chat with you for a bit."

Voices warred in his head. Who should he trust? How much should he share? When he rocked on his heels, the drive dug into his toe. He tried to concentrate on the pain instead of on the fear building inside him that he was screwing up.

After dropping his messenger bag on the coffee table, Eddie sat on the sofa, leaned in, planted his elbows on his knees, and pointed at the armchair. "Please."

What if he was the one person who could bring her home? It wouldn't hurt to hear what he had to say, would it?

Dave positioned himself in the chair.

An approving smile stretched across the agent's tanned features. "Thank you. We need to talk about the visit you had fifteen minutes ago. Tell me what you know about him."

What the hell was he supposed to say? The weight of his decision bore down on him, and the idea of running away seemed very appealing. "Nothing."

Eddie squinted and assessed him as he rubbed his hands together. "Nothing?"

Dave kept his face as expressionless as possible and nodded.

"So, he appears out of the blue, hangs out with you for approximately twelve minutes in your office, and you learned nothing about him?"

Jerry moved behind Eddie's sofa, glaring at Dave. With two predators casing their pending kill—him, he shifted in his seat and pulled out the bent card.

Edil Ghani

Office of Terrorism Analysis, CIA

"Okay, well let me tell you what I've learned about your friend. In the past five years, Dr. Nasif Abassi has come to the States on three separate occasions seeking medical treatment for his wife and paid for it all in full. Doctor or no doctor, how does someone come up with well over a million dollars in cash?"

Dave remained silent, hoping Eddie would answer his own question.

"So we did some digging. Turns out he's the personal doctor to Sayeed Irfani, a person of interest for the CIA. And most likely, the one fitting the bill for our good doctor's expenses. Did you know about any of this, David?"

Acid burned his throat, leaving a sour taste in his mouth. He swallowed it and rubbed the dampness of the hardened muscles at the nape of his neck. "No, I didn't. Is there a purpose to these questions?"

Eddie shrugged his shoulders and unzipped his bag. "Just making sure we're on the same page. That's all."

He pulled out a file and placed a picture on the table. "That is Sayeed Irfani."

The man in the photo was dark haired and bearded. His thick brows raised, he smiled at the camera with a look of satisfaction. A look that said "she's mine." Even drenched in sweat, Dave's body chilled.

"Irfani has ties to terrorist organizations. The question is, in what capacity? I hope you can enlighten us."

Dave's fingers clenched the fabric of the chair while the walls seemed to close in. With a long, slow intake of air, he counted to five and released it, the way Ally used to do.

"The plan was to take you to the agency and discuss this matter there. Dr. MacIntosh has put his neck on the line for you and said that wouldn't be necessary. That you're a friend of his, and if he trusts you, I trust you too."

"David's wife's been missing for over two years. Nasif told him she's alive," Jerry said, handing Eddie the Blackberry.

The room fell into a heavy silence. His mouth dried as two sets of eyes waited for him to respond.

"Nasif told you that your wife, Alisha Dimarchi, is alive?"

Uncomfortable with the fact that Eddie obviously knew everything about his life, Dave kept his focus on the phone in the agent's hand and cleared his throat. "He said I need to be careful who I trust because the man who took her has some powerful friends in America."

"Did he tell you who that man was?"

He glanced at Eddie and stared at the bastard's picture on the table but didn't respond.

Jerry answered for him. "Sayeed Irfani."

"Irfani took your wife?"

Dave nodded.

"Did he tell you anything else or give you anything?"

"Just the phone and her wedding ring." Dave pulled out his

hand and showed him the band on his pinky. "I'd like the phone, please."

"Of course." From his bag, Eddie slid out a tablet and a cable. In seconds, a wire was connected to the cell and his device. After a few clicks on the keyboard, he turned the monitor so Dave could see and her face popped up. "That's your wife?"

She looked different on the bigger screen. More real. His lungs felt like lead, but he managed to respond. "Yes."

"So, Irfani took her?"

Her hair covered, she stared back as if pleading for help. "Yes," Dave whispered.

"Sayeed Irfani's personal doctor seeks you out to tell you that your wife has been kidnapped by his boss, and what?"

"I need to go find her." He tried to memorize the face on the screen.

"He gives you a couple of pictures and her wedding ring. Nothing else?"

There was a scar on the top right corner of her forehead he'd never seen before.

Eddie cleared his throat. "The thing is, I get the feeling there's more to this story. If he wanted you to find your wife, he would have given you additional information on how to get to her. Is there something you've forgotten to mention?"

"David, you can't do this on your own. Let them help you," Jerry interjected.

A shiver ran down his spine. He shook his head of her images and eyed the man in gray, considering his options. Maybe there was a way.

Eddie clicked to another picture, and another. Each one was a punch in the gut. Dave's eyes watered.

"Dr. Dimarchi, I promise I will do everything in my power to bring her home. You have to trust me."

"There's more," he whispered. "Addresses, names, his American contacts, and some other stuff."

"Where?"

"First bring me my wife."

Dave's muscles tightened at the heavy weight of silence that followed.

Eddie cleared his throat. "Excuse me?"

With a deep breath, he stood up and Eddie rose as well. "Bring Alisha home and I will give you everything."

The man didn't say a word. At first, Dave wondered if he needed to repeat himself. Before he got the chance, Eddie walked to him. So close, in fact, that he could smell the coffee on his breath. Although a few inches shorter, there was no doubt in Dave's mind that man could cause him serious bodily harm. He gulped and stayed frozen.

"Why don't you give me what you have, and you have my word I will bring her home." His words were spoken, each syllable drawn out for emphasis.

"No. Ally needs to be safe, then you can have the information." As he spoke the words, his fear slipped away. This was about her and he'd do anything he needed to keep her safe.

The scrunched-up skin between Eddie's brows turned beet red. "You should reconsider your decision, Dr. Dimarchi."

"There's nothing to reconsider."

Besides the darkening shades of red on his forehead, the agent's face stayed emotionless.

"You ever lost anyone before, Eddie?"

Although he didn't answer the question, the corner of the man's eye twitched.

"This man, Sayeed, you mentioned. He's a monster, isn't he?" Anger warmed his chilled muscles as Dave considered the next question. "What kind of things do you think he's done to my wife?"

Eddie didn't respond and again the muscles in his face twitched.

"Alisha has been held against her will by this bastard for two years. God knows what kind of hell she must be going through. You can torture or even kill me, but I assure you, until she is safe, you will get nothing."

So focused on Eddie, it took Dave by surprise when Jerry squeezed his shoulder. His boss stepped between the two of them, making Eddie move back. "No one's going to hurt you. We're on the same team here. Right, Eddie?"

The man nodded but didn't say a word.

Jerry cleared his throat. "Eddie, why don't you go to your office, try to figure out where Alisha might be and call us when you find something?"

The agent's gaze stayed fixed on Dave. "Don't leave town. I'll be in touch."

CHAPTER NINE

THE PLAN

FOUR MONTHS POST KIDNAPPING

Ally glanced at the clock on the wall. One fifteen

With her ear pressed against the door, she listened. Silence.

It had been three months since the move into her new room...since the rapes started. Three months of planning to get to this day. A trickle of sweat ran down the back of her neck. She sucked in a breath, opened her door slowly, cringing when the hinges squeaked, and peeked into the hallway.

Empty.

Her pulse raced as she entered the long corridor. Hitching the sides of her abaya up a few inches to keep her bare feet from tripping on its length, she closed the door. As she snuck down the hall, her mind flew through the checklist. Sayeed should be at the other side of the courtyard, Alyah deep into her nap, the servants home for their afternoon break, and Reema should be outside on laundry duty. Lots of should-bes.

If anyone saw her, if he figured it out, he'd kill her. Or worse. He'd kill David. Her fingers throbbed from their vice grip on the fabric, but it helped steady her shaky hands.

At the door to her destination, she pressed her ear against the wood and listened. Again, silence. Both hands covered the knob, one to turn and the other to steady the first. She twisted, cracked it open and peered in. The kitchen was empty. After closing it behind her, Ally rested her back against the frame and exhaled. Somewhere in this process, she had forgotten to breathe.

Next to the sink were clean dishes and knives. She picked up a blade and ran a finger over its sharp metal edge. The perfect size and edge to cut Sayeed into small pieces. Ally shook the thought away and returned the knife. Her plan was much more covert. In order to get out alive, it had to be.

She filled a glass with water, placed it on the counter, and started rummaging through the bottom cabinets. The first set revealed soap, rags, and pots. Behind the next pair of doors, she found mixing bowls and more pots. She started second guessing herself.

What if I imagined it? No. It's here. I saw it. I know I did.

She slid her glass of water down the counter and squatted in front of the third set of cabinets. Bottles of cleaners and bags of scouring pads stared back. When the supplies were pushed aside, her heart leapt to her throat.

The box was small and the words written in Urdu, but the picture of an ugly black rat said it all. After grabbing the prize, the other products were returned to their rightful spots and the cabinets were closed.

Back on her feet, she glanced at the door to make sure it remained sealed before pulling up her dress and tucking part of its hem under her chin. She tugged on the brown belt tightly wound around her waist.

During one of Sayeed's visits to her room, she had managed to kick it under her bed. With the help of a ballpoint pen and some sleepless nights, she created new notches in the brown strip until it fit snugly against her. She sucked in her stomach and tried to squeeze the box between the leather strap and her skin, but the package was too thick to fit.

During her second attempt at shoving it down, a shadow floated across the back corner of the room. She held her breath and looked up, locking gazes with Reema.

The girl's large hazel eyes switched from Ally, to the poison pressed against her skin, then back to her face. Reema stepped closer and then hesitated.

Ally had planned for such a situation, but now as everything unraveled, her brain slowed to a crawl. She couldn't remember what she was supposed to do. Explanations for why the abaya was hiked up and why there was a box of rat poison under her dress didn't materialize.

"Reema," Alyah's voice down the hall caused both of them to jump. The woman's footsteps and voice grew louder by the second as she spewed orders to the young girl. But neither moved. Box still against her stomach, Reema and Ally continued their silent staring match.

A voice deep inside whispered to drop the skirt and act as if nothing happened. But her limbs refused to comply. The child knew; Ally could see it in her face. Her chest tightened as a tear rolled down her cheek. Sayeed would kill her.

Reema nodded, as if agreeing with Ally's conclusion, and rushed to her side. She grabbed the poison out of her shaky hands. Heart in her throat, Ally cringed and waited for the girl to go running to Alyah with the evidence. Instead, the child yanked the white bag out of the box and pushed the sack under the leather belt around Ally's waist. Stunned, she watched as Reema tugged the fabric out from under Ally's chin, adjusted the gown, and tossed the empty box back into the cabinet before closing the door. Reema wiped the wetness from Ally's cheeks and gave her arm a quick squeeze before heading to the stove.

By the time Alyah entered the room, Ally leaned against the countertop, holding the glass of water for dear life while Reema made the afternoon tea. As usual, the woman's eyebrows formed almost a straight line when she glared at Ally. Grateful the marble counter braced her weight, Ally's heart pounded. She worked on making her breathing slow and normal. With her brain finally working, she took a slow swallow of the liquid.

Will Reema tell?

Alyah waved her hand and spewed Urdu as she approached. The all-too-familiar words "*mujhae akela chore do*" fell from her lips. She was pretty sure it meant "get the hell out of here," and although every bone in her body told her to do as the woman commanded, she knew it would look suspicious. Instead, she took another sip of water.

~

In her room, seated on the bed, Ally stared at the paper bag resting on her lap. From inside it, she pulled out Rodenticide—her retribution. Torn strips of old newspaper were stacked on the sheet beside her. She folded one, shaping it into a square pouch about two inches in size.

With the tip of a spoon, she scooped a little of the powder from the bag, poured it into the tiny pouch, and sealed it shut. She rolled a rubber band just above her elbow, high enough to be covered by the long sleeves of the abaya, and popped the packet into place between her skin and the rubber. When she waved her arm around, it didn't budge. A rare smile stretched across her face.

Success.

Another piece of newspaper was folded like the first, then she worked meticulously on creating nineteen more packets.

After he'd raped her the first couple of times, Ally's thoughts had gone from revenge to suicide. The stolen knife currently taped under her drawer was intended for that purpose. But when the cold blade touched her wrist, a sinking realization hit. She was replaceable. He'd find another woman to steal and lock away in this hell. That was unacceptable. There was only one way to end this story: Sayeed had to die.

As she creased the edges of the paper before folding it into a perfect envelope, she thought back to the documentary that had inspired this idea. It was about a battered woman in Africa who slowly poisoned her abusive husband. No one knew until the widow confessed to the crime years later. Hopefully this story would be the same, except she had no plans of confessing.

The contents of the packets would be added into his morning tea. Just a small amount every day, enough to hurt. Not to kill, at least not immediately. If she planned this right, he'd be dead by the end of the month and no one would know why.

Her hand trembled as she filled the tip of the spoon with poison, almost spilling it on the bed. She shook away the fear and focused on her ultimate goal. Sayeed's death was all that mattered, and it would happen slowly. He would mysteriously become sicker and sicker as the amount of poison increased.

Putting it in his chai would be easy. The bastard loved pretending he had a happy home. Which was why every morning at six thirty, Ally walked down the hallway, unsupervised, and served him his breakfast. Plenty of opportunity to taint his tea.

Ally was always watching, discreetly paying attention to everything he and the others did. In the past couple weeks, she'd even picked up on some Urdu words. All of it with the hope that one day it would help her get home.

She checked the clock on the wall and worked faster. Sayeed would arrive soon. It was something else she'd figured out. He loved routine. After his morning meal, he would stretch out his hand and lead her to the courtyard for their walks, their talks. If all he did was hold her palm and talk to her, she knew she was safe until the next day. But on walks like this morning, when he rubbed her arm and back repetitively, there was no doubt he'd be in her bed by sundown.

During those walks, when he only held her hand and spoke little, his lust was for Alyah and Ally was safe. A shiver rippled down her spine. The nights he spent with Alyah were the most traumatic for Ally. Since their rooms shared a common wall, she heard everything. Alyah's screams were hard to take. The words she yelled at Ally during the day, "mujhae akela chore do" were heart-wrenching to hear at night through her sobs.

His first wife hadn't pieced together the things she had, like how the pleas aroused him more. Some nights were so bad, it took every ounce of self-control Ally had to not rush in and help Alyah. By the morning, there would be purple tinged bruises on the woman's cheek or wrist. She'd considered pulling her aside, to tell her to keep her mouth shut and turn her emotions off. But it was too risky. In so many ways, his first wife was similar to Sayeed. Both enjoyed wielding their power, but unlike her husband, who killed and tortured, Alyah's pleasure came from terrorizing the innocent souls in the compound. It was the age-old theme: The victim becomes the bully.

Ally worried the woman would use the information against her. Alyah made it obvious just how much she hated Ally. The addition of a second wife meant the addition of a second in command. If the second wife provided the child, there would be a serious change in power, leaving Ally in charge and Alyah out in the cold.

Her mind drifted to another worry. The boys. There were ten or fifteen of them, not even old enough to shave. They wandered around the courtyard, laughing, playing. "My children," Sayeed called them, and they acted the part as they followed him around as if he were their shepherd and they the sheep. Every day after his walk with her, he disappeared behind the metal doors of the large two-story concrete building behind the compound, the boys in tow. Why were they here? What purpose did they serve?

The thought of what he might do with them sent a shudder rippling through her. She couldn't screw this up. Too many lives depended on her succeeding. Ally placed the filled packets and the supplies into the paper bag just as the grandfather clock on the other side of the building chimed nine times. Sayeed would arrive any second. His voice down the hall confirmed her prediction. She pulled the rubber band off her arm and tossed other supplies in the sack before shoving it under the bed.

Tomorrow.

There were no more tears. The panic attacks had diminished as well. Only a constant state of fear and hate remained. She had survived the unimaginable, the unsurvivable, and the realization made her stronger.

Dressed in a white cotton gown with her hands in her lap, she reminded herself of what she'd figured out about him. At some point in his life, Sayeed must have been sexually abused. The signs were there. His need for sexual control. How he stepped back sometimes and looked almost scared when she reached for his erection. An accidental touch the first time, but once she saw his reaction, it became very intentional.

Nights when his flashbacks were intense, he pushed her away and left quickly. On unlucky nights, the ones when the memories weren't as painful, none of her tactics stopped him. In the end, she'd lie there and escape to a safe place in her mind where he could never hurt her as he used her body.

"Sara." Sayeed closed the door behind him. Dressed in his typical white cotton pants and matching untucked shirt, he approached. She pretended not to notice that he kept something hidden behind his back and rose from the bed. The more compliant she appeared, the less interested he was and the quicker he'd leave. Pulling her dress over her head, she let the soft cotton crumple to the floor and stood naked before him.

His eyes raked her body over and over. He smiled his approval. When he was beside her, cold plastic brushed against her shoulder. Fear gripped Ally's throat when she finally realized what he had in his hand.

~

Leaning back in the shower, she allowed the cool water to wash away all traces of Sayeed. Her pulse raced against her ears. She'd left him on the bed staring at the pregnancy stick on the nightstand.

"Go take your shower while we wait for the results," Sayeed said. But there would be no celebration tonight. What would he do when he found out? A shiver ran through her.

Swallowing the fear, she poured a handful of shampoo and massaged it into her hair. If she had started with the poison a week earlier, he might have been too sick to even...

"Sara!"

Her hands froze in mid-scrub. Sayeed, red faced and still naked, grabbed her arm, pulling her out of the shower. Shampoo dripped down her forehead and into her eyes, burning them. The pain from that was less intense than the terror consuming her.

He dragged her to the little white stick on the corner of the table. "Read it," he growled.

Her heart pounded as she tried to think of the right words to say. "Sayeed, it takes some people years."

His fingers tightened around her arm as he pulled her closer, his mouth so close to her cheek that when he spoke his lips brushed against her slick skin. "Read. It."

Ally brought the stick closer. The pink minus sign trembled in her hand.

"What. Does. It. Say?"

She swallowed the terror rising in her throat and choked out the answer. "Negative."

His grip tightened. "Speak louder, Sara. What does it say?"

"Negative. It's negative."

"What does that mean?" He knew what it meant. They both did.

"I'm not pregnant." Before she said more, he threw her against the wall. Her body slammed against the concrete surface and she slid to the floor.

His slippers squeaked as he approached. "Look at me." Although the voice was low, the rage in his words was clear. "Why are you not pregnant?"

She trembled as she repeated her earlier statement. "These things take time, sometimes years..." His kick to her side silenced her explanation. Curled in a ball, her arms covered her head as she gasped for air.

"Answer the question. *Why* are you not pregnant?"

"I...don't know," Ally wheezed.

When his foot met her ribs a second time, pain exploded through her chest.

"Liar."

Heaving for air and desperate to make the violence stop, she said the first thing that popped into her mind. "Maybe it's you. Maybe you are infertile." As soon as the words flew out, Ally knew it was a mistake.

Another kick to her already tender spot and she couldn't breathe. He twisted her wet hair around his hand, pulling her to her knees. Her head tugged back, he glared at her. "Don't you ever say that again."

Gasping, Ally tried to calm him. "Sayeed, please..." When he yanked at the hair, a cry escaped her lips.

"Shut up! Shut your filthy mouth." With his free hand, he fondled himself, his erection growing under his touch. "If filth comes out of your mouth, then filth must enter it. Open your mouth, Sara."

With a hand on either side of her face, he pushed himself into her mouth. Breathing through her nose, she gagged each time he slammed himself to the back of her throat. The pain, his hips crashing into her face, it all became too much. The room spiraled. When she fell, she didn't feel her body hit the floor. Instead, what greeted her was a peaceful sweet darkness.

~

"Sara?" Nasif's voice and the loud raps on the door wakened her. Her naked frame shivered from resting against the marble floor. When she stretched, the fire in her abdomen reignited and with it the memories of the night before returned.

Ally's eyelids flew open. Her hair was dry. She must have been out for hours. As she scanned the space, her gaze rested on the crumpled bag poking out from under the bed. The sack needed to be moved, and put somewhere no one would find it. Fighting wave after wave of nausea, she sat up and waited for the pain to ebb. When it didn't, she bit her lip, climbed on all fours and began the painful trek to the bed.

The distance between her and the poison seemed to increase. Every move sent her to another level of agony. Sweat dripped down her face on to the marble. It was becoming harder and harder to swallow the screams.

The door squeaked open and Nasif poked his face in. He scanned the room, her bed, the bathroom, finding her on all fours behind the bed. "Sara?" He closed the door behind him and rushed to her side.

"I'm not dressed. You shouldn't be here," she wheezed out.

"Sayeed sent me. What happened?"

"My ribs, he broke my ribs." Her voice was a whisper. It hurt to breathe, much less talk. When she lifted her arm to point to the spot, the room spun out of control.

He grabbed her before she toppled over. Squeezing her eyes shut, she focused on short pants of air and ignored how his fingers stabbed like blades into her body as he felt her for injuries.

"I need to put you on the bed." He lifted her arm, wrapped it around his shoulder, and pulled her up. Ally cried with each agonizing step as Nasif guided her to the mattress and sat her down.

He muttered in Urdu while he examined her back. "I think you have two or three cracked ribs. But since we have no x-rays, I can only guess."

Out of his backpack, he pulled a black leather pouch. "He's never hit you before. I don't understand," he whispered. Sifting through the foil-lined trays of pills, he popped out two white disks and handed them to her. "Take this. It's for the pain."

She placed them on her tongue and swallowed while pointing at the pregnancy stick still lying on the floor. Confusion turned to guilt as he picked it up and analyzed the white plastic. "This is my fault. I shouldn't have..."

"I'd rather he beat me to death than have his child."

He avoided her gaze and threw the stick in the trash. Ignoring her body's painful reminders that speaking was not an option, she gritted her teeth and pushed out the words. "Nasif, this is no longer about you and your guilt. Do you understand?"

Instead of responding, he squatted and collected her dress from the floor. When he didn't rise, she looked at him, worried he'd discovered the bag. To her relief, he just seemed lost in thought, as if considering his options.

"If you even consider stopping the Depo shots, I will make sure he is made aware of your involvement. Is that clear?"

Nasif brought the fabric to her and pulled it over her head. Although he tried to be gentle when he threaded her arm into the sleeve, a groan escaped her.

"The medicine should take effect and give you relief soon. I will get Reema to take care of you." With a hand on her back, he guided her until her head rested on the pillow. She hissed through the ache when he turned her onto her broken side. "Take deep breaths. The pain will ease soon... Good. That should feel a little better."

And it did, with little being the key word. "Why is Reema even here? What happened to her family?" she grunted out.

"The same as the rest of us. Sayeed happened."

Nasif tucked pillows behind her shoulders and sat on the bed beside Ally. "Reema was from a very rich family before this. Her father, Jamil, was Pakistan's Minister of Industries. A successful businessman, he believed the government should be run without corruption.

"Sayeed tried to bribe Jamil. That is how he gets his power. He pays powerful people under the table. In return, they give him what he wants. But Jamil refused. Sayeed felt insulted and made a lesson of him by personally having Jamil and his family killed.

"I heard Sayeed made the poor man watch while his men raped Jamil's wife. Then he killed them. First the son then the mother. Both shot in the head one by one." A shudder ripped through Ally, but this time it had nothing to do with the pain.

"We hid Reema's identity and pretended she was the servant's daughter, otherwise she would have been shot too."

"*We* hid her identity?"

He smiled. "You're feeling better I see. I had to hide her. It was the only way to keep her alive."

Things were becoming a little foggy. Ally tried to stay focused. "She must have been scared."

He nodded and sat silent for a moment before answering. "She was for a very long time. Reema had never worked before. She used to cry a lot in the beginning until Alyah beat it out of her. I fixed her broken arm and stitched her up a few times. Eventually, she stopped crying. Stopped speaking."

"Why hasn't anyone come for her? The police? Relatives?"

Nasif laughed. "He would kill them. Anyway, why the sudden

interest in the girl?"

"I'm not sure if I imagined it, but I think she spoke to me."

Nasif's eyes widened. "No."

"She called me Didi that first night."

A slow grin stretched across his face. "Selective mute. I'm sure you didn't imagine it. And you know why she called you Didi, not Baji?"

Ally shook her head.

His smiled widened. "Because I told her you're Indian not Pakistani. What a brave, smart girl."

Anger and a strong need to protect the child filled Ally's foggy consciousness. "But not smart and brave enough to save?"

His grin vanished and a sadness replaced the pride that was in his eyes just moments ago. "This is Reema's fate."

The words left a bitter taste in Ally's mouth. "Really? Is that what you think, Nasif? That it's Reema's fate to be treated like a dog? Is this my fate too?"

He patted her head. "Sara, the only way she can survive here is if she learns to adjust with Alyah, and she has. She is Alyah's property now. Don't get in Alyah's way. She's looking for a reason to come after you, and if you interfere, you will only make Reema's life more difficult."

She ignored how he referred to the child as a possession and focused on a bigger worry. "What has Sayeed done to Reema?"

"Done? Why would he... Oh, I see. No, he hasn't touched her, if that is what you mean. She's not his kind."

"But I am." An uncomfortable silence filled the room. So many lives damaged because of one man. "Someone has to stop him."

Nasif climbed off the bed and packed his bag. "Yes, Sayeed must be stopped. There is no question. But not yet. If he dies, there will be no more help for Hasna. The treatments will stop."

Anger warmed her chest. As much as Ally tried to keep her emotions in check, the medication was making it hard to rein them in. "So to keep your dying wife alive, I need to continue being raped and beaten. And Reema? She needs to be tormented for the rest of her life too? What about those boys he trains every day? You know what he's training them for, don't you? And no one can stop him until when, Nasif? After your beloved wife dies?"

His face paled. “I have two daughters I still need to marry off and a wife who is dying. Please understand my situation...”

“Your situation?” she snapped. “My bones are broken because I’m not pregnant, Nasif. What should I do the next time he brings in a pregnancy test and it’s negative? And the next and the next? Allow it to happen? Pray he doesn’t kill me? Or should I pray for Hasna’s death? Is that what you would like for me to do?”

He rested his backpack beside her and stared at his hands. “You are right. I am a selfish man. My Hasna, she is my world and she is dying. I am not ready to lose that world yet.” Nasif squatted down and reached under the bed. Picking up the brown paper bag of poison, he tossed it into his backpack. Zipping it up, he put it over his shoulder and walked to the door. “I’m sorry, Sara.”

CHAPTER TEN

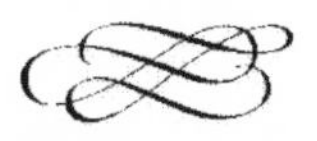

THE PRICE OF LOVE

TWENTY-SIX MONTHS AFTER ALLY'S DISAPPEARANCE

Seated on a couch in a cheap hotel, Dave returned the phone to its cradle and ran his nails through his hair. Other than the two messages left by Kate, his voicemail was empty. He let out a breath. What the hell was he supposed to tell her?

Kate, my wife's alive. Thank you for the past six months. Let's forget it ever happened.

He cringed at how stupid it sounded. Not that he needed to say anything, anyway. By now, everyone he'd ever met was probably being questioned by the government. Images of men in suits sitting in his parents' living room flashed through his head. He swallowed hard, trying to stop the five cups of caffeine he'd consumed from continuing their ascent to his mouth.

His knee bounced under the coffee table, hitting the glass. Items on the table shook and fell from the impact.

"Will you stop that?" Reya growled beside him. In her hand was a cup of diet soda she saved from the impact of his overactive knee.

"Sorry," he muttered. He got up and paced the suite.

After leaving Jerry and the CIA agent at the office, Dave's paranoia of being watched had gotten the better of him. He'd tossed his cell, withdrew cash from the bank, hailed a cab, and spent some serious money at a local electronics store before calling the only two people he could trust: Ally's siblings.

He looked over at the guy stretched out on the bed. Dressed in basketball shorts and a baggy 76ers shirt, Nikhil lay with his back propped against the headboard and a computer on his lap. His thick black hair was parted to the side, and the round glasses he wore framed his tanned face. Since he was their older brother, Ally and Reema called him Bhai, and since Dave wasn't Indian, he just called him Nik. Although a doctor by profession, Nik was also the most computer-savvy person he knew. Within minutes of entrusting the flash drive to him, he had the contact list downloaded to everyone's notebooks. Two hours later, they'd searched almost all of the names.

Dave's sneakers squeaked against the faux wood floor as he paced. Questions filled his brain, none of which he had answers to.

Will the CIA help? And if they don't, what then? How are we supposed to go to Pakistan and do this? None of us even speaks the language.

"No fucking way." Reya's eyes were the size of hockey pucks, and her gaze was glued to the screen. "Boys, remember how I said these people were the shadiest of the shady? Well, I was wrong. Come check this out."

He slid next to her on the couch and stared at a picture of a long-faced, bearded man with a white turban. "Do you recognize him?" she asked, jabbing her finger at the screen.

Before he could respond, Nik spoke up. "That's Ibrahim Ayoub, right?"

She nodded and read from the screen. "The leader of the second largest terrorist organization in the world. Ayoub has a fifteen-million-dollar bounty on his head by the FBI and is number four on their list of the ten most wanted terrorists."

Dave rested his head against the sofa and stared at the ceiling. From leaders of radical groups to military defense contractors, every name they'd researched had added to the sinking feeling inside him.

We're fucked.

"We need to talk." Nik squeezed his shoulder. Dave glanced up at him, noticing the worry lines creasing his forehead. "There's nothing I wouldn't do for Alisha, but let's be realistic here. This Sayeed guy is obviously a terrorist." He pointed to Reya's monitor.

"And his friendly sidekick over there happens to be Satan. If we try to take them on, we'll be dead before the flight attendant has a chance to say 'Welcome to Pakistan.'"

Dave's stomach gurgled and twisted. The words that had been running through his brain were finally spoken by Nik.

"I guess what I'm trying to say is we need help. You need to call that CIA guy."

As if tapping into the other voice in Dave's head, Reya barked back, "No. We have information the CIA wants. They need to make the next move, not us."

Nik let out an exasperated sigh and returned to his spot on the bed. "Come on, Rey, if he doesn't call, then what?"

"He'll call. Give him time," she snapped.

As the two bickered, Dave closed his eyes and pressed his fingers against his brows to ease the throbbing. Rey was a risk taker and Nik the calm voice of reason. Both of them made sense. What the fuck was he supposed to do?

"What if you called and gave them Sayeed's address?" Nik asked.

Dave turned on the sofa to stare at his brother-in-law. "Do we have it?"

Eyes glued to the monitor, Ally's brother smiled while he typed. "The house is in Lahore, Pakistan. And here's the address."

As his fingers flew across the keyboard, Dave and Reya hunched over his shoulder, watching the activity on the screen. And soon a layout of an L-shaped building appeared, each of its rooms labeled.

Unable to speak, Dave stared at the hand-drawn image on the screen.

"Oh. My. God," Reya turned the laptop for a better view.

Nik's fingers moved across the lines and stopped. He zoomed the screen to the hand written word in the little rectangular box. *Sara.*

"Di," Reya whispered, squeezing Dave's arm. "Even if they don't help, we know where she is."

"Come on, Rey. Think." When Nik closed the file, the screen shifted to the drive's menu. "Yes, we have an address, but even if she's there, she's probably surrounded by the most dangerous people in the world."

Dave scanned the list on the monitor while they argued. One of the folders caught his eye. "What's in this file?" He pointed to the first item on the list labeled pictures.

Nik hesitated and glanced over at his sister. When Dave looked over at Reya, she averted her gaze. He glared at both of them. "You're keeping things from me? Show me the fucking pictures. Now."

When Nik clicked on it, Dave sucked in a breath as he took in the image. The bastard stood smiling with his arm around Ally's shoulders. She stared ahead, her face expressionless and eyes lifeless.

His stomach tightened. Heat snaked through his veins and his fists clenched. "Son of a bitch."

"There's more." Nik slid out of the way, letting Dave take his spot.

A click of the arrow revealed the second image. It was a picture of him sitting in the park down the street from his apartment. "What the...?"

"Keep looking," Nik urged.

He clicked on the next and the next. Dated pictures of himself flew across the screen.

"We think these were given to Di." Reya put her hands on Dave's shoulders and squeezed.

That didn't make any sense. Fear built in the pit of his stomach. He followed the progression of dates and clicked past each. Why would they show her pictures of him?

As soon as he thought the question, the answer popped on the screen. Every organ in his body turned to ice as he stared at Kate and him lip-locked in front of the hospital's service elevators.

His hands shook at the thought of Ally sitting in some dark room looking at this. Not only had she suffered because of that bastard, but he had added to her misery.

"There's one more," Reya's voice pulled him back.

This time the image was through the half shuttered blinds of Dave's office. They were kissing, his hands pressing Kate's hips into his. Dave's mouth dropped and his heart tried to burst through his chest as the world around him spun.

The mixture of coffee and acid inched up his throat. He leapt off the bed and sprinted to the bathroom. After spewing every drop of liquid he'd ingested in the past eight hours, Dave rested his forehead against the wall.

All this time...

While she went through hell, he'd been screwing someone else.

Dave screamed silently into the plaster.

The bastard had taken her away. Raped her. Beat the life out of her and threw Dave's stupidity in her face. She'd seen the picture; he could see it in her eyes.

Clenched hands pounded the drywall as tears spilled. There was nothing he could do about any of it except fucking cry.

His fists broke through the surface. Instead of calming him, the hole and his throbbing knuckles fueled his rage. Another punch and another until his hands pulsed and he heaved.

"Nice."

He jumped around to face the familiar voice. Still dressed as he had been that morning, the agent leaned against the door, cross-armed, with a smile tugging at his lips.

Aching fists still clenched, Dave stepped forward. "What the fuck do you want, Edil?"

The man straightened and raised his hands in front of him. "Take it down a notch there, Hulk man."

The firmness in the agent's voice made him step back.

He nodded his approval. "That's better. Call me Eddie."

The two men eyed each other. Neither spoke. Voices warred within Dave's head about whether to beg for the man's help or to tell him to leave. Not sure what the hell he was supposed to do, he sat on the side of the tub, rested his forehead in his palms, and focused on the tiled floor. Soon the sound of plastic hitting porcelain filled the space when Eddie shut the toilet lid and sat on it.

"Can I look at that?" he asked and took a stack of washcloths from the metal rack over his head.

Dave glanced at the man in confusion.

"Your fists that are obviously not made of steel. Mind if I check the damage?" Eddie leaned over the counter, wetting one of the towels. Without waiting for permission, he grabbed an injured wrist and wiped away the blood and debris.

He flinched as rough fabric scraped the cuts, turning the

already burning skin into an inferno of pain.

Eddie chuckled as he tended to the wounds. "You might want to breathe because I'm going to need you to stay conscious while we talk."

Dave didn't bother responding. He had nothing to say.

"Let me guess, you just realized that Sayeed is Goliath and you're David." He laughed and shook his head. "Get it, David and Goliath?"

Dave rolled his eyes. "If he's Goliath, I'm a pathetic lizard whose legs have been cut off."

Eddie cleared his throat and worked on Dave's other hand. "The proper name for that, my friend, is a snake."

"I'm timing you!" Reya's high-pitched voice resonated through the closed door.

Eddie tilted his head in her direction. "She said she'd give us ten minutes before she kicks my ass out the door."

Dave pulled his hands away and sent a silent prayer to the heavens as he stared at probably the only person on the planet who could help him. "What do you want?"

"Well, after you left this morning, the good doctor and I had a chat. Actually, he threatened and I listened. He told me you are a stubborn son-of-a-bitch and will most likely jump on an airplane and get yourself killed."

Dave clenched the terry fabric and fixated on the pain instead of his growing impatience.

"He then proceeded to tell me if I let that happen, he would find me and cut my balls off while I sleep." Eddie shook his head and smirked. "The thing is, I believe him."

"You showed up in my bathroom to tell me this?"

Eddie scanned the room as he considered Dave's question. "It is a little strange, isn't it?" He leaned forward, resting his elbows on his knees. "I wanted you to know that I did some digging on Sara Irfani."

Every cell in his body focused on the agent's words.

"My sources tell me Sayeed does have a second wife named Sara. The problem is, at this point it's just speculation that she is *your* wife. Even if it is, we have no reason to believe she's there against her will."

Dave's chest tightened at the tone in his voice, at the way the guy stared at his feet. "What are you trying to say?"

"The CIA is refusing to be involved."

With the only hope for Ally ripped from his fingers, anger pulsed through his neck, making it hard to get out the words. "They're just going to leave her there?"

He nodded. "The CIA will not help you."

Dave's mind raced. There had to be a way to change their minds. "And the memory stick? Don't they want that?"

Eddie cleared his throat. "They already have the information."

After all the work he did to keep them off his trail and to keep the information safe, the words were a slap to an already bruised ego. He had failed again. "How? I tossed my cell, didn't use a credit card. What did I do wrong?"

Eddie leaned back against the toilet tank and shrugged. "Do you remember this morning when I connected the Blackberry to my computer to show you the pictures? I placed a microchip in the device. It tracked your location and the internet activity of all the electronics within a twenty-foot radius of it."

Dave placed his hands over his head. He had screwed up before he ever left the fucking building. There was no anger left—just sadness and the realization of how pathetic he was.

"It's not something I'm proud of. But it was a matter of national security and needed to be done."

"Nobody's going to help her," Dave whispered.

"That's not what I said. What I said was the CIA won't help."

Their gazes locked. The agent leaned in close. "I know Lahore. The people. The language. The culture. I have connections. If anyone has a chance of getting her, it's me."

Dave's breath stuck in his chest, he stared at the man in disbelief. "Why?"

He shrugged. "I don't think she's there of her own free will and want to help."

"You're expecting me to believe that you're going to go against government orders to play mercenary?"

A smile tugged at the corners of his mouth. "That's exactly what I'm expecting you to believe."

Dave searched his face for a clue of what the man was hiding, but he gave nothing away. So he tried another angle. "What's in it for you?"

Eddie placed the unused washcloths on the counter and dried his hands. "Money. I need the money."

He eyed the man, waiting for him to continue. Yes, there was more to this than what Eddie was saying, but he didn't care. The guy knew what to do and had a plan.

"This requires tapping into some of my informants. It won't be cheap. There's a house across from Irfani's that's perfect to set up shop. We'll need to purchase some surveillance equipment..."

"How much?"

"Half a million dollars, give or take."

Dave's brain throbbed. Where the hell would he get that kind of money? The image of the room labeled *Sara*, and the thoughts of what must have happened to her there crashed into his mind. He shook his head. Nothing else mattered except bringing her home. "I'll get it to you, but I'm coming with."

Eddie chuckled. "I expected as much. So here's how this will play out. I'll take only you. No one else. And you"—he jabbed a finger into Dave's shoulder—"will do everything I tell you. You're not allowed to think. I am the brains, do you understand?"

"Get my wife and I will do whatever you want."

"If you try to undermine me and go at this on your own, I will leave you behind."

Dave nodded as adrenaline pumped through him. They were going to bring her home. "Deal, but once we're there you will tell me what's really going on."

He chuckled. "Agreed."

A loud banging sent Dave jumping to his feet. "Two minutes left," Reya screamed.

He stared between the door and Eddie, trying to figure out how to handle the two on the other side. "I need to talk to them."

~

"What the hell is wrong with you?" Reya glared at both Dave and Nik as they paced the small space. "Are you really buying this shit he's selling?"

"We have no other choice," Nik said. "We don't know anything about Pakistan, and he has resources we don't."

"Do you think the CIA will sit on their asses and be okay with him taking money under the table like this? He's a slimy piece of shit bastard trying to take advantage of our situation. If he can lie to the U.S. government, what makes you think he wouldn't lie to us? And how do you know he's not one of the guys the old man warned you about?"

Dave ran a hand through his damp hair. Everything she said was true, but it was the only shot he had. "I trust him. And like Nik said, he's all we've got. Unless you have any other suggestions?" He cut her off as soon as she opened her mouth. "Wait. Do you have any *realistic* suggestions? Because none of us has a clue what the hell we're doing. The last thing we want is to take a seriously messed-up situation and fuck it up. She's alive, Rey, and if we do something stupid that gets her killed..." He didn't finish his sentence, didn't have to.

Reya sealed her lips and gazed across the room at him. "I just want my Di, and I'm tired of people screwing with her and us." Nik tugged her into his arms and held her close as she cried.

"Is your sister like you?"

Everyone turned to face Eddie standing at the bathroom entrance.

Reya wiped her cheeks and stared him down, her voice choked. "She's nothing like me. She's patient and gentle. Beautiful in every way. She means everything to me."

"If she's there, I'll find her. And if she wants to come home, I will bring her home." Eddie kept his gaze fixed on Reya. "You're not sure if you can trust me. I get that. So tell you what, come up with two hundred fifty now and pay me the other half when I bring her home. Consider it payment for services rendered."

"What guarantee is there that you won't take the money and disappear?" she asked.

He shrugged. "There isn't. But what if I do find her and bring her home? Would it be worth it?"

"My dad will give us the money." Nik turned his cell phone on and punched the keys. Minutes later the phone dinged and he smiled, reading the screen. "You will have the cash in about a week."

"Great, I'll tell you where to send it." Eddie walked to the front door and grabbed the knob. "As soon as it's in my account, the good doctor and I will leave. In the meantime, I need to get you a new identity and passport."

Before he walked out, he turned to them. "A man by the name

of Tim should be here in an hour to take care of the bathroom. You don't have to be here. He can let himself in." He shut the door behind him.

Dave fell onto the couch. Reya and Nik followed suit on either side of him. They watched the door Eddie exited in silence. "What just happened?" Dave finally asked.

Reya put her head on his shoulder. "Fuck if I know." She pointed at her brother. "But Bhai agreed with it. So if this goes to pot, it's his fault."

CHAPTER ELEVEN

THE GAME

FIVE MONTHS POST KIDNAPPING

"Pink?" Dressed in only a bra and long, brown cotton skirt, Ally gaped at the orthopedic tape in Nasif's hand.

He grinned and winked at Reema. "I saw it at the shop and thought of you. It's colorful, rebellious like you."

With her arms raised, she watched him work. He pressed the tape below her bra and stretched the bandage around her torso. The pull of the fabric against her ribs no longer brought tears. For the first time in a month, Ally inhaled without pain.

"I'm locked away from home in a fortress on the other side of the world. Colorful and rebellious are not words that come to mind." The bitter edge in her voice was purposeful and the flash of guilt on his face, her reward.

He shook his head and continued taping in silence.

Things had been different between them since the day he discovered the poison. Colder. As much as she hated him for doing it, she hated losing her almost friend and missed his company.

"How's Hasna?"

"Better. The pain seems to have eased. We took her in for tests last week, and they think her tumor may have stopped growing. "

"That's wonderful, Nasif. I'm happy for you."

He flashed her a look and kept working. "Are you?"

When she tried to respond, he waved her off and grabbed the pair of scissors Reema held. Nasif cut the end of the tape from the roll and tugged at the fabric, stretching another layer around her trunk. "Sayeed is waiting outside for you." He avoided her gaze and concentrated harder than necessary on wrapping her.

Ally's breath caught in her throat. Sayeed had banned her from his presence since the negative pregnancy test. Alyah now brought him his breakfast, and their morning walks had ceased. All of which was a relief to her. Until now.

"Is he planning on killing me?" The words were barely a whisper because she already knew the answer.

Nasif avoided her gaze and cut another strip of tape. "I don't know."

Stunned, she spent the rest of the time lost in thought as he worked. Knowing Sayeed, there was no question in her mind he'd make her death painful. As she considered what that end might be like, she realized the idea of her death no longer stirred fear or anger. Nothing.

She eyed the little man beside her and his thick glasses. The sad reality was that their situations weren't very different. They were both puppets in an evil man's game. Sometimes her resentment got the best of her, making it hard for her to see how bad his life was as well. After securing the tape, he packed up the supplies, zipped his backpack shut, and turned to leave.

"Nasif." She considered her words carefully as she waited for him to face her. This might be the last thing she'd ever say to him. "I said some harsh things to you, and I want you to know that I would never wish ill on Hasna or you or anyone else in your family."

Although silent, the corners of his mouth quivered. "I will pray for you." With a squeeze of her elbow, he walked out the door.

Reema closed the door behind him and walked to Ally's side. Although just a child, in the past month, she'd nursed Ally back to health. Her silent, emotionless face, and even lack of eye contact, had been oddly comforting.

An ache tugged in her chest. *What happens to her once I'm gone?*

"You will have to go back to Alyah and kitchen duty now."

The girl unfolded a brown, long-sleeved abaya from the bed and pulled it over Ally's head.

"Remember, she's like one of those little dogs. All they do is bark, bark, bark." Reema's cheeks twitched for a second and then nothing. "I know you understand English." Instead of responding, the girl wrapped a light blue hijab around Ally's head. When she turned to leave, Ally grabbed her wrist. "Reema, I am grateful for all you have done. You never deserved this life." The child's eyes filled with moisture. She nodded and disappeared from the room, leaving Ally alone. To pace. To think.

Yes, her life was hell and she'd found herself praying more times than not for death, but it didn't feel like the end. She thought about Reema and Nasif and what they'd gone through because of one man. Their stories couldn't end like this.

What if she was the one person who could change all of that? The question sounded ridiculous the second it popped into her head, but still...there it floated, challenging her.

Manipulate the monster, a voice whispered from within.

It was what she needed to have done all along. Too lost in fear, she had cowered from him and hidden away in her room, reinforcing Sayeed's opinion that she was weak and useless.

She rolled her shoulders and walked to the door. Too many lives were at stake. It was time to play the game.

~

When she entered the courtyard, the rays of the sun stung her eyes. Ally sought shade under a nearby tree, letting the sounds of birds and the rustling of the trees soothe her.

The building itself sat in the middle of ten acres of land. Thick banyan trees overflowing with dark green foliage shaded most of the property. Their pale, twisted trunks provided the eerie illusion of an imprisoning forest. As imposing as they were, the trees provided comfort when juxtaposed against the twenty-foot concrete barricade that encircled the compound and its land.

The ugly gray wall was topped with shards of glass. Although hard to see, thin wires snaked around the jagged pieces, buzzing with current, ready to strike with the slightest touch. More than one poor, distracted bird had met an instant death by coming into contact with the electrified glass. For Sayeed's added security, there was only one way in and out of the grounds—the ornate iron-gate.

Two young men in jeans and T-shirts sat on plastic patio

chairs on either side of the gate. Their machine guns rested against thick concrete columns to which the gates were hinged. When they stood and nodded in reverence to an approaching figure, her muscles tightened. Sayeed had arrived.

He had long since abandoned his three-piece suits for linen pants and matching light-colored cotton shirts that hung over his hips. As he spoke, he patted each man on the shoulder. To the untrained eye, Sayeed seemed encouraging and respectful. But ever so slightly, the men stiffened under his touch and avoided his gaze. The pride in his eyes—an indication he noticed their fear. He continued talking with them, relishing in their discomfort.

Ally made a mental list of the people he allowed in his life. Being part of his circle meant knowing he could kill you at any moment. As long as you served a purpose, you were safe. Although believed to be barren, Alyah ran the house and understood his routines and expectations implicitly. She was valuable. Nasif, the trusted doctor. Amir and Kadeen, the guards he trusted with his life. Those four people Sayeed would not kill...yet.

And Ally? He'd already broken her bones. She wasn't pregnant. Why keep her? Too scared to talk, their walks had been quiet and unsatisfying for him. He'd told her as much. Obviously, his patience had run out. She needed to figure out how to make him believe he needed her before it was too late.

As if sensing her gaze, he turned and smiled, assessing her for a reaction. Her breath caught in her throat and her body shook. No matter how hard she tried to prepare for him, the effect he had on her was immediate. Which was fine as long as he didn't realize it. She nodded but kept her face emotionless despite the erratic thudding of her heart.

While he made his way to her, she focused on the one thing she knew could calm her. With each approaching step, Sayeed's round body transformed. He became taller. Leaner. The once circular face lengthened. His neatly trimmed beard and the acne scars beneath disappeared into smooth clean-shaven skin. The most beautiful smile stretched across a pronounced jaw line. Instead of piercing dark brown eyes, hints of blue surrounded by a sea of green stared back. David.

An ache, a hunger for him to be real crawled through the depths of her, along with a need to feel his arms around her. She gripped the tree for support. If only in her imagination, her hero had arrived.

He stretched out his hand to her, and she watched the long fingers that had brought her pleasure more times than she could count fade away. In their place were shorter, plumper ones. The hunger from moments ago was replaced with a wave of nausea as reality hit. No amount of fantasizing would bring him back.

The harsh realization brought with it the reminder that there would be no heroes coming to her rescue. Ally searched Sayeed's face for clues he'd noticed her bout of craziness, but he seemed oblivious. She accepted his outstretched hand and allowed him to lead her into the forest.

"You seem well."

With a quick prayer for courage, she forced her response. "I'm surprised you noticed."

The dark, thick commas over his eyes rose. A lump formed in her throat. Was she pushing too quickly? She lifted her own brow and met his gaze. Instead of annoyance, a smile spread across his face. Sayeed pulled her hand to his lips. "I missed you, Sara."

His kiss flipped a switch in her. Every organ on overdrive, her muscles warmed and tightened, ready to run. A natural reaction, considering the things he'd done to her. Instead of succumbing to her fears, she tugged her hand away and walked down the narrow uneven path, hoping she was doing the right thing. The crunching of dead leaves and his laugh gave her all the assurance she needed.

Thick fingers wrapped around her hand and he walked alongside. "You have nothing to say?"

"I'm not sure what to say."

When he tightened his grip, she focused on the tree roots underfoot, fighting the urge to pull away.

"Let me be more clear. I've missed our talks from before."

"Before?"

He chuckled. "Yes, in Philadelphia."

The acidic taste of the morning's tea mixed with bile rose to her mouth. She swallowed it down and tried to keep emotion out of her voice as she lied. "I don't understand."

Sayeed stood in front of her, forcing her to stop, his dark eyes probing for a reaction. Sirens roared in her head, announcing danger, but she fought the reflex to look away. The sounds of nature faded while her heart pounded faster, louder. With his free hand, he wiped a bead of sweat from her brow. He trailed his knuckles against her cheek and traced his thumb across her lips.

Ally cleared her throat. "Why the games, Sayeed?"

He scrutinized her and stayed quiet for a painfully long moment. Just as she began to second guess herself, a slow smile stretched across his face. "And what game would that be, my love?"

"This intimidation game. Say what you need." Again, his gaze bore into her. A battle of emotions raged within, fear and hate challenging each other for dominance. Focusing on the hate, Ally allowed the other to ebb and stared at his ear, waiting for his next move.

"Now, I am the one that is not understanding," he said.

"You understand completely."

His jaw dropped at her challenge. He looked to the sky for a moment and laughed. Sayeed folded his hands as if in prayer and pointed them at her. "This is the part of you I've missed. And this is why I fell in love with you." His palms sandwiched her face seconds before bearded lips scratched against her forehead.

He rested his head against hers. "If anyone else ever said the things you say, I'd kill them. But you, when you say them, it's exciting. Just when I'm ready to give up on you, here you are. Back for good?"

The smell of coffee and garlic on his breath and the threat laced in his words fogged her thoughts. Ally swallowed hard, forcing herself to stay on task. "As long as you don't break any more of my bones."

He laughed so hard he had to wipe tears from his eyes. Once he had regained his composure, he pulled her into a hug and squeezed. "Deal. Now come, let me show you something."

They wandered off their regular path toward the mysterious two-story building hidden behind the trees. The graying concrete house with soot stains along its sides was small in comparison to the one she shared with Sayeed and Alyah. There were no glass windows on this home, just openings with brown wooden shutters.

Boys in matching navy shorts and pale blue, short-sleeved shirts sat in three rows of five on the gravel outside. An older man wrote on a chalkboard with his back to them while the children watched.

To the side of the building was a smaller, one-room structure. Seated on a chair by its front door was Amir. A machine gun rested against the wall beside him. When their gazes locked, he averted his.

She pointed to the students. "Who are they?"

Sayeed wrapped an arm around her shoulder and gave her a quick squeeze. "They are my boys, and I have you to thank for them."

"Me?"

"Let me show you something." He pulled out a small black spiral notebook from his side pocket and handed it to her. She touched its wire binding and tried to process how she, the book, and the boys were connected.

Sayeed whispered, "Do you know why I picked you?"

Ally's fingers froze. She'd asked the question a million times since the nightmare began. "No."

"I was at a convention and heard you speak about depression and some other emotional nonsense. The minute you opened your mouth, I knew you were the one. So I made an appointment to meet the great doctor." He laughed and rubbed her back. "Back then in your office, everything out of your mouth was a gem, a pearl. I would leave our meetings and write down all of it because I didn't want to forget. So many of my decisions were based on the things you said. But since you've come, you've been different. Until today."

"You dragged me away from my home and locked me up. How exactly did you think I would react?"

"True." He kissed her temple while his fingers traced a path down her spine. "Whatever the reason. You are back now and *that* is what matters."

She tried to draw the conversation to the children and their purpose. "And them?"

"Ahh, yes the boys. Do you remember our first session?"

"No," she lied. How could she not? She'd relived each of their two sessions over and over the past five months. His vague reasons for coming. The way he asked her personal questions. Everything screamed danger. If she had only followed her gut sooner.

He positioned himself behind Ally and circled his arms under her chest. Resting his chin on her shoulder, Sayeed's breath burned against her ear as he flipped through pages of scribbled writing, stopping halfway through the book.

"See here?" He pointed and read. "To build healthier relationships, I need to stop intimidating people and work on developing relationships of mutual respect. The only way they will do anything for me is if they feel safe with me."

He scraped his bearded skin against her cheek. "And *that*, my love, is exactly what I'm doing."

Ally stared at the blue letters on the page, trying to ignore the way her gut twisted at his words. The lives of fifteen boys were ruined because of her?

"You were right. Once I pretended to care, they started to listen, to respect me."

"You told me you were having trouble at your job. I thought we were working on how to build a better relationship with your colleagues."

"Ha! You do remember. Well, I lied about the job, but your lessons were still very relevant."

One of the kids in the back row turned to stare at Sayeed and Ally. Smaller than the rest, his enormous eyes and smile caused an ache in her heart. Everything about him screamed innocence.

Sayeed laughed and waved. "They are so naïve, no? Easy to manipulate."

The child raised his palm. When Ally returned the gesture, his face brightened and he rocked his thin hips in excitement.

"Umber!" the teacher yelled, snapping the child back to attention.

Ally tore her gaze away from the child and looked over at Sayeed. "Why are they here?"

He flipped through the pages and shrugged. "I bought them."

"What do you mean, you bought them? They're not loaves of bread." She cringed at the anger she heard in her voice and braced herself for his wrath.

"I love when you question me like that." He chuckled and nipped at her ear. "They are from an orphanage in Islamabad. All twelve years old and all orphans. They needed a place to live." He shrugged. "So I bought them and gave them a home and food and school. In return, they call me Sayeed Babba."

"Why?"

"Because they consider me their father."

"No, why are you doing this?"

"Because of you and what you taught me. If they felt safe and respected, then one day they will do something for me."

"What do you want them to do?"

"Ah, that's another story for another day."

Goose bumps swept across her skin. "I have seen them with weapons before. Normal children don't use weapons."

When he laughed, the heat of his breath burned her skin. "Well, normal is subjective, no? You taught me that. Here let me show you."

He flipped through the pages while Ally pushed the topic further. "What are you grooming these children to do?"

"See, what one culture believes to be normal, another might consider abnormal. Such pearls."

The fear of what might become of the children was making it hard for her to stay in control. She needed to rein it in. "I asked you a question."

His arms tightened and her still-tender ribs screamed out in pain. "You did and I chose to ignore it. Just because I allow you to speak like this does not mean you control me or have a right to know everything, my love."

With a sigh, he waved at Amir, who in turn stood and entered the building he guarded.

"Can I tell you a secret?"

Although the room was dark, the afternoon sun filled the space enough for her to see. Shelves filled with guns lined the back wall. "Are you really asking for my permission, Sayeed?"

"No." He laughed. "I'll give you a hint. Amir is in that room preparing for something. Do you know what he's preparing for?"

A shiver ran down her spine, but Ally said nothing.

"Your execution."

Every muscle in her body stilled. All emotion shut off.

"He is supposed to kill you, love."

Amir exited carrying a black duffel bag and closed the door. He placed it on the ground and stared back. A knife. A gun. One weapon would make sense. Why a bag of them? Did it matter? No. If she had to pick her killer, it would be Amir. He seemed to be the most merciful. She hoped.

"But no worries. I think I'll keep you around for a little

longer." Sayeed waved at her executioner, who nodded and returned to the room with bag in hand.

Still frozen and unable to breathe, she watched on. He kissed her cheek. "Consider today your birthday, love. Your second chance at life. What gift would you like for your birthday? Money is no object."

Amir locked the door and returned to the chair. His shoulders relaxed as if a weight had been removed from them.

Ally stared at the boys. Somehow she needed to help them. Amir's gaze locked with hers.

"Well, what do you want?"

A pawn with the help of other pawns can sometimes overthrow the king.

"I want Reema."

BOOK TWO

CHAPTER TWELVE

INFIDELITY

TWENTY-FIVE MONTHS POST KIDNAPPING

Dressed in only a shirt, Sayeed stood over her bed, staring at Sara. He chewed on his lower lip. The tips of his mustache curved into a smile. Stripped of her clothes, she wore only the ropes tying her arms to the posts.

"Beautiful." His voice was husky. When he climbed on top of her, she stared at the wall to hide the fear shuddering through her body. The smell of perspiration mixed with Scotch permeated through him, choking her. Swallowing back the bile, she waited for him to begin and to finish...

After an eternity, he finally rolled over and went to sleep. Sara's limbs remained tied to the bed, and she gazed at the ceiling. Tonight was the worst, not only physically but emotionally. When he violated her, her body ripped under his assault. Hours later, blood poured from her still-spread legs as sweat beaded her forehead. The wetness chilled her.

Even if her core wasn't consumed in a blaze of fire, she would be awake. The loud snores of the man passed out beside her were one reason. The pictures he brought of David, the other.

Usually those were sent through Nasif, but last night was different. The images from the two prints scattered across the floor had been seared into her brain. When she closed her eyes, she saw him. His lips pressed against that other woman's.

After everything she'd lost, knowing David moved on speared her—a punch to an already bruised and battered body. Yes, it had been two years. At some point everyone healed. Even David. This was what she wanted, wasn't it? So why did it feel like her soul had been ripped from her body?

When Sayeed showed her the images, the realization crumbled Sara's wall of self-preservation and her tears pushed through. The way his eyes sparkled at her pain and the smile of satisfaction across his face were clear indications she had fallen into his trap. Knowing him, her visual display of emotion would only arouse him further, guaranteeing a vicious attack. But no matter how hard she tried, she couldn't stop the onslaught of tears.

"Proof you are mine and no one else's. There is not a soul in the world who wants you but me," Sayeed said while he tied her up, and for the first time, she believed him.

The bed shifted when he turned, pulling her back to the present. He groaned and, when he stretched his limbs, froze. His hands wandered to her legs and then over the mattress. Seconds later, Sayeed leapt to his feet and looked down. The bottom half of his once white tunic was crinkled and the most beautiful shade of dark red. He glanced over at the stained sheets and finally at Sara. His mouth moved, but she couldn't hear a word he said. Darkness closed in. Maybe this time, it would stay.

~

TWO WEEKS LATER

The burn between her legs pulled her awake. An intricately carved wooden table sat next to the bed, and on its corner laid the two large pills Nasif left to numb the ache. When Sara tried to swallow one, it lodged in her throat. She washed the medicine down with the few drops of water left in her glass but it wasn't enough.

Her gaze dropped to the floor, to the girl asleep on the mat. The covers kicked aside, her skinny frame was curled in a ball. A thick braid of hair stretched like a baby python from her head and rested beside her. The child's round face, the color of chai, made her look younger than eighteen. Enormous eyes under heavy black lashes stared back for a brief second before exhaustion sealed them tight again.

I could ask her to bring me some water.

She shook her head. Reema had restrained her hands while

Nasif sutured her rip. Nursed Sara as she healed. When the fever came, the girl sat by her side until last night when it finally broke.

No, it's three in the morning and she needs rest.

She grabbed the glass and pulled herself from the bed and exited the room. The empty hall was dimly lit. Fire shot from Sara's stitches with every step, and she gripped the wall for support, treading gingerly. Unlike the inferno that threatened to consume her two weeks ago when he hurt her, this heat was bearable. Or it could be the pill taking effect.

A door closed somewhere from behind and startled her. She stumbled into a dark open room and bit back the scream of pain that threatened to escape. From the shadows, she watched.

Sayeed?

Sara hadn't seen him since the night he hurt her, and Nasif had made it clear to him that she needed time for her wounds to heal. The thought of running into him now sent her heart racing. Her body couldn't handle any more of him. Not yet.

She wiped the fear beading over her lip. *Can't be him.* He wasn't expected back for another week. Nasif would have told her if he'd returned sooner.

When she peeked into the hall, she caught a glimpse of Alyah. Her head lowered, the woman walked past the kitchen and continued to the other side of the building. Odd. Nothing of importance was there, just empty rooms and the guards' quarters. What was she up to?

Sara followed from a safe distance and ignored her body's protests to slow down. A thick column stood proudly in the corner of the hall. She waddled over and squeezed between the marble post and the wall.

Wassim exited from a door Alyah passed and approached the woman from behind. Tall and muscular, he was the newest addition to the guards. His job was to watch over Sayeed's first wife while Amir's was to guard Sara.

When the dark-skinned protector walked beside Alyah, Sara's eyebrows rose. Odd. They were expected to keep an appropriate distance from the wives at all times. He stretched his arm and grabbed her rear, giving it a quick squeeze before passing and disappearing into his room.

Sara's jaw dropped. She leaned from behind the safety of her column to get a better view of Alyah's wrath. The woman's colorful words were amusing when they weren't directed at her or Reema. But it didn't come as anticipated. Instead, Alyah followed him into his bedroom and, when she turned to shut the door, noticed Sara standing openmouthed in the hall.

The woman's eyes widened and face flushed, erasing any question Sara had of what she might be doing with him.

A jittery rush of adrenaline coursed through her. One day, her knowledge of Alyah and Wassim would be a powerful weapon. Sara smiled and waved her empty glass at her before waddling back to the kitchen.

CHAPTER THIRTEEN

FOR THE LOVE OF THE FATHER

Sara's body seized with fear, mercifully awakening her from the night terror. She bolted upright and grabbed handfuls of the sheet. The room glowed from the dim light of the bedside lamp. Feeling her wrists for rope burns, she scanned the area for Sayeed.

Empty.

The only sound was her heart slamming into her chest.

Just a dream.

She released a breath. If the real life torments weren't enough, Sayeed also terrorized her dreams. By five thirty every morning, she was wide awake, gasping for air, feeling like she'd run a marathon. With the back of her head against the cold cement wall, Sara hugged her knees to her chest and squeezed. Once the tremors subsided, she grabbed a stack of pictures from the drawer in the nightstand and got lost in them.

Seated on a park bench, David stared out into space. As selfish as it was, the dark circles under his eyes and the sadness etched in his face comforted her. It was proof he existed, and the pain she saw in him was evidence that he once loved her. Her conscience raised its brow, and to appease it, she flipped through the six and stopped at the ones of him with the blonde, embraced in a kiss. Most of his features were covered by her frame, but there were no more dark circles. He didn't seem lost anymore. From the way his hands set low on her back, her body was one he felt very comfortable with. Sara's eyes moistened.

Was the woman a doctor like him? Did he love this woman the way he once loved her? Well, not her but Ally, the woman she once was.

She considered tearing the photos into tiny pieces but as usual didn't. They served as a reminder that Philadelphia was no longer an option. She lingered on the image of the couple embracing. Too many hearts would break if she ever went back—as would hers. Sara shoved the images into the drawer for the next time she needed a reality check and ran her fingers across the edge of the table.

Aside from the prints, it sheltered something else in a hollow leg—a blue pill. Her one guaranteed end from this nightmare. It was Nasif's silent gift to her last month after Sayeed left her bleeding. She'd considered swallowing it more times than she cared to count but stopped for the sake of those she now considered family. That didn't mean she wouldn't use it. The pill would serve a higher purpose. One day, when the stars aligned, she would feed it to the monster responsible for ruining so many. She just needed to be patient for that moment to finally arrive.

Resting her cheek on her knees, Sara closed her eyes and imagined a world post-Sayeed. It was a fuzzy image, but one that kept her focused. A home much smaller than this somewhere in Lahore for Reema and the boys. As far as she was concerned, they were all her children. Now that Hasna had passed away and his girls married, even Nasif wandered into her fantasy. All of them were misfits, each broken in their own way. Together, with her love, they would learn how to heal—to be a family.

"Didi, why are you smiling?" A soft voice pulled Sara out of her thoughts.

She climbed out of bed and squatted next to Reema's mat. Pulling the thin sheet to her neck, Sara tweaked her nose. "Because I'm proud of how well you speak, in both Urdu and English. Now, go back to sleep. I'm going to take a shower."

~

Showered and dressed, Sara inspected herself in the mirror. The reflection staring back was not one she recognized. Her cheeks had hollowed and shadows hugged the skin under her eyes. Once upon a time, she'd considered herself attractive. She touched the raised scar running across the side of her forehead. Those days were long gone. After tucking in a stray hair, she left the room and headed to the kitchen.

Rays of the morning sun seeped into the halls through little slots on the top of the walls that ran the length of the building. Servants meticulously scrubbed and mopped every inch of the hall, including the concrete walls and marble floors. The vapors from the cleaner burned Sara's nose as she approached them. When she walked past, they stood and bowed their heads in deference. With a nod, she continued on. Since they believed she only spoke English, the need for small talk was unnecessary.

Aside from Sayeed's torments, life in the compound was...bearable. Her discovery of Alyah and Wassim's affair a few weeks earlier kept the woman at bay. Even her snide comments and aggression toward Reema had stopped. Sara took advantage of the cease-fire and made some changes. The biggest one being that Reema would no longer dress in salwar kameez. Instead, she would be expected to wear an abaya and hijab like the two wives and keep her face covered whenever she left the building. It was the only way she knew to keep the girl safe. The men who stood guard outside were different from the ones who shadowed her and Alyah.

She'd heard stories from the female servants about how the guards heckled them when no one was watching. There was no doubt in Sara's mind they would do the same to the beautiful, shy girl if she was ever alone in their presence.

Since everyone knew the painful consequences of disrespecting Sayeed's family. She hoped by having Reema dressed like them, the guards would leave her alone. So far it had worked.

Since the servants were not things Sayeed cared about, he didn't stand in her way. Of course, Alyah mumbled under her breath whenever she caught sight of Reema in an abaya, but for the most part she kept her mouth shut. Although they'd never be friends, there was finally a silent understanding between the two wives. Now, the woman's lover was an entirely different story. Whenever Sara crossed his path, his eyes slanted and stayed fixed on her. Luckily, her trusty guard seemed to pop up whenever Wassim was around. It just took one raised brow from Amir to send the other shuffling back to his hole.

At the kitchen entrance, she stopped and inhaled the smell of warm bread before poking her head in. Relaxed and enjoying each other's company, the women sat cross-legged on the floor eating their breakfast. Obviously, Alyah hadn't arrived yet. Upon seeing Sara, they started to rise. She waved at them to stay down and then left the room. They deserved some time before the female tyrant appeared, and there was something else on Sara's mind.

She headed into the living room where floral sofas lined a windowed wall, and flat screen televisions hung across the other side. Walking to one of the oversized windows, she scanned the grounds until she found the boys in the middle of a game of cricket in the courtyard. Sayeed threw a ball at one of the boys, Sameer. The gangly teen hit it with his flat bat and ran. The roar of boys mixed with their father's laughter filled the grounds and twisted her gut. Amazing how a killer could look paternal.

Sara scanned the players for Umber. The smallest and most timid of the children, he would be easy to find if he was there, but he hadn't been in days. She squinted and moved closer to the glass to search for the child who'd stolen her heart.

The consummate scapegoat, the others blamed him for losing their games and fussed over whose team would get stuck with him. A few months ago, when the kids got really angry at him, he hung his head and disappeared into the banyan trees. Sara had followed a safe distance behind. Umber's little frame weaved around the trunks until he reached the farthest corner of the compound and crumbled into a crying mess. The sharp corners of his elbows protruded as he hugged his boney knees. When she sat beside him and smoothed his hair, his moist hazel eyes widened and lip quivered. She held him close while he sobbed.

The child spoke of not fitting in with his adopted brothers and the ache of losing his mother years ago. Every word dripped with pain and loneliness. Her heart broke for his loss. When he talked of the kindness and love of Sayeed Babba and his hunger for the man's approval, Sara bit her tongue. Instead, she held Umber close and poured all the love she could into him. That afternoon, they made a pact under the banyan tree. If he never told anyone about their friendship, then he could always send word with Reema when he needed Sara, and she would come. She didn't explain to him why they needed to keep it a secret, and thankfully, in all the times they'd met since, he'd never asked. If Sayeed ever found out...

A victory cry from the kids jerked Sara out of her thoughts and back to the activity outside. Whether in games, school, or combat practice, Sayeed expected all the children to actively participate. Odd that Umber's absence didn't seem noticed. She raked the courtyard for the hundredth time but couldn't find him. Suspicion gnawed at her. Something wasn't right.

The voice of an American anchorwoman from one of the flat screen televisions pulled her attention from the game. "Pictures of the suicide bomber just moments before he entered the Egyptian mall have just been released."

People walked in and out of the electric doors of a building. The anchor pointed to a short, thin man dressed in jeans and a loose tee. A baseball cap shaded his face and a backpack too big for his frame rested against his arm.

"...reports from witnesses indicate he was about four feet eight inches tall and in his early teens."

As an image of a boy's face froze on the screen, the blood drained from Sara's face. Wide, hazel eyes brimming with fear stared back. *Umber?* All her senses focused on the anchorwoman, willing her to tell Sara she was wrong.

"The food court was full of weekend shoppers when the bomb detonated. Rescuers are sifting through the rubble for survivors. Egyptian officials anticipate the death toll from this attack could be as high as a hundred. There are unconfirmed reports that the terrorist group, As-Sirat, is taking credit for the bombing."

A shudder ripped through her. Grasping the wall for support, she turned back to the window and searched frantically, but the quiet and awkward little boy was nowhere to be seen. Sara's fingers touched the glass while she counted heads. The tally was always the same. Sayeed looked up from his game. Their gazes locked for a brief moment before he threw the next pitch.

"Sara?"

She jumped hearing Nasif's voice behind her, but she kept her focus outside, willing the child to appear.

"Where's Umber?" she squeaked.

When Nasif didn't respond, she turned to face him. Her heart pounded and the words spilled out in a breathless rush. "On the news, they showed a suicide bomber in Egypt. He looked like Umber. Nasif, where is he?"

From the way he stared back, wringing his hands, she knew the answer. The walls seemed to encroach on her. Sara's chest tightened, making it impossible to breathe. Tears tumbled as a painful shudder ripped through her. "Did you know?"

He avoided her glare and rubbed the back of his neck. "I had my worries."

As if an invisible hand was reaching within and twisting every organ at once, pain overtook her. Sara fell to her knees. The image of Umber's frightened face from the screen etched in her mind. She sobbed.

Hungry for Sayeed's approval, Umber did the unthinkable for the love of a man incapable of loving. And he died afraid and alone.

For what? Sayeed?

Heat shot through her veins, filling every limb, and propelled Sara off the floor. In a few quick strides, she found herself staring down at Nasif. "How could you let this happen? He was a fourteen-year-old child!"

He glanced at the door and whispered, "How could I have stopped it? Tell me?"

When she opened her mouth to speak, he held his hand up. "And I did not know for sure until now." When he reached out to touch her, she jerked away. "Sara, listen to me, we have a bigger problem. Umber was just the trial. This afternoon Sayeed will meet with the As-Sirat to see if they will buy the other boys."

"To buy? Why would anyone want to...?" Sara's voice trailed off and the pieces fell into place. Their lives were expendable for a cost. Sayeed's greatest weapon, sold to the highest bidder. Anger pulsed through her neck. "Son of a bitch."

A male voice on the television captured her attention. "Suicide bombers like this teenager are brainwashed to hate..."

Hate?

Umber wasn't capable of hating anyone or anything.

With the back of her sleeve, she dried her face as she listened to the man analyze Umber as the monster he never was. Through clenched teeth, she whispered her promise. "Sayeed will not live to see another sunrise."

CHAPTER FOURTEEN

SURVEILLANCE

It was as if he were on a different planet instead of in a foreign country. Seated on a metal folding chair, Dave looked around the barely furnished room on the top floor of the three-story concrete home. Accented with marble flooring and intricately carved teakwood doors and banisters, it was the kind of house he hoped to one day own, after some minor alterations— like the location, dropping the concrete walls, and adding centralized air conditioning.

Forty feet below, a busy street lined with single-family homes and businesses snaked around the city. From restaurants to clothing stores, people and cars sped up and down its length at all hours. It had taken a few days, but he'd learned to ignore the constant chorus of blaring car, truck, and bus horns, religious music, and voices. The mixture of diesel fumes and savory meats cooking nearby no longer overwhelmed his senses either.

The slight breeze that circulated through the space barely rustled his hair. Dave grabbed his sweat-soaked towel, mopping the moisture dripping down his face and the back of his neck for the millionth time. He looked at the screen of one of the two laptops sitting on the table in front of him. Both of the computers, as well as the large PC located in Eddie's technology room on the first floor, were live streaming images of the fortress across the street.

Dave checked the clock. Ten more minutes. It felt like an

eternity. Every morning, she appeared in the courtyard. And when she did, his heart and the ability for coherent speech stopped. Mesmerized by the sight of the one person he thought he'd never see again, all he could do was stare and pray for her to feel him, to know he was near. Although brief, each vision left him frozen. Eddie had to remind him to exhale.

A fly whizzed past his face, and he watched as it dove kamikaze-style into his glass of steaming chai. Its wings fluttered for a little before the buzzing stopped.

"Fuck." Eddie rose from his spot across the white plastic café table. "You need to keep your drinks covered." After spouting a couple more curses under his breath, the man picked up their cups and disappeared down the stairs.

Dave glanced out the window to the terrace, where an old lady Eddie referred to as Usma Aunty was currently hanging laundered clothes to dry. The woman wrung out each item and pinned it to the line overhead while she hummed a tune. He cringed at the sight of her twisting water out of his white briefs. She looked up and, when their eyes locked, grinned a toothless smile before nodding and returning to the task of pinning his underwear.

The woman managed the home, and from the pictures on the walls, she had lived in it for years. Odd, considering Eddie claimed he needed some of the two-fifty to buy the place. Unless he'd bought the house *and* the owner with the money. And it was interesting how the guy and said owner shared similar facial features.

Things didn't add up.

His fingers tapped and his knee bounced at the thought of Eddie. The man had promised answers before they left and still evaded every question. Today he'd push the subject and get Eddie to talk. As if hearing Dave's thoughts, the dark-haired man climbed up the final few steps with a covered pitcher of water and steel glasses in his hands. When he finally got himself situated, he turned to Dave.

"Problem?"

"It's been two weeks. You owe me the truth."

He leaned back and sighed. "We've gone through this already. We're here to save your wife."

"I'm tired of hearing the same bullshit story from you. I deserve to know what's really going on. Ally's life and mine are in your hands. My father-in-law gave a chunk of his savings to you." Eddie stared into the laptop and typed while Dave's irritation heated to anger. "I am in another country and haven't even tried to make contact with anyone since we've landed. All of this because of a hunch that I can trust you."

Instead of acknowledging anything just said, Eddie continued to click on the keyboard. Dave rose from his seat, closed its lid, and leaned forward until their noses almost touched. "Talk. To. Me."

Eyebrows raised, Eddie locked gazes with him. "I'm all you got. You want to screw this up?"

The man didn't move, much less fucking blink. Dave, on the other hand, did both as the threat cooled his anger. He sat back and rested his head in his hands. "You're right. You're all I've got." His voice cracked, so he cleared it and continued. "There's nothing I wouldn't do for her, and I'm just fucking tired of the secrets."

Eyelids closed, Dave curled his fingers into his hair and tugged. The asshole was right. He had all the control and Dave needed him. Which meant he needed to stop pushing and be okay with whatever happened. As long as he got Ally, that was all that mattered. Wasn't it?

Metal scraped against marble when Eddie shifted in his chair.

He looked up and watched the man shake his head and let out a puff of air. "What do you want to know?"

"Are you really CIA?"

Eddie stretched back in his chair. "Yes. Well, sort of."

Dave's jaw tightened. "What the fuck do you mean 'sort of'?"

Eddie grinned. "I can't get into all of that. It's confidential. But I'll tell you this much: I was born in Pakistan, moved to the States when I was seventeen, and a year later I enlisted in the Army. Since I speak and blend in with most of the Arabic cultures, and because I'm a bad ass, I moved up pretty fast in the ranks."

"So that means you do have connections. You know people who can help us."

The proud smile plastered on Eddie's face fell. "Well yes, I have connections but no, there isn't anyone willing to help. Like I said before, the CIA can't get involved. There's no proof Alisha Dimarchi is here against her will."

Dave cut him off. "You've seen her. I've seen her. There's no question she's here, and it is against her will. Ally would never disappear like that."

He raised his brows. "No? A year before she vanished, didn't she leave you?"

Dave's stomach clenched and face warmed, but he didn't lower his gaze.

Eddie shrugged. "I don't get involved in something without doing my research."

Dave leaned back and fidgeted with the corner of his wet towel, remembering the time long ago. "She left me, but she told me first." Although painful, the memory made him smile. "Ally doesn't just up and leave. That's not her style. She gave me one week's notice before she moved out. And there is no doubt in my mind she is here against her will. So stop with the bullshit. What's the real story?"

Eddie looked out toward the compound and played with the rim of the empty metal glass as if considering his options. After what seemed like an eternity, he turned the cup over and leaned forward. "You're right, there is more. This thing is bigger than your wife." When Dave opened his mouth to argue, he held his hand up. "I know she's the most important thing in the world to you. But this is about more than just a couple lives. It's about thousands."

Dave shook his head, not understanding what the man was talking about.

"We're pretty confident that Sayeed is the one supplying illegal arms to the As-Sirat, but we have no proof. Their leader, Ibrahim Ayoub, is a smart motherfucker. He's responsible for five different terrorist attacks that have killed hundreds of people. Just this morning there was a suicide bombing in a mall in Egypt. Guess who took credit for it?"

Dave mouthed Ayoub's name and he nodded.

A fly flew past, landing on the table between them. Eddie raised the empty cup and trailed it. "He's created this following throughout the Middle East, and every time Ayoub pulls a stunt like this, his support increases tenfold. But we can't seem to get our hands on the slippery son of a bitch. We're hoping Irfani may be the key."

He positioned the mouth of the cup over the fly and slammed it down. The insect leapt away and shot into the air right before it was captured. “Fucking fly,” he mumbled.

“It’s too risky for the government to get involved. If they stepped in and things backfired, we’d look incompetent and Ayoub wins. So the compromise was that I come here with you as your hired mercenary. If things go wrong, they can claim ignorance and say I went rogue. If they go right, not only will we be able to get your wife out of there, we’ll get Sayeed alive and squeeze him for information.”

Dave sat open mouthed, digesting what he’d heard. Something didn’t make sense. “Why would you risk your career? What’s in it for you?”

“I’ve been tracking Irfani and his people for a while now. He and I have a past.”

“That’s where this house and your aunt come in?”

He smiled and glanced at the woman. “She’s my mother’s older sister, and the only family I have left. I bought this place when it came on the market years ago. Let’s just say I’ve been waiting for the right opportunity to pay my neighbor a visit, and thanks to you I may have finally found it.”

CHAPTER FIFTEEN

THE TREAT

The heat of Sara's rage was all consuming. Her fists clenched as the images of Umber replayed across the television. The world labeled him a killer, while the real demon ran free.

"Hasna's gone. No more excuses." Her voice rose with each word. "I will kill him and if you try to stop me this time, I'll..."

Nasif pulled her away from the windows, and his salty hand cupped her mouth before she could protest. He looked over his shoulder at the open door, before returning his attention to her, his eyes flashing with anger. "Lower your voice."

After she nodded, he removed his hand.

"*We*. Will. Kill. Sayeed. There is no 'I'." His eyes brimmed with tears as he pointed at her. "You have endured hell for me. If it is the last living thing I do, I will make sure that man dies. Do you understand?"

"I've already lost Umber." Her voice cracked when she spoke. "I can't let anyone else die."

"Agreed. But we have to do this wisely. His guards..."

A rasping from the entrance quieted them both, and they turned to find Reema standing in the hall, her eyes lowered.

Nasif leaned closer to Sara while keeping his gaze on the child. "Just give me an hour to think before doing anything, please?" Without waiting for a response, he folded his arms behind him, turned, and walked out the door.

Reema smiled when he walked past and then raised her brows at Sara. Had they been in her room, an interrogation would have ensued. Fortunately, they weren't.

Sara shook her head and returned her attention to the news coverage of the bombing. Nasif was right. Sayeed's execution had to be done carefully. The children deserved to finally experience freedom. But was she really capable of taking a life?

As soon as Umber's face filled the screen, the answer flashed in her head. She wiped a stray tear. No one else would die; she'd stake her life on it.

After pasting a smile on her face, Sara rushed out of the room before Reema had a chance to see what was on the television. The less she knew the better, and it was time to feed the guards.

Hot bread and spicy aromatics consumed Sara's senses the moment she and Reema entered the kitchen. She scanned the room, finding Alyah seated at the table eating her breakfast. Typically, the woman acknowledged her arrival with a nod, but today she kept her attention on her meal, ignoring Sara's gaze. It was odd, but Sara didn't have time to think too deeply about Alyah's moods.

Next to the woman was a tray piled high with food and plates for the guards. Sara picked it up while Reema grabbed a carafe of tea and some cups. She followed the young woman out of the kitchen and down the hall as her mind drifted to the pill hidden in her room. Somehow she needed to get it down Sayeed's throat. Putting it in his food was impossible since Alyah was in charge of all his food delivery, and he hadn't shown up in her room demanding sex in a long time. To top it all off Kadeen, Sayeed's guard, rarely left his side except at night.

As they headed toward the back door, Sara looked up to find Amir leaning against the wall, awaiting her arrival. The tall, skinny boy she first met had transformed into a giant whose T-shirt stretched with muscles beneath. The mustache that seemed so out of place two years ago now fit the face of the man in front of her.

He wore a thick, black belt around the waist of his jeans, a gun holstered against his right hip. When he noticed them, he stood straight and smiled. His grin widened as Reema inched closer. When his gaze lingered on her partially scarfed face, the visible parts of the girl's cheeks colored.

Sara took a step back, allowing Reema and Amir their moment. There was a time in her life that the idea of encouraging a relationship between a girl who was barely eighteen and a man in his mid-twenties would have disturbed her. But this was a different time and of the men, Amir was the best option. He had a gentleness to him, a respect for women the rest lacked. Her chest tightened. By this time tomorrow, he might be the only person Reema would have left.

~

The blinding morning sun and blaring car horns from the street outside the gate burned her eyes when she exited the building. She stopped and stared at the brown-pebbled yard, giving her vision time to adjust.

Shoes crunched against gravel as little feet ran across the lawn, and the sounds of laughter grew louder as they approached. The children must have noticed her. She shielded her eyes to look, and sure enough they were making a beeline toward her. The boys came, eager to see what treat Sara had, and like always, they weren't disappointed. The cooks had provided a plate stacked high with fifteen orange golf-ball-shaped buttery sweets. Amir took the heavy tray out of Sara's hands. She removed the plate of treats before he and Reema continued on their way to serve the guards their breakfast.

"Ledu!" Fourteen lanky boys cheered. With buzz cuts, shorts and tank tops, their big eyes and huge grins remained fixed on the platter she offered. Each took a ball from the plate and mumbled "thank you" before returning to their game. When they had been adopted, they could barely read their own names and now they were fluent in several languages, including English.

Emotion burned her eyes as she looked down at the one Ledu still left on the plate. These were Umber's favorite. She used to keep a secret stash of them and a bag of pistachios in her armoire for when they met.

"Sara Mummy, why are you crying?" Razaa, tall with big ears, stood in front of her, his treat still in his hand.

"The sun hurts my eyes," she lied.

Sayeed's laughter echoed through her ears seconds before his hands grabbed her shoulders, giving them a firm squeeze. She stiffened, almost dropping the brass plate as the scent of sweat mingled with pine burned her nose.

In Urdu, he spoke to the boy. "Razaa, you will find that women are the weaker species in every way. Even the sun makes them cry."

She swallowed the rising bile and fixed her gaze on the black fuzz above the child's upper lip. Sayeed's thumb scraped against Sara's cheek, wiping the tear. "Now go take a shower. Your teacher will be here soon."

The child smiled his understanding and ran off, disappearing into the entrance of the two-story building.

His hands ran down the length of Sara's arms. Goose bumps and dread spread when he rubbed her back. After two months of ignoring her existence, why the sudden interest in her?

He wrapped an arm around her waist and rested his chin on her shoulder while pressing her back against his hips. The ends of his beard, like needles, pierced her cheek as she fought to hide her disgust.

Sayeed picked up Umber's treat. "You know when I was a child, I loved these things, but my mother would never get them for me. Smell it."

The scent of butter and cardamom overpowered her nostrils when he shoved the food into her nose. When she stepped back, directly into his groin, he let out a low moan and held her tight against him.

As his erection ground into her, Sayeed returned the crushed orb to the plate. Out of his pocket, he pulled a handkerchief and wiped the crumbs from her nose and upper lip. "Heavenly, no? The smell is just as divine as the flavor. You know, every party I went to as a child, I would go in search of these and eat as many as I could."

His nose traced circles on her cheek. "The aroma, the feel, the taste, it was something I craved constantly. I had what you would call an insatiable appetite for it."

Digging her palms into the edges of the brass plate, she focused on the sharp pain that resonated through her hands and reminded herself of her mission.

"Then one day, I got sick of it. The thing I once thought was tantalizing became disgusting. Its texture, smell, taste repelled me, and so I stopped."

She held her breath. He wasn't talking about the Ledu. Sayeed picked up a piece of the food and traced it along her lips. "It's been so long since I've tasted it that now, I'm intrigued. Maybe it was the time away. Or maybe it is the question of 'what if I still don't like it' that thrills me? Whatever it is, I am ready for another bite."

She watched from the corner of her eye as he bit into Umber's treat. A morsel of the orange stuck to his beard. Sara's fingers twitched to yank it, and the hair it clung to, out of his skin.

"It was never yours to take," she said, as emotionless as possible.

His brow rose, and when he smiled, the crumb sunk deeper into his growth. "The treat? Of course it was."

"There were fifteen pieces, but only fourteen were eaten. Where's the fifteenth boy?"

He paused for a moment before savoring another bite. "One of my sons is missing? Which one?"

"Umber."

"Hmm." He dropped the last piece into his mouth.

"Where is he?"

"You know, you are right. He has left us for a much better place." The popping sound his lips made when he sucked the remnants of the treat off his fingers made her press against the plate even tighter.

"Funny thing. The grounds people told me about this pile of pistachio shells they kept finding in the same spot over there in the farthest corner." He waved toward the patch of trees. "Do you know anything about that?" Sayeed rubbed his cheek against hers, waiting for a response they both knew wouldn't come.

He chuckled. "I didn't think so. Where was I? Yes, Umber. Such a timid boy, no? I talked to him on the phone yesterday."

She blinked and fought back the tears.

"He was a little nervous about going into a big mall by himself. But I told him someone he loves very much would be waiting for him with a bag of pistachios."

Sara's stomach lurched. A desire to rip that tongue out of his filthy head overwhelmed her, and as she fought with the urge, a cell phone rang. She looked up to find Kadeen standing a few yards away. He answered the call while his gaze stayed fixed on them, as if reading her thoughts.

"It was so nice," Sayeed continued. "He sounded excited. Hmm, I wonder whom he thought he would meet. Any ideas?"

A tear slipped from her eye. Before it got farther than her cheek, his tongue captured it.

"You should get inside, it seems the sun is still in your eyes. Oh, one more thing. Good news, actually." His lips grazed Sara's ear as he whispered. "Alyah is pregnant. It looks like I will finally get my beloved son. So if I were you, I would spend some extra time getting ready for tonight. Let's see if you can thrill me."

CHAPTER SIXTEEN

THE PERFECT TEAM

Movement on the monitor captured Dave's attention. A tall woman exited the building and walked into the clearing, a tray of food in her arms. Between the long-sleeved dresses and the scarves she wore, only her face was ever visible. Expressionless, she turned to the two who were typically beside her, an armed man and another woman. The woman was younger, maybe even a girl, and completely covered by her clothes except for her eyes and forehead. They grabbed the tray and left the graceful, beautiful woman's side.

He leaned his head onto the screen and fought the urge to run to her. She seemed close enough that he could call out and she'd hear him. It didn't matter how often he'd seen her, the impact was the same.

As the bastard approached her, Dave clenched the edge of the table. A man of average height, Sayeed appeared to be in his forties. With a thick mustache and beard, his repulsive face looked too big for his portly body. He stood behind her and snaked his thick arm around her waist. Rage burned through Dave's veins.

In all these weeks, he had yet to see the man acknowledge, much less approach her. That alone made it easier for Dave to pretend she was safe. But now he couldn't. Heat filled his stomach, his chest, his face. Muscles tightened. The voice in his head screamed to go break the son of a bitch's neck.

Sayeed pressed his filthy cheek next to hers and spoke in her ear. When Dave pushed out of the seat, Eddie reached over, grabbed his arm, and pulled him down. "It's not time yet."

The agent clicked a couple buttons on his keyboard, zooming in on their faces. Sayeed's lips pressed against her skin while Ally stood rigid, staring out. When he took the orange dessert from her tray and pushed it into her nose, her eyes slammed shut.

Blood pulsed through Dave's neck and pounded behind his ears. Eddie's grasp tightened. A lone tear fell onto her cheek. She contained the shudder rippling through her as his tongue licked the drop away. The smirk on his pathetic face when he turned and walked away, the terror that flashed across her face before she disappeared into the compound; Dave watched all of it, and like a bull, his chest heaved as he shook, ready for attack.

"Son of a fucking bitch," Eddie muttered. "By the time I'm done with that motherfucker, his dick and his balls will be in two different continents."

"When." More of a demand than a question, Dave was on his feet, staring at the man who was supposed to help. "You've done a lot of talking. But where's the action? How long is she going to have to go through hell before you step in?"

The man rested his forehead on the tips of his fingers and closed his eyes. "It's complicated..."

Before he got any further into the explanation, Dave ran down the two flights of stairs as images of the ways he'd torture Sayeed played in his head. Finally on the first floor, he headed for the door.

A few feet before the entrance, his back was slammed against the wall and an arm pushed into his neck, holding him in place. Eddie's face was inches from his. He clenched his teeth as his eyes bore into Dave's.

"Do you think I don't know how hard it is to wait? To go to sleep every night, knowing that bastard is still walking free after everything he's done to the people you love?" His voice shook and spit bubbled on the edges of his mouth.

The pressure against Dave's windpipe increased, making it harder to breathe. So he stopped fighting and glared. The little patch of skin between Eddie's brows turned a deep purple and his body shook. "Four years. Not a day goes by in the past four years when I don't think about him. Now that I'm this close to getting the bastard, not you or anyone else is going to screw that up for me." Eddie leaned in close. "Do you understand?"

The musical notes of a bell made them both freeze and stare at the door. Eddie placed a finger on his mouth before removing his arm from Dave's throat. He pointed to the study across the hall. Dave nodded and walked to it as Usma ran down the stairs. Wide-eyed, she wiped her hands on her shirt and smoothed down her hair while continuing to the door.

Dave holed himself up in the library and rested his back against the doorjamb. His heart pounded wildly. He took deep, slow breaths and tried to listen. To think. Ear glued to the door, he searched for the voice of the visitor. When he finally heard it, fear turned to excitement and his mouth dropped.

Nasif.

~

The two men sat across from each other on floral sofas speaking in Urdu, unaware of Dave's entrance. His sleeves rolled up, Nasif's elbows rested on his thighs. His mercenary, for lack of a better term, laughed at something the old man said.

Dave stared suspiciously at the pair. For strangers, they seemed comfortable with each other. Usma Aunty placed cold glasses of orange juice on the table and sat next to her nephew. When Nasif looked up to acknowledge her, his gaze rested on Dave.

How was it that the old man knew where Eddie lived? If they did know each other, why the hell had Eddie been sitting on his ass staring at videos for the past two weeks?

"David?" The old man's brows rose and mouth opened seconds before the man stood and embraced him as if a beloved son. "You came." Unlike when they first met in Philadelphia, his touch was no longer repulsive. Dave returned the affection. If they got her out of this hell, he would forever be in the man's debt. "Hello, Nasif."

He tugged on his arm. "Come. Sit next to me." He rested his hand Dave's shoulder. "I am happy you found Eddie. You two will make the perfect team."

Dave's attention shifted between the two men. "So how do you know each other?"

Nasif smiled at Eddie. "We met how long ago? Three years?"

The information had Dave raising his brows and staring at his mercenary. There had been way too many secrets. Eddie cleared his throat. "We have more important things to discuss right now, like who told you we were here?"

The old man jutted his chin at Eddie's aunt. "Usma."

Three pairs of eyes landed on the woman, who fiddled with the hem of her shirt.

"She hangs a red scarf outside each day you are here," Nasif finished.

Eddie shifted and spoke to his Aunt in Urdu. The woman sat up straight and glared back. Her arms waved as she responded, her words increasing in pitch and speed. Whatever she said had him glaring at the old man.

Dave swallowed the building anxiety and inched closer to Nasif. If there was a fight, Eddie would beat the shit out of both of them. But the man was the one who led him to Ally, and for that reason alone, Dave's loyalty was to him. "What's happening?"

Nasif patted his arm. "Usma is explaining why she would tell me about Eddie's comings and goings."

Eddie glared at Nasif. "If you've known all this time, then why wait until now to pay me a visit?"

"Because I am desperate and it was not until today that I felt safe reaching out to you."

"Go on," Eddie ordered.

"Sayeed, his first wife, and two of his guards are about to leave the compound. They will be on their way to the airport where she and her guard will board a plane to Afghanistan. Sayeed is not expected to return until the evening and has told the workers to take the rest of the day off as well. The only people in the building right now are Sara, her servant, three guards, and the children."

"What do you mean desperate?" Dave interjected.

The old man's sad eyes locked with his. "He has made a deal with the devil."

"I thought Sayeed was the devil," he muttered.

Nasif shook his head. "No. He is a demon. Ibrahim Ayoub is the devil. Have you heard of him?"

In spite of the Pakistan heat, Dave's feet were turning to ice.

"Some. Go on," Eddie urged.

Dave swallowed and tried to flex his toes. Instead of thawing, the frigid sensation worked its way up his knees while Nasif explained.

"Sayeed has some things Ayoub wants."

"What could a man like Ibrahim Ayoub want from Sayeed?" Eddie asks.

Two of the deadliest men he had ever heard of were coming together, and Ally was stuck in the middle. But he'd known this for weeks. So why was it affecting him now? He rubbed his hands against numb thighs.

"Weapons," Nasif replied.

Dave tried to stay focused despite the frozen tundra crawling its way into his stomach.

"What kind of weapons?" Eddie pressed as Dave balled and released his fists.

"Surface-to-air missiles and suicide bombers."

Dave's fingers froze in mid-clench.

"He has his hands on several of them, and Ayoub is willing to pay cash for them."

Eddie leaned forward. "What do you mean by suicide bombers?"

"About two years back, Sayeed adopted fifteen boys. He bragged about it being a humanitarian gesture and raised them on the compound as his own. You must have seen the boys."

Eddie's face revealed nothing. Dave swallowed his terror and steadied his voice. "The ones Ally brings food to?"

Nasif nodded. "This morning one of them carried a bomb into an Egyptian mall. Last I saw, they are still trying to find survivors in the rubble."

Suicide bombers. Satan and his spawn. All the evil in the world would soon be scurrying around his wife. Blood drained from his face. He closed his eyes and worked on remembering to breathe. How the hell were they supposed to get her out?

His eyes flew open. "Wait. If Ayoub is involved, the CIA will step in. Isn't that what you said?"

Eddie ignored the question and continued his interrogation. "So Sayeed plans to sell the weapons and the kids to Ayoub?"

"The plan is for Ayoub to arrive at the compound tonight to examine the missiles and the boys. If he likes what he sees, then..."

Tonight? Adrenaline pumped through Dave, thawing every

limb and organ in its path. They'd get her out of there tonight.

"...Sayeed will make a sizable profit and shift his residence to Afghanistan with the family."

"He's taking my wife to Afghanistan?" Although he whispered the words, it was obvious everyone heard.

Nasif took a drink of his juice. "That is the reason I am here. Sayeed will not be taking Sara with him. He knows Sara will not sit still and let him sacrifice the children." The old man stood and moved over to the other sofa. He sat in the spot Usma had occupied. So engrossed in their conversation, Dave hadn't noticed her leave.

"He plans to kill her tonight before Ayoub arrives."

Stunned silence filled the room. Dave pressed his fingers into his temples as Nasif's words repeated in his head. "But he won't because the CIA's going to help us get her out." He waved his hand at Eddie. "That's what you said. If Ayoub is involved, the government will help." When the agent didn't reply, he pushed it. "Tell me they'll help Ally."

Again, he ignored the question and probed Nasif. "What time will this meeting with Ayoub happen?"

Nasif glanced at Dave and hesitated. "Seven tonight."

The mercenary rose up from his seat. "I need to make a call. Both of you stay put," he ordered before disappearing into his room.

A mix of anxiety and sheer terror played havoc within Dave. *Why didn't he answer my questions? What if they won't help Ally? He probably needs to get things set up first.*

With nothing else to do but think, he paced the floor while Nasif watched. "They have to go in there and get her out, don't they?" he said out loud to no one in particular.

"If they don't, we will," Nasif replied with a shrug. He tapped the floral cushion next to him. "Have a seat, David. I have a plan."

CHAPTER SEVENTEEN

THE PLAN

Sara didn't notice Reema and Amir had returned until the girl squeezed her arm. Lost in thought, she was rooted in the same spot they'd left her, as Sayeed's summary of Umber's final moments repeated in her head. Each word, like a knife, pierced every part of her being, making it hard for her to breathe, much less think.

Tiny, feminine hands took the platter from her fingers and placed it on the tray with the others. Sara allowed the girl to guide her into the building, down the halls, and to their room. Once inside, the red-faced, wide-eyed Reema locked the door and began to search the space. Her words flew in whispered Urdu as she moved past Sara.

"Sayeed plans to kill you tonight." She grabbed a large canvas bag from the corner and opened the armoire, pulling out a shoebox. Gold and diamonds sparkled in the light as she poured all of Sayeed's expensive gifts into the empty sack.

"Amir has been told to dispose of you." She rushed to the nightstand, opened the drawer, and tossed the pictures of David in with the valuables.

Numb, Sara sat and watched the girl tremble as she worked. She opened her mouth to argue but shut it. After months of helping Reema heal and calm her fears, she could no longer offer promises of a future together.

"Didi. Are you listening to me?"

After Sara nodded, she continued. "Kadeen, Sayeed, Wassim, and Alyah will all be gone soon. That leaves Amir and the guards at the gate. We have to get you out of here as soon as Sayeed leaves tonight."

Her eyes filled at the fear she saw in Reema. This was her fault, she should have never waited this long to act. Umber was gone, and in the end, Sayeed used her relationship with the child to lure him to his death. No one else would be hurt or used because of her.

"Reema, I'm not running away."

Ignoring her, the girl continued to pack Sara's things. "Amir will help, I know he will, and you can sneak out while I keep the guards..."

Sara grabbed her shoulders and faced her. "Reema, I am not running away."

Her face paled while she processed the words. In a hushed voice she responded, but this time in English. "Didi, he will kill you. Tonight."

"Think about it, Reema. This is Sayeed Irfani, the man who massacred your parents and brother because your father said no to him. Do you think he will just let me pack up and leave? First, he will kill everyone I ever loved. You, Nasif, my family in America, everyone. Then he will come after me, torture me, and only then let me die."

Reema gasped and dropped the bag. Seating herself on the bed, tears spilled while her eyes darted around the room as if hidden within its walls was the answer to their dilemma.

Sara dropped to her knees in front of the girl and grabbed her hands. "Reema, look at me." When their gazes locked, she continued, "I have to kill Sayeed. Tonight. There is no other way."

A flight of emotions passed through Reema's face before finally, her lip trembled and she was sobbing in Sara's arms. "He has killed everybody I love. I can't lose you too."

She stroked the young woman's hair until the crying stopped. After a long while, she pulled the girl away and wiped her wet face. Sara rolled her shoulders back and tried to sound confident. "Have I ever broken a promise to you?"

Reema thought about the question for a while before shaking her head.

"I promise you, he will die for everything he did to you and your family."

CHAPTER EIGHTEEN

SHOW TIME

After Dave's twentieth lap around the sofa, Eddie returned to the living room, walked past him, and headed straight for the study. Once there, he opened the door and stared at him. "David, we need to talk."

A spasm of fear shuddered down his spine. Nothing good ever came after "we need to talk." Nasif smiled his encouragement and Dave followed the mercenary in. Eddie closed the door and turned to face him.

"What's there to talk about? They're going to go in and get Ally." Dave's voice rose ten octaves higher than normal because the answer scared the shit out of him.

"Sit down."

Nervous energy turned to irritation. "I don't want to sit down. Tell me what the fuck is going on."

Eddie positioned himself on the corner of the wooden desk and finally made eye contact. "Delta Force will infiltrate the city in the next two hours and make their way to the compound. Their mission is to capture Ibrahim Ayoub."

The words were just what he wanted to hear, but the hesitant way they were spoken set off alarms. "That's good, right? They'll get Ally out."

"In order to ensure they get him, they will not go in until they have confirmation Ayoub is in the building."

Anger tightened Dave's throat as the pieces fell into place. "What? You heard Nasif. My wife will be dead before that man shows up."

Instead of answering, Eddie looked away.

Dave clenched his jaw, and the room spun. He held onto the wall and steadied himself. When things stopped moving, he finally found his voice. "They are going to let her die because Ayoub's life is more valuable?"

Eddie's silence fueled his rage.

"Who the fuck gives them the right to make that choice?"

Instead of responding, the agent stared down at his folded hands.

"That's it? After all of this? You're going to let her die?" His body shook. "There are a lot of things I can deal with. But allowing the woman I love to die without trying to stop it is not one of them. I don't care what it takes, I will get her out."

Dave stared out the window into the gated courtyard. How the hell was he supposed to go up against them on his own? With the back of his hand, he wiped away the tears spilling on his face and edged close to Eddie.

"I can't do this alone." His voice was a whisper as he searched the man's face for a reaction. "Name your price. Whatever it is, I'll pay it. I'm a doctor. Her brother's a doctor. Her dad has a shit load of money."

Eddie closed his eyes and sighed. "I can't. I have my orders."

"For God's sake, do *something*. Don't just let her die."

"He won't let her die." Nasif announced from the doorway behind them.

The old man walked over to them and rested his hand on Dave's shoulder. "I'm sorry, but I couldn't help overhearing. I promise you she will not die and Eddie will help."

Dave stepped aside and prayed he was right.

Eddie shook his head. "Ayoub is responsible for the deaths of thousands of innocent people and will kill more. We have a responsibility to the world to contain him."

Nasif nodded. "All true, but why can't you do both? Keep Sara safe until Ayoub arrives."

"I have my orders. We do not get involved."

"What if I told you Sara would not be the only one killed if you do not get involved?"

Eddie rose from his spot, put his hands on his hips, and looked at the two of them. "It doesn't matter who's in there. That's a risk we will have to take."

"And if your sister was one of the lives that would be lost?"

Dave sucked in a breath and watched the anger flash across Eddie's face. The agent slammed his eyes shut and filled his lungs several times before speaking. "She's dead and it wouldn't make a difference if she was there. My hands are tied."

Nasif's answer was in Urdu, and whatever he said had an impact. Eddie tilted his face and scanned the room as if looking for something. Seconds later, he grabbed the old man's collar and slammed him up against the wall.

Dave grabbed a hold of Eddie and tried to pry him away. "What the hell are you doing?"

His eyes never left Nasif's and his teeth clenched. "Let go of my arm, David."

Instead, he pulled harder.

"If you don't fucking get your hands off me, I will break them."

"It's okay, David. He won't hurt me," Nasif wheezed.

"Hurt you? I'm going to break your neck." Eddie pointed his finger at Nasif. "You kept her a secret from me all these years."

"I had no choice." Nasif then switched to Urdu. The old man discreetly waved a hand at Dave, pointing to the door while he continued answering Eddie's questions.

With a nod, Dave stepped away. Completely wrapped up in the conversation, Eddie was unaware of anything except the interrogation. Things were going according to Nasif's plan. Dave smiled and backed away quietly while the two men argued.

Once Delta Force was in place, there was no way he'd get anywhere near the compound. This was his only chance.

Usma ran in, joining the chaos. Seconds later, Dave slipped into the living room. With careful steps, he made his way out of the house.

The noon sun streamed overhead as he shut the door behind him and turned away from the place that had been home for the past two weeks. Flipping the metal latch of the iron gate, he squeezed through and closed it behind him. Immediately he found himself swallowed up in the throng of people on the sidewalk. He walked in the direction opposite of Alisha, just as Nasif had told him to do earlier when Eddie left them alone. Ducking into an alley, Dave leaned against the wall and waited in the shadows. The flood of emotions he'd felt in the past few weeks drained away as a sense of calm blanketed him. He wiped the bead of sweat on his forehead and stared at the metal gate a hundred feet away, waiting for the only person who could help him.

Eddie.

~

Head down and drenched in sweat, Dave walked among the crowd of patrons along the street for a second time. His destination loomed ahead. After a peek at his watch, he stopped in front of a clothing store and peered into the glass display. It was too soon. A couple of mannequins adorned in deep purple and maroon bridal attire smiled back. He pretended to admire their clothes. The details of the conversation he had over half an hour ago ran through his head. Screwing up wasn't an option.

"Why are you helping me?" Dave asked while Eddie adjusted the time on a watch.

The man shrugged. "The reason's not important." He handed over the timepiece. "Here, put this on. There's a tracking chip on it, so make sure it stays on your body at all times. At exactly twelve thirty, all electricity to the building will be cut. The generators should kick in thirty seconds later. Nasif will shut those down at twelve forty. By twelve forty-five, you need to be distracting the guards. At which point, I will climb over the rear fence. If everything goes according to plan, I'll be on the grounds and your ass will be at my place ten minutes later." He scanned the alley they were holed up in before continuing.

"And if you're wrong?" Dave buckled the brown leather onto his wrist.

Eddie pulled out a small metal flask from his pants pocket and unscrewed the lid. "I won't be. Just stick to the times and don't try to be a hero. I'll do the rest." He splashed Scotch on Dave's bearded face and handed him the container with the remaining liquid.

"But if you are wrong?"

"If I'm wrong then you'll either be dead or I'll be toast. Literally. But I'm not wrong." With a slap on Dave's shoulder and a nod, he walked out of the security of the shadows and disappeared into the sunlight, leaving Dave alone.

The blaring of horns from the street brought Dave back to the present. He looked at his watch. With a deep gulp of air, he turned and made his way to the compound.

Two guards leaned against the iron rods conversing, unaware of his approach. He sucked in a breath. It was show time. As loud as possible, Dave began to chant the Pledge of Allegiance and staggered to the gate.

CHAPTER NINETEEN

THE DRILL

The shaded area under the banyan tree calmed Sara's tightly wound nerves. She could still sense Umber's presence there. Like a magnet, the spot pulled her out of the building and into the forest. Possibly drawing her here to grieve or to feel connected to a life that was no more. Whatever the reason, it helped.

Squirrels ran along the branches, ignoring her existence. Even the birds seemed to sing a sweeter song. As if they knew that by tomorrow an evil would no longer exist in their world. An evil Sara would efface.

"Time to get ready for Sayeed," she whispered to the creatures before wiping the grass from her back and heading to the compound. Like a sea serpent, the trees' roots weaved in and out of the earth. She walked over them and made her way to the open perimeter of the fortress.

With every step, the calm waned and fear built. The blue pill had been ground into a fine powder and poured into a packet that Reema had stitched into the hem of her dress. It was all she had: a pouch of dust and a lot of "what if's." What if she didn't get the chance to poison him? What if he realized what she was doing? What if it didn't work?

A pulsating ache planted itself in the middle of her forehead, worked its way to the nape of her neck.

At the clearing to the compound, with his palms planted on his hips, Nasif waited. His face relaxed as soon as he set his eyes on her. He tipped his head to the side before walking in that direction.

The old man asked for an hour this morning and then disappeared for at least three. What had he been up to?

Sara's muscles tensed as she followed. In a moment of grief, her guard had lowered and she shared too much. When he gave her the poison, it was with the intent that she take her own life, not another's. He never said it in so many words, but she understood. As much as she needed his help, he couldn't be trusted. The last time she tried to kill Sayeed, it had been Nasif who stopped her.

He led her to the rear of the building, away from the guards, and leaned against a tree. A few yards away, the boys attended their outdoor class. Seated on benches at wooden picnic tables, they snickered and whispered while the bearded teacher translated the parts of the body from Urdu to English.

Sara propped herself against the trunk of another tree and gazed on Umber's empty seat. Her chest tightened. *How can everyone move on as if nothing happened?*

Nasif pretended to listen to the lecture with a smile painted on his face. "I have been looking all over for you."

She copied his pose, minus the smile. "I needed some time alone. To think."

He nodded. "Sayeed is gone for the day and has taken Alyah with him. He told you she's pregnant?"

The boys exploded into laughter when the teacher drew a picture of a chest and labeled the different regions. The instructor looked over in her direction, and she bobbed her head, waving him to continue.

"Well, he's put her and Wassim on a plane to Afghanistan. With the As-Sirat wandering around, he does not believe Lahore is a safe place for them."

The most intimidating person she'd ever met was sending his pregnant wife off, with the man who was most likely the father of her child, because he was intimidated? The irony of the whole situation made her laugh.

Nasif shot her a questioning glance.

Covering her mouth, she cleared her throat. "Sorry."

"That means both Kadeen and Wassim are off the property..." Voices of men arguing erupted before he could finish. They both turned to the source.

Seconds later, sneakers crushing against the pebbled earth approached. A gasp escaped her lips when Amir rushed toward them, gun in hand.

His voice roared through the grounds. "Safety positions, now!" Emotionless, Amir looked behind him while he sprinted to the children.

In a single-file line, the teacher led the silent, wide-eyed boys into their two-story building. They'd practiced the drill so many times; everyone understood what to do. But this was different.

When Sara turned to question Nasif, he was already halfway across the yard. He rushed past Amir and disappeared around the wall of the house toward the angry voices.

There was only one force that could cause this much fear. The As-Sirat. If they were here, she needed to get to Reema fast.

Unable to move, her heart pounded as she scanned the empty grounds for Reema. The pain in Sara's head throbbed, increasing tenfold. Her chest tightened and muscles contracted, the beginnings of a panic attack.

Amir rushed to her side. Grabbing her arm, he tugged her along as he spoke in Urdu. "Didi, we need to go. Now." In all this time, he'd never uttered a word to her.

Before she could ask why they needed to go, two loud pops and a man's agonized howl filled the air. A chill shuddered through her. A need to rush to the voice overwhelmed her and when she tried, Amir yanked her away.

Sara's brain ordered her to go into her assigned spot, Sayeed's safe room, but her body struggled to go to the gate.

Amir's grip tightened. "Didi, please. It's not safe for you."

Another pop filled the air, but this time, Nasif's terrified voice followed with one deafening word. "Reema!"

Both she and Amir froze and the girl's name echoed in her ears. The young guard stared wide-eyed at her.

"Reema!" Nasif screamed again.

The world went silent. Everything stopped moving. Only the sound of her heart thumping wildly was audible. Sara mouthed the girl's name.

"I will take care of her. You have to get inside, now." He dragged her forward. Instead of complying, Sara hoisted her skirt, twisted her arm out of his grasp, and ran toward the gate.

A few seconds later, Amir had his arms wrapped around her waist and, like a bag of laundry, hurled Sara over his shoulder. He darted in the other direction, away from the gate and the safe room.

With her world upside down, blood filled her head, along with the memory of Nasif screaming Reema's name. Kicking Amir's stomach and punching his spine, she yelled at him, no longer trying to keep her knowledge of Urdu a secret. "No! Reema needs help. Let me down."

Amir tightened his grip and moved forward, despite her hysterical pleas and attacks.

When he finally stopped, keys jingled. Door joints creaked. "I'm sorry, Didi. Reema wants me to keep you safe. I promise you, I will protect her." He tossed her onto a cement floor and slammed the door shut. Metal scraped against metal, locking the light out and Sara in.

Immersed in absolute silence, and night so dark that it made no difference if her eyelids were open or closed, images of Reema's bloodied body flashed through her head. She scrambled to her feet and banged against the metal surface. "Amir! Let me out! I need to go to her!" The thought of her out there alone made Sara pound and yell harder until her face was drenched with tears and sweat. But no one came.

Out of breath, her knuckles were bloodied and her throat was hoarse. Pain radiated through her shoulder and toes from the multiple times she slammed and kicked against the bolted entrance.

"She is all I have!" Sara wailed. Sliding down the length of its cold surface, she fell to the ground and rested her cheek against the dusty floor. For the first time in a long time, she gave into self-pity and sobbed.

Sayeed had taken everything—her identity, her sanity, her family. The life she once had was gone. The life she learned to accept—gone as well.

Her lungs felt like they were being sucked into her throat. First Umber. Now Reema.

After what seemed like an eternity, the tears ran out and the heaving stopped. Dust from the floor scraped against Sara's cheek and lips, some drifting into her eye. Grasping the hem of her abaya, she wiped the speck away.

The packet Reema stitched into the bottom grazed against her fingers. If the As-Sirat were out there, then Sayeed would no longer be her issue.

They would.

Images of what might await her flooded her brain as shivers ran up her spine. No one would ever be allowed to do what he did to her.

With a tug, the folded paper popped out of the threads. She circled her fingers around it. What difference did it make now anyway? Everything that mattered was gone. Why not put herself out of this misery?

She closed her eyes. How would it feel to sleep and never wake up? To escape to a place where monsters could no longer hurt her? Sara stroked the folded edge. Amazing how a small amount of dust could become so powerful.

Nasif said it would take about an hour. "*It will mix with the acid in your stomach. At first feeling like indigestion, then the pain will intensify. Organs will burn. After a while, it will become unbearable and you will beg for relief, pray for death.*"

She ran her finger inside the opening of the packet.

Am I thinking this through? What if Reema isn't dead? What about the boys? If I swallow this, what happens to them?

No.

The boys needed her and she would protect her family. No matter the cost. If there was no family to protect, she had a way out. Wiping the tears off with her sleeve, she tucked the pouch into her bra.

On all fours, Sara felt her way to the wall she'd attacked earlier. Pressed against its cool metal, she pulled herself up. Her palms glided across the surface. There must be a way out. Moving over a few inches, she continued until her fingers connected with smooth plastic, and an inch farther—a button. As soon as it was pressed, darkness was replaced with soft fluorescent light. She rested her head against the wall and waited for her eyes to adjust to the brightness.

There were only two rooms with dead bolts on the outside of the door. One—the prison, which held her two years ago. The other she had never been allowed to enter...until now.

The armory.

CHAPTER TWENTY

THE ARMORY

Gray and black metal boxes of varying sizes lined shelves and cluttered the floor. Dozens of holsters, similar to the ones worn by Amir and the others, hung on the wall. In the middle of the room, three gray trunks lay like coffins alongside each other. Sara unlatched the one closest to her. She hooked her fingers under the edges of the lid, forcing the heavy material off, and rested it against the wall.

Encased in blue foam lay a weapon almost as tall as her and as thick as her thigh. With unsteady fingers, Sara touched its hard, metal surface. As she traced the curved trigger at the end, images from an old movie flashed in her head. Resting a similar contraption on his shoulder, a man in the desert had aimed it at a helicopter in the sky. A missile, much like the three that lay wrapped in blue foam alongside the weapon, flew out of its mouth. The man walked away as hues of yellow, orange, and red exploded in the sky and pieces of metal fell to the sand behind him.

A shudder ran the length of her spine. She shook off the fear and continued. One by one, she opened and searched each container. Inside were weapons, some Sara had never seen, and others she recognized. Mostly, there were guns: long, short, and medium-sized, along with cartons of bullets, packed and waiting.

The perfect tool for groups like the As-Sirat, who used religion as an excuse to terrorize and kill innocents. Just as he had with Umber, Sayeed would profit from their hate. He was evil to the core, but unlike them, he had no religion. His hunger was for money and power. He preferred to display his wickedness in the shadows, out of the watchful eyes of others.

From one of the canisters, Sara traced the outline of the weapon it hugged. When she tugged, a small gun slid out of the containment. Its steely weight felt powerful in her grasp. She pulled out a magazine of bullets tucked in the box and gazed at the weapon in one hand and the heavy black rectangle in her other.

If the As-Sirat had really taken over, they'd make sure the children fulfilled the mission Sayeed had groomed them for. The boys were doomed unless someone stepped in to help.

She slid the clip into the black handle of the gun and, with a push, snapped it into place. The sound of scraping metal and a final click, her reward as the magazine seated itself.

~

A bead of sweat trickled down Sara's temple and followed the path of others to her jaw, along her neck, until it was lost in the collar of her abaya. The spun cotton of the dress seemed more like wool, and everything beneath the heavy fabric was drenched, clinging to her.

An hour, at least, had passed since Amir left, but it felt more like days as she waited for the door to open...if it opened. The spot on the wall she leaned against had warmed from her body heat. Careful not to jostle the contents in her palm, she shifted over a few inches and savored the coolness of the untouched surface against her cheek.

Shaped like a perfume bottle with a sprayer, the blue ball she cupped in her hand was far from delicate. Instead of smooth glass, hard steel chilled her skin. The tips of Sara's fingers slid up the lever to the ring and traced the circular metal. As she hooked her finger into the loop, she closed her eyes. One pull was all it took.

Circled around her feet were more blue globes. Fear sat heavy in her chest. Would the explosion of the one in her hand be enough to set the others off? Enough to destroy everything in the armory?

She exhaled a long, slow breath, pushing down the emotion. If her hunch was right, the As-Sirat would want the three missile launchers behind her more than they would the boys. And if placed in a position to choose, she prayed they'd pick the lifeless metal, allowing the children and Reema to live.

If she was lucky.

But she wasn't naïve. Even if they agreed to her demands, they'd never let her leave the property alive. Which was why, under the abaya, a heavy black belt hugged her waist—latched to it, a gun. Once the kids were safe, she'd put a bullet in her head. A much less painful death than whatever they'd plan.

When the door to the room rattled, terror tightened its grasp around her throat. Sara stood straight, wiped the sweat off her forehead, and tucked her hair behind her ears. She'd come too far to hide now. With the pin still looped around her knuckle, she waited for the visitors to make their entrance.

The door's hinges creaked their complaint when it finally opened. Bright light poured into the darkness, forcing Sara to turn away.

"Didi?" The shy whisper echoed through the hard walls, warming the frozen core of her soul. She searched the entrance, where Amir held the door open. Sara's heart stopped and tears of relief mixed with sweat flowed as she focused on the person standing in front of him.

Reema.

Safe.

Breathing.

"You're alive." Her words trembled, as did the rest of her body while she scanned the woman. "I heard the guns. Then Nasif said your name. I thought..." Frozen in her spot, sobs of relief washed over her and her legs weakened. She rested her back against the wall for support and cried. *I thought...*

When the girl advanced, Amir grabbed her arm, pulling her behind him while his eyes and gun stayed fixed on Sara. He moved forward, speaking his words slowly. "Reema, get out and lock the door behind you."

Instead, she closed the door, shutting the three of them in, and stood between his gun and Sara, staring up at him.

"Put it down." Reema waited until he lowered his weapon before turning to face Sara. "I'm fine, Didi. Everybody is fine. A crazy man..."

When she inched forward a second time, Amir grabbed her wrist, pulling her back again. "No. If she pulls the ring, we die."

Reema tugged out of his grasp and stretched out her hand to

Sara. "Didi, give it to me."

Still in shock, Sara looked down at the forgotten grenade in her palm. Her hands shook as she unhooked her finger from the loop.

Amir swooped in, grabbing it before she had a chance to think. But she didn't care. The only thing she cared about was standing in front of her. Sara stepped over the deadly ring of grenades and sandwiched Reema's face in her hands. Her fingers shook as they moved to her shoulders, arms. Nothing seemed injured, out of place.

Metal boxes opened and slammed shut behind her as Amir returned the grenades to their home.

Reema wrapped her arms around Sara's waist, pulled her into a tight embrace. "Didi..." She stopped mid-sentence when her small hand brushed against the hard metal strapped under Sara's abaya. The gun dug into Sara's hip while Reema explored it.

Goose bumps pebbled Sara's waist and arms and she pulled away. When Reema tried to speak, Sara shook her head, looking over at Amir. The girl nodded and grabbed Sara's wrist instead.

"How could you lock her away like this?" Reema snapped.

He stopped putting away the weapons and stared dumbfounded at her. Amir ran his fingers through his black, wavy hair. "I was trying to keep your Didi safe." He waved in Sara's direction. "She wouldn't listen to me."

"She was scared. She thought I was hurt. Instead of understanding, you caged her in here like a dog." Hearing the selective mute child speak outside their bedroom, much less reprimanding an armed guard, had Sara staring wide-eyed at Reema.

"What would you have preferred? I let her go to the gate while that crazy man was running around? I kept my promise. She is safe."

Sara glanced over at Amir while his words sunk in. "What about the As-Sirat?"

"The As-Sirat? What about the...?" His brows rose and a smile spread across his lips as he shook his head. "You thought you could fight the As-Sirat with a few grenades?"

Reema wiped the sweat off Sara's cheeks with her sleeves. "Didi is tired. I need to get her home and let her rest."

"Of course she is. She was going to single-handedly take down a terrorist group." Amir chuckled and walked past them. When he reached the door, he stopped and looked Sara over. "Do you have any other weapons?"

The pounding in her chest sounded like drums beating in this vacuum of a room. Unable to speak, she stared past him, shaking her head.

Reema grabbed Sara's wrist and thrust her chin out. "Haven't you shamed her enough? Will you search her too?"

He laughed as he opened the door. "It is pure admiration, not shame."

Sara hesitated, peering into the courtyard for any signs of danger. The grounds were oddly quiet, with not a soul in sight.

"It was just a drunk, Didi, nothing more. You are safe," he assured her and urged them along. "I need to tell the boys. Go to your room for now."

She stared at the man who until that day hadn't spoken a word to her. "Amir?"

He stopped in his tracks and turned to her.

"How did you know I understood Urdu?"

Amir glanced at Reema. "You are not the only one with secrets, Didi. Now hurry before the guards see you." With a nod, he jogged toward boys' compound.

She looked over at the pink-faced Reema. Instead of responding, the now silent woman tugged her to their room. With each step Sara took, the hunch in her shoulders straightened and the tremors subsided. Power and hope surged through her veins. So much had changed in a short amount of time. Amir made it clear the As-Sirat weren't on the grounds. But Sayeed would be soon. Now armed with not just poison but also a gun, she no longer worried about holes in her plan.

Everything seemed brighter, better. Even Reema. Not only did she speak, she stood up to Amir. This side of her was far different from the passive girl Sara knew. Strong. Confident. Defiant. Any worries Sara had about what would happen to Reema after tonight dissipated. But first, there were some very important questions she needed answers to.

As soon as the door to their room closed, Sara started her interrogation. "What happened at the gate?"

Reema poured a glass of water and handed to her. "A drunk man made some trouble. The guards shot him. But Nasif and I treated his wounds, he will be fine."

Satisfied with the answer, she gulped down all of the cool liquid before continuing. "What's going on with you and Amir?"

Reema lowered her gaze and fiddled with her sleeve. "When the fighting started, I was coming to find you, but he stopped me. He told me to stay inside and promised he would keep you safe." Enormous hazel eyes searched hers, begging for approval. "And Didi, he did. He shouldn't have locked you up, but it was for me."

"How long has he known that you can speak?"

A red hue crept across Reema's cheeks. "A week, maybe two. But I make sure no one is around when we talk. Are you angry?"

The emotion Sara felt was far from anger, more like relief but first she needed to be sure. "Should I be?"

"No."

"Has anyone else heard you?"

"No." Her eyes widened. "We are careful. I never talk when people are around." A shy smile stretched across her face as she returned to playing with her sleeve. "He says he likes hearing my voice."

Sara blinked away the emotion and squeezed Reema's hand, encouraging her to continue.

"Didi, he is a good man. He says he wants to marry me and take me away from this. He will take care of both of us."

Sara pushed away the sadness. There was nothing she wanted more than to experience the ending Reema narrated, but as long as he lived, Sayeed would never leave them alone. Instead of stating the obvious, Sara pulled Reema into an embrace and discreetly wiped away the one tear that had escaped. "I'm so happy for you."

She ran her hand over the back of the Reema's head and tried to memorize everything about her as they hugged. The heat of sadness choked her, making her voice husky when she finally spoke. "You need to leave."

Reema rested her hand on the gun still on Sara's hip. "What are you going to do with this?"

Sara stepped away from her touch and walked to the door. "You know what it's for."

"You have never used one before."

"I know enough." With one hand on the knob, she pulled Reema with the other. "I have to get ready for tonight and you need to leave. Find Nasif or Amir. Stay with one of them at all times no matter what happens. Understood?"

When she protested, Sara raised her palm. "Reema, I have to kill him tonight."

Her mouth opened and eyes widened.

"He had Umber killed, and I won't let him hurt anyone else. So please go. I need time to think."

Reema wrapped her arms around Sara and rested her head on her shoulder. "Didi, you are all I have."

Shuttering her lids, she fought away the tears as she slid a palm over the back of Reema's head. "That's not true, you have Nasif and Amir. And never doubt my love and loyalty."

When her body shook in quiet sobs, Sara stepped away from the embrace and stared down at her.

"Hey, look at me." Sara tipped Reema's tear-stained face up and stared into her eyes. "This is not goodbye. We will walk out of here together, tonight," she lied. "Just promise me you will stay with one of them at all times until I come for you."

After Reema nodded in agreement, Sara pushed her out and shut the door behind her. Standing against its frame, she blew a breath and closed her eyes.

She reminded herself that killing Sayeed would be the greatest gift she could give Reema and the boys. Her body no longer shook. It was much easier being brave for the sake of others than herself. Sara glanced at the clock on the wall—one o'clock. She had about six hours before Sayeed showed up for his after-dinner entertainment—her.

Peeling the thick abaya over her head, she tossed it to the floor. Her sweat-soaked undershirt and pants clung to her skin. Soon they would be discarded as well. She tied her hair up and unhooked the belt, laying it across her bed.

Magazines in pouches ran the length of the strap. A holster in the middle contained the loaded weapon. A smile tugged at her lips. It would be more than enough to kill Sayeed and his guard.

The gun pulled easily from its sheath. Her hands wrapped around the handle. How could something that weighed around two pounds be capable of taking a life? Sara rested her finger on the trigger and positioned it. She'd seen the guards do it hundreds of times during the boys' weapons training classes.

Images of Sayeed flashed in her mind: the beatings, the rapes, his smell, and the noises he made when he slammed his lust into her. Then there was Umber. Her sweet, brave Umber. What did he think when he walked into that mall and didn't find her waiting for him? The knife Sayeed thrust into her chest when he sent that child to die, twisted.

A shadow in the corner of her right eye caught her attention. Sara's senses went into overdrive. She held her breath and turned to face the unwelcome guest with her gun aimed at the direction of the shadow.

Sayeed?

CHAPTER TWENTY-ONE

TRUST

A tall, dark-haired man stood in front of her. His stubbled cheeks stretched when he flashed Sara a crooked smile. He slowly moved his arms up into the air and waved his hello.

Her stomach twisted and sweat beaded her lip. The weight of the gun increased with every second it was pointed at his chest. She took a breath and attempted to hide the fear building within. "Who are you?" she asked in fluent Urdu.

"A friend," he responded, stepping forward.

Her finger tightened on the trigger and she inched away. "You're not my friend. Don't come any closer. I will shoot you."

He shook his head and moved closer. The corners of his mouth twitched as if fighting a smile. "No, I don't believe you will."

The sound of her heart racing behind her ears was deafening.

With a steady hand, she aimed at his forehead and inched toward him. "What makes you think I won't?"

He jutted his chin at her weapon. "Your safety's on."

Her focus shifted to the little orange dot on the side of the gun. Dividing her attention between him and the safety, she moved her thumb to slide it.

He lowered his arms and took another step closer. "Trust me, that's not a good idea."

Sara swiped at the top of the lever as he lunged forward. In seconds, her back was slammed against the wall, legs forced apart by his, wrists pulled over her head, all while his cheek pressed into hers. Fortunately, three of her fingers still grasped the butt of the gun.

"Told you that wasn't a good idea," he whispered.

The proximity of his body. The way his hips pressed into hers. The warmth of his breath against her skin. It all transported her to the hundreds of times Sayeed violated her.

Rage seeped through her, heating her muscles, and for the first time in two years, she tried to fight off the attack. She squirmed and twisted her body against his as she inched the gun farther into her hand. "Do you have any idea who my husband is?"

Undeterred by her, the man laughed in her ear. "Yes, actually I do, and that's why I'm here."

"He'll kill you when he finds out you're in my room." Her fingers inched up the handle.

He twisted her wrists behind her and grabbed them together into one of his. With his free hand, he pulled the weapon from her grasp, tossing it to the other side of the room. Sara watched as her chance for escape slid under the bed. When she tried to slam her head into his, he pressed his cheek to hers, immobilizing her head against the wall.

The warmth of his breath tickled her ear when he spoke. "He's the one that sent me."

Sara's stomach dropped. Sayeed? The man responsible for her hell was paying a stranger to end it? That didn't make any sense. She stared down at the blue vein snaking around the side of the assailant's tanned neck. An idea popped into her head.

"Will you stop fighting and listen to what I have to say?" The vulnerable skin flexed when he spoke.

She nodded and waited for her chance.

When he shifted his weight, releasing the hold on her head, she bit down on the target. The taste of sweat burst into her mouth. Teeth punctured skin. Soon the metallic flavor of blood mixed with his salty flesh spread across her tongue. She pushed away the desire to gag and worked to deepen the wound.

"Fuck!" He groaned, shoving her away and jumping back.

While he pressed against the injured area, she ran for the door. Before she could open it, arms encircled her, lifting her off the floor. Sara kicked and twisted as he dragged her to her bed and tossed her on to it.

Out of breath and ready to fight, she climbed to her knees. He pointed a finger at her, panting. “I don’t give a fuck who your husband is. Move off that bed and I’ll fucking tie you down, understand?”

His words got her attention. Not because of what he said but how he said it. He spoke clear English. The accent-free kind she hadn’t heard in years. Sara stared at him as he grabbed a handkerchief from the pocket of his jeans and put it on the gashes of red beading on his neck. “David sent me. So can you please keep your incisors inside your lovely lips and listen?”

That name hadn’t been spoken out loud in so long, it sounded foreign. Her throat dried and breath caught in her lungs. She wiped the remnants of the man’s blood from the corners of her mouth and gestured for him to continue.

“So please, no more guns, vampire attacks, or anything else until I’ve finished my job. Okay?”

She rested on her haunches as her mind raced.

David sent him?

David knew she was alive?

It didn’t sound right. This was Sayeed’s doing. Just like how he lured Umber into that mall with lies, this was an entertaining story he’d created to lead her to slaughter.

Sara jutted her chin out and rose to her knees. “You have the wrong woman. I am Sara Irfani. Second wife to Sayeed Irfani.”

He grinned, making her wish she had bitten him harder. “Really? So you don’t know who David is?”

The man dug into his jean pocket. Unsure of what weapon he’d pull out, she prepared to lunge at him. “Wait, just look at this first before you drink me dry.” He tossed a thin, palm-sized television screen onto the bed.

A chill ran through her the moment she saw the face staring out from the monitor. David. His face was bearded and he looked tired, but she’d have recognized him anywhere. She grabbed the device and leapt off the bed. “What did you do to him?”

His palms in the air, the man moved away. “Nothing. I swear. Press the arrow in the middle of the screen.”

“If you’ve hurt him...”

"Then you'll kill me. Hit Play and find out." The man shifted to the side of the bed and squatted. When he pulled the gun out from under it, her heart hammered against her breast.

She opened her mouth but he raised a finger and stood. "If after you listen to the video, you still think I'm the bad guy"—he slipped off the safety and handed her the gun—"then shoot me."

Sara's gaze shifted between him and the weapon in her hand, unsure of what to do next.

"We don't have a lot of time. Please." He pointed to the device.

She brought it closer and pressed the arrow. When David blinked, she gasped. In all this time, there had only been pictures, frozen images of him. As the weeks turned to months then to years, it became harder to remember the details. The mix of blue and green in his eyes. The way his mouth lifted his cheeks when he talked excitedly as he currently did.

"Ally, it's me." The deep baritones sunk into the crater in her chest, filling her. Tears built, but with an audience, she swallowed them and worked to look unaffected. She pulled the recording closer and tried to memorize every detail of David. His face. His voice. Although his words were rushed, each syllable warmed her.

"Nasif told me everything. By now, you've met Eddie. He's a mercenary. Your dad's paid him a lot of money to get you out of there. Do whatever he says, trust him. He'll keep you safe. We're bringing you home, baby. I promise. Reya, Nik, your parents, we're all waiting for you."

The screen froze on his face, ending too soon. A hunger for more—to touch him and feel his embrace rocked her.

"I'm Eddie, in case you were curious."

Sara kept her gaze locked on the screen as David's words repeated in her mind. He was still waiting for her? Still wanted her?

The heat of emotion burned her eyes with the reality of her situation. He didn't want her, none of them did. They wanted the naïve, unbroken Ally who disappeared two years ago. The person she'd never be again. Sayeed's damage couldn't be undone.

She handed the video and the gun to Eddie and backed away. "You need to go home and tell them she's dead."

When he didn't accept either, she tossed them on the bed and walked to the far corner of the room, seating herself on a chair. Sara placed her hands in her lap and tried to figure out how to convince the man to leave.

He mumbled things under his breath and followed her. Standing in front of her, Eddie planted his palms on his hips. “My job is to bring you. Once you’re there, you can tell them whatever the hell you want.”

Sara grabbed the bag Reema had packed that sat on the floor beside her. She picked through the pounds of jewelry, selected the most valuable, and handed them to Eddie. “Here. Whatever they’re paying you, I’ll double. Gold, diamonds. More than enough to cover your expenses.”

He squatted in front of her, staring into her eyes as if trying to read her mind. “Why?”

She dropped her gaze to the valuables in her lap. “Alisha died two years ago. I’m not that woman anymore. I have a family here that needs me. I can’t leave them.”

He blew out a breath and muttered some more.

Sara lifted the bag to him. “Isn’t this enough?”

Eddie reached into the tote, grabbed a handful of jewelry, and inspected it. “How’d you get all of this?”

She laughed. “Gifts from my husband.”

He returned the stash and took another fistful. “That doesn’t make any sense. Sayeed keeps his wives completely covered and inconspicuous. Jewelry would draw attention.”

She tugged at the thick gold choker studded with diamonds in Eddie’s hands. “In public, he expects us to be covered and without makeup and jewels. But there’s a part of him most don’t see. The part that likes his sexual conquests adorned in gold and diamonds and nothing else. It’s a fetish of his.”

Eddie returned the jewels to the bag and pulled out David’s pictures. One by one, he laid them on her lap. “Your real husband wants you home. And I can do that. Get you out of here and away from that motherfucker.”

Instead of sharing her plans or explaining that the “motherfucker” in question wouldn’t just sit idly by and allow that, she returned the pictures and the jewels to the bag, handing it all to Eddie.

He shook his head and put them on the floor. “I don’t need this. They’re paying enough. I’ll tell them you’re dead, if that’s what you want. But first, I need your help. One of my associates has been shot and is being held here. I need to get him out."

Sara thought of Reema's description of earlier events. "The drunk?"

He smiled. "He wasn't drunk. But yes, we were on the same mission when things got a little crazy."

An idea began to take form in her head. Sara locked gazes with Eddie. "I'll help you on one condition."

"Besides lying to your family? What more could you possibly want?"

"There are some others I need your help in getting out of here."

Eddie stood up and laughed. He walked to her bed and sat down before answering. "Others? As in plural?"

She nodded.

He dipped his handkerchief into her water glass and cleaned his neck. "How many?"

"Sixteen."

He chuckled and shook his head. "You want me to get sixteen people and my injured partner out of here?"

Her chest tightened. This could work. "Yes."

"Alive?"

"Yes."

He continued cleaning his wound as if they were talking about the weather. "Who?"

"My servant girl, Reema. Nasif and the boys who live in the house outside."

Eddie flashed her a crooked smile. "The suicide bombers in training?"

She bit her lip and fought the urge to snap. "Like I said, I'll help you if you help me."

"And they'll come willingly?"

"I'll make sure of it."

His brows rose as he stared at her in disbelief. "How exactly do you expect to manage that?"

Sara headed to the side of the bed, picked up the gun, and passed it to him. "Sayeed will arrive soon. We need to get them out before he shows up. I will get Reema, Nasif, the boys, and your friend. Your job will be to take care of the two men at the gate. I'm assuming you can do that much?"

He rolled his eyes.

Amir's face popped into her head. "The other guard, I'll take care of."

Eddie scanned the room and laughed. "You're joking, right?"

When she didn't respond, he sobered. "I'm supposed to sneak out the entire compound except for you. What happens to you?"

Fear fluttered its wings, making its ascent within her. She quickly turned her thoughts to Umber, squelching the emotions attempting to smother her. "Sayeed and I have some unfinished business we need to address. I can only do that once everyone's safe."

A rasp at the door silenced their conversation. Eddie rushed to the armoire, squeezing his muscular body into the small space and shutting himself inside. The mirror on its frame caught Sara's attention and her face flushed. Dressed in a paper thin white T-shirt and one of the boys' white linen pants, much too short for her, Sayeed would beat her to a pulp if he found her like this.

"Didi, open the door."

She forced the almost-dry abaya over her head and rushed to let Reema in.

The young girl hurried into the room with a tray of food. The smell of warm bread and lentil soup filled the space. She placed it on the bed while Sara closed and locked the door.

"I told you to stay with Nasif and Amir. You shouldn't be here," Sara whispered. Ignoring her, the girl filled a bowl with the steamy yellow liquid. She tore a piece of the bread, scooped the lentils onto it, and popped it into Sara's mouth when she opened it to tell the girl to leave.

"I know what you said, but I've discovered something important you need to know. First, eat."

Sweet, soft wheat mixed with garlic and peppers melted on her tongue. Sara's stomach rumbled its approval.

"See..." Reema nudged her chin at Sara's waist. "You haven't eaten since last night and you need energy for today."

"Thank you. I will eat but you need to leave. Now." Sara steered her to the door.

Reema twisted around, inserting another morsel of the warm food into Sara's mouth. "I will. Let me tell you about what I've found first. The man they have is an American." Before Sara had a chance to finish her second bite, another was shoved in.

She cupped her mouth to prevent further additions.

"They have him in the same room they locked you in. Sayeed is on his way. Amir says the American will be killed tonight."

Sara stopped mid-chew, lost in thought. Sayeed would be back sooner than expected. Her head throbbed with all the things that had to be done before he showed up.

Reema let out a gasp. Her plate of food fell to the floor. Mouth covered, the girl looked past Sara at the armoire. Sara turned to see Eddie staring back at them.

"Reema, it's okay. He won't hurt you. This is..."

"Edil Bhai," Reema whispered as tears flowed. Sara wrapped her arm around the sobbing girl's shoulders, searching Eddie's face for answers.

His reddened eyes stayed glued on Reema, and when he spoke, his teeth were clenched. "Her name is not Reema, it's Farah. She's no one's servant."

He reached for Reema. "I'm here to take you home."

"Home?" Reema snapped, stepping deeper into Sara's embrace. "What home? You left me. My home is with Didi, not with you." She rested her head against Sara's shoulder as she wept.

"Farah..." he whispered, inching toward her.

"Don't come any closer." Sara pulled her back, suddenly regretting that she gave him the gun. "Reema, who is he?"

The girl wiped her face with the sleeve of her gown. "It's okay, Didi. He can't hurt me any more than he already has." With a deep gulp of air, she continued. "Edil Bhai is my elder brother by fourteen years. He was my hero. My everything. Then one morning when I was nine, he and Pappa had a big argument. I never saw him again. I begged Pappa and Mommy to bring him home, but he never came."

Eddie ran his fingers through his hair and looked at the floor.

"After everyone was killed and I was brought here, I used to pray he would rescue me. That he would kill Sayeed for all the things he did to me and our family. But he never came." Her voice cracked as words became incoherent through her sobs.

When Reema's legs buckled, Sara gently slid them both to the floor. Eddie squatted beside them and pulled his sister into his embrace. Instead of resisting him, Reema rested her forehead against his chest and cried.

"I came, Farah," he whispered. "I promise you I did, but they lied to me. I didn't know." Eddie kissed the top of her forehead and pulled her scarf off, resting his chin on her head. "They threw their bodies in a pit and left them there to rot," he said.

She moaned softly as his lip quivered.

Sara moved away from the two, seating herself on the bed as she wiped away her own tears.

"I took them home and buried them. There were five bodies. Pappa, Mommy, Raza, the servant and a little girl. All this time, they let me believe I buried you."

"Nay Bhai, that was Reema, the maid's daughter," the child whispered.

Their voices became distant sounds as thoughts ran through Sara's mind. Between Eddie and Amir, there was no doubt Reema would be cared for. But what about the others? With Sayeed arriving at any moment, how could she save them? Now that he found his sister, would Eddie and the man in the prison even help?

"Didi?"

Reema's voice pulled her out of her head. Sara smiled at how at ease she looked wrapped in her brother's arms. How long must it have been since she'd felt that way?

"You two talk. I need to find Nasif and Amir. If Sayeed's on his way here, we're running out of time. I need to figure out who's going to help and how to get everyone out of here before he shows up."

Before Sara got to the door, Eddie grabbed her arm. "No, you need to stay in this room until I tell you otherwise."

She jerked it away and reached for the handle. "This is too important. We only get one chance."

He pushed against the door. "I get that, and I know what you want. I'll make sure it happens, all of it. But you have to trust me and stay in here. This is bigger than you think, and there are others involved. Let us do our job."

Sara raised her brows. "Us?"

"Trust me."

CHAPTER TWENTY-TWO

CONCUSSIONS

A hammer pounded against the back of Dave's skull. When he moved his fingers to the targeted spot, fiery currents of pain shot throughout every inch of his body, making him groan.

"Can you hear me?" A man's thick accent broke through his foggy trance. Dave nodded but stopped mid-movement because it made him wince. He cracked his eyelids open, adjusting to the light before opening them all the way and staring into the round face peering down at him.

"David, do you know who I am?"

He squinted at the familiar-looking stranger, waiting for his brain to click on. When it finally did, the events that led to the present flashed in quick succession. How he staggered to the gate and banged against it. The two guards who flashed their guns and threatened him in broken English. Instead of walking away, he hurled insults and rocks at them until finally they rushed out of the compound after him. The bigger of the two slammed the butt of his gun against Dave's head while he tried to pull the other guard's weapon away. The last things he remembered were the ear-splitting sound when the gun went off, the pain that coursed down his leg, and his head being used for batting practice.

How did it all go so wrong?

"Do you know who I am?" The old man's voice rose a few

octaves, bringing him to the present.

Dave swallowed through the pain. "Yes, Nasif, I know who you are."

Nasif released a breath and flashed his plump finger in Dave's face. "Good. Now follow my finger."

At first, Dave trailed the digit to the left but then turned his attention to the room. Four gray walls stood over ten feet tall, creating an almost perfect square. Void of furniture except for the bed on which he rested, it boasted two closed doors on opposite sides. Halogen lighting and a lack of windows added to the prison appeal.

Shit.

Dave hoisted himself up and leaned against the wall, a difficult task considering his left leg was currently lifeless. The denim on that leg had been torn off from mid-thigh down, and white gauze wrapped around the area just above his knee.

The plump brown finger returned in front of his face.

"Pay attention, please."

He nodded and did as he was told. "Where am I?"

"You're in the compound. Now, what's your name?"

A question like that would have typically made Dave's eyes roll, but with the way his head throbbed, he didn't even bother. "David."

The old man squeezed his shoulder and smiled before continuing his exam. As he pried open each lid and flashed a light into his eye, Dave pushed for more information.

"What happened?"

"Well, instead of distracting the guards, you decided to fight them. The end result is, you have a gunshot wound to the thigh and a concussion." Nasif sat on the bed beside him and pointed to the injured leg. "Lucky for you, the bullet went straight through, missing your femoral artery by a millimeter. You should have full feeling of your leg in a few minutes."

Dave ran a hand over the throbbing area of his skull. "And my head?"

"The guards hit their guns into the back of it. Your occipital bone appears to be intact, although it's probably bruised." He handed him a towel. "Here, put this on the area. It should help."

He took the wet cloth from the old man and placed it on the

spot, instantly the pain cooled. "And Ally?"

Before Nasif had a chance to respond, something slammed against the door. The old man leapt off the cot and when Dave tried to do the same, Nasif pushed him back down.

Before they could argue, a woman's high-pitched wail erupted from the other side of the room.

Ally?

Dave's heart raced. He jumped off the bed, forgetting about his injury until his thigh suddenly felt like it was consumed in fire. By his second step, the room spun and his knees buckled. Nasif grabbed him before he hit the ground and guided him back to the bed. When Dave tried to argue, the old man flashed a palm, silencing him. Outside, keys jingled against the door and muffled voices floated through the thick wood.

Unsure if it would be Ally or Sayeed on the other side, Dave sucked in a breath and watched as the knob turned and the door creaked open.

As soon as he caught a glimpse of the woman at the threshold, his heart sank. It wasn't Ally. She rushed in and Eddie followed behind, dragging the body of a man by his leg into the room with him. The woman shut the door and rushed to the dead or unconscious man on the floor, resting his head in her lap and pressing her cheek against his face.

Eddie glared at the couple as he walked to Dave, grumbling something in Urdu.

"What the fuck is going on?" Dave asked as he watched Nasif rush to the man on the floor and check his vitals.

The mercenary planted his hands on his hips and shook his head at the scene. "Nothing good."

Nasif rested his hand on the girl's shoulder and spoke to her. The way he talked in a soft, fatherly tone, wiped her face, even kissed her forehead, made Dave's throat tighten. *Had he soothed Ally like that?*

He shook the thought away. That didn't matter right now. All that mattered was bringing her home.

The room slanted when Dave climbed off the bed a second time. But this time Eddie caught him before he hit the ground.

"What the hell happened to you?"

Dave grabbed his arm and waited for things to stop moving. "I fucked up. But I'll be okay. A superficial wound and a concussion. Did you find her?"

He looked at Dave as if trying to figure something out before he answered. "Do you want to sit down?"

"No, it's not spinning as much. Just give me another second." Once everything stopped, Dave let go of his arm and twisted around to face him. "Did you find her?"

He averted his gaze. "Yeah."

Dave's breath caught in his lungs. "Does she know I'm here?"

"Sort of."

A mixture of excitement and irritation bubbled to the surface. "I don't pay you for answers like that."

Eddie sat on the bed, glaring at the couple on the floor. "She knows my *associate* has been captured, and I'll be getting him out but not that it's you."

His mouth dropped. "What? Why didn't you tell her?"

The agent pulled the shoulder strap of his tank top aside, exposing red swollen skin and teeth marks. "She wasn't too happy to see me. Went all Vampira on me."

Dave's bruised head throbbed when he clenched his teeth and tried to rein in his anger. "Because she fucking bit you, you decided not to tell her?"

Eddie flashed him a scowl before returning his attention to the couple on the floor. "No, because she said she didn't want to leave."

Dave shook his head, trying to process Eddie's response. He sat on the bed as his blood ran cold. "Ally wants to stay here?"

"When I told her you sent me, she tried to pay me off. Said to tell you and the rest of the family she's dead. Between the biting and the bribing, I figured it wouldn't be a good idea to share that you were the one locked up in here."

The pain in his head and leg dulled while he tried to make sense of the agent's recount of events. *She knows I sent him and she said no?* "Why would she do that?"

When the woman on the floor gasped, Eddie jumped off the bed and reached into the waistband of his jeans, pulling out a gun. "Looks like our friend's finally awake."

The now-conscious guard moved his head, grabbing the back of his skull. With Nasif and the woman's help, he sat up and scanned the room until his gaze landed on Eddie and the gun currently aimed at him.

Nasif positioned himself between Eddie and the man. "Put it down. Amir is a friend."

Eddie jutted his chin toward the man on the floor. "Any forty-year-old man who thinks it's okay for a child to fall in love with him is no friend."

Nasif shook his head. "Reema..."

"Her. Name. Is. Farah."

"*Farah* is older and wiser than her eighteen years, and let me finish." Nasif's voice rose when Eddie began to argue.

The old man walked over and squeezed Amir's shoulder. "He is only twenty-three, and you owe him your sister's life. He found her hiding in the servants' quarters the day they attacked your family. For me, he lied and told Sayeed she was the servant's daughter. That's the only reason she was spared." Nasif cleared his throat. "Sayeed gifted her to Alyah and hasn't thought twice about her since."

"I don't owe any of you anything," Eddie snapped back. "If you'd told me the truth from the beginning, we wouldn't even be having this conversation."

Dave climbed onto his feet and hopped closer to them.

"When she came here, she was scared and with good reason. These men are not moral, God-fearing people. Their loyalty is to Sayeed and each other. Amir made it clear to them she was his, and if they touched her, he'd kill them. Even though he was only a teenager himself at the time, they respected him enough to honor that wish."

"He staked his claim on a child. On what planet is that considered acceptable?" Eddie stepped around Nasif and pointed the gun at Amir. "He's a disgusting piece of shit."

The old man planted his hand on Eddie's wrist. "He staked his claim of protection, nothing more. What's blossomed between them is very new and pure. You owe them a chance to see where this leads."

"Again with the *owe* bullshit. *He* is one of Sayeed's men. His loyalty is not with us."

"Nay, Edil Bhai." Farah rose to her feet, standing in front of the gun. Her lover was up seconds after her, pushing the woman behind him. She poked her head around his side. "Amir is different. He would never hurt us or Didi. See? His loyalty *is* to us."

Eddie scowled at her, and when Amir spoke something to him in Urdu, the agent growled back his response, quieting the guard.

Unable to keep his desperation and anger under control any further, Dave hobbled into the middle of the reunion, glaring at them. "Somewhere in this building is my wife, and Sayeed plans to kill her tonight. I'm pretty sure that when he sees me, he'll kill her sooner. We need to get her out of here, alive, now. There is no time for this bullshit, and we can use his help."

"David?" Farah's eyes widened. "You're Didi's David?" When she stepped toward him with her hand outstretched, Amir grabbed her, positioning her again behind him.

"Stop fucking touching her," Eddie snapped. Seconds later, his hand was wrapped around Amir's neck while his gun jabbed at the man's temple.

Dave hobbled over to the agent, who for the third time that day was pushing someone against a wall. Amir stretched his muscular arms out and made no attempt to fight.

"For God's sake. He was trying to protect your sister," Dave hissed.

A few frozen seconds later, Eddie lowered his gun and stepped away. Farah ran into Amir's arms, who kept his attention on the brother while he pressed her against his chest. A spasm of pain flashed across Eddie's face as he watched the two. "You're right, we need to get out of here before Sayeed shows up."

The guard inched his face closer to hers, wiping the tears from her face. Eddie rolled his eyes and looked to the ceiling as if waiting for divine intervention, infuriating David even more.

"This debate and reunion is going to have to wait. I need to find Ally and talk some sense into her."

Eddie tucked his gun in his pants. "She's not coming and we've run out of time."

In stunned silence, Dave watched the man search the room. *After everything that's happened, to be this close, he's walking away now?*

The heat of anger flooded him, and this time it was Dave pushing Eddie against the wall. "We're not leaving without her. I paid you to..."

Eddie shoved him off, and with only one healthy leg, Dave fell onto his ass.

"Don't ever do that again." He glared down at him before leaning over and offering his hand.

Ignoring his help, Dave crawled over to the bed.

"First of all, the whole money thing was a cover. And for the record, you paid me to find her, not rescue your ass out of here, and I'm already doing way more than I ever agreed to. I told you from the beginning she might not come. I'm not risking everyone's lives by trying to make her do something she doesn't want to do. Second, I'm already neck-deep in shit for not following orders. We need to get out of here before all hell breaks loose."

Dave hoisted himself onto the bed as Eddie finished his rambling. "Fine, then go. Just know that no matter what she says or does, I'm not leaving my wife. Do you understand? He is going to kill her. Even if she doesn't want me, I'm not going to let that happen."

"She plans to poison Sayeed tonight." Farah's quiet voice chimed in, silencing both of theirs.

Dave's gut twisted as he turned to face her. "What?"

"She said that if he is left alive, he will never let any of us live in peace."

The puzzle fell into place. Why Ally refused to run away and why she wanted Eddie to tell him she was dead. She didn't think she'd survive the night. "I won't leave without her," he whispered.

"Then, my friend, this is where we say goodbye, because I need to get my sister out before Sayeed shows up." When Eddie grabbed Farah's arm, she pulled away and returned to Amir. The guard wrapped his arms protectively around her and spoke to her very unhappy big brother. Farah nodded at whatever the man said.

Dave looked between all of them, desperately wishing someone would tell him what the hell was going on. He locked gazes with Nasif. The old man smiled reassuringly and walked to him. He grabbed Dave's arm and guided him back to the bed. "What the fuck is he saying?"

Nasif grinned as he rummaged through his backpack. "That we're not leaving without your wife."

Dave let out the breath he'd been holding.

Nasif filled a syringe with clear liquid from a vial. "This is a cortisone shot. It'll help numb the pain."

As he leaned over the bandaged leg, Dave focused on the activities in the room, trying to ignore the sharp pain of the needle when it penetrated into his wound.

Everyone froze when Amir's cell phone started to ring. The guard pulled it out of his jean pocket and everyone listened to his one-sided conversation in Urdu.

After he hung up, Nasif translated. "It was Sayeed. He's pulling into the compound now."

Dave's body turned to ice. They were too late. Eddie wrapped his arms around his sister and kissed her head.

"He's promising to never leave her again," Nasif said with a smile. The old man grabbed his backpack and squeezed Dave's shoulder. "Don't worry. We'll get your Alisha home safe."

Dave watched as Eddie handed Amir a gun. The guard, Farah, and Nasif all left the room, leaving him and Eddie alone.

When Dave slid off the mattress, Eddie pushed him back on. "Sorry, buddy, you're the prisoner he's coming to visit. We don't have a lot of time, so listen. Sayeed's sharp, probably already suspects who you are. So whatever you do, don't tell him. We have to play on his doubt until I come up with a way to get us out of here. Understand?"

Dave nodded while his heart tried to take flight. He wiped off the perspiration dripping from his forehead with the back of his hand.

Eddie pulled a gun from the back of his jeans. "I'll be here the whole time so don't worry about anything." He checked the magazine inside his gun before lying flat on his back on the floor next to the bed. "Now move your feet."

Dave lifted his legs. "What are you doing?"

He grinned as he slid under the bed. "Waiting for the guest of honor."

CHAPTER TWENTY-THREE

LUNCH

Keys jingled for the second time in thirty minutes on the other side of the door. Dave's throat tightened, and he clenched and released his fingers as the voices from the hall floated into the room. Seated on the floor against the farthest corner from the entrance, he waited. The brass handle turned and the dark wood door creaked open. With a deep breath, he reminded himself of the goal: not fucking up and getting everyone out alive.

He glanced over at the black wing-tipped shoes now visible at the threshold, up to the designer gray pinstriped slacks and jacket which covered a heavy set body. Finally higher to the round, bearded head that crowned the thick frame. When their gazes locked, the man nodded and approached.

Hate tightened around Dave's throat. He swallowed it and leaned against the wall to look up at the man who had tormented his wife for two years.

"Why am I here?" The words came out drawled and as Southern as possible.

Sayeed folded his hand over his gut and smiled. "I was going to ask you the same question." His voice grated in Dave's ears, tightening his chest.

More footsteps approached. A Goliath of a man over six foot seven, muscle-bound to the point that he waddled, entered the room. He was dressed in traditional long shirt and pants like the rest of the Pakistani men, but compared to him, they looked like weeds. The scar that snaked across his cheek seemed to smile when Goliath scowled. The sweat stains around his armpits and neck and the gun strapped to his waist raised his intimidation factor exponentially. The creature leaned against the wall and silently glared.

Sayeed cleared his throat. "Now, let's try this again. Why are you here?"

Dave eyed the man in front of him. Ways of beating the fucking bastard's brains into his asshole swirled in his head. Instead of revealing those thoughts, he shrugged, repeating the story Eddie had made him practice since they'd boarded the plane in Philly. "I'm a tourist and was backpacking across the country the past few weeks."

Sayeed seated himself on the bed and leaned forward. "Backpacking?" The corners of his mouth twitched. "Where all have you been?"

"The Chitral Mountains, Peshewar, and now Lahore for a few days before I go home. The people I'm with will notice I'm gone and notify the American Embassy. You should let me go before this becomes an international incident."

By the time Dave was done with his speech, the man was laughing. "What's your name?"

"Jordan. I'd give you my passport, but for some reason I don't have it anymore."

Sayeed pulled the navy book in question from his jacket and thumbed through it. "Jordan Campbell. Place of birth, Atlanta, Georgia." He flipped several pages and turned the book sideways. "You arrived almost two weeks ago to Lahore."

Dave kept his face stoic. "This is where I started. You know how hard it is to find liquor in Pakistan. Well I got my hands on some today, and I guess I went a little overboard 'cause I don't remember anything else. And like I said before, my buddies must be worried about me."

"Yes, you did mention that." He tossed the passport and it landed next to Dave's injured leg. "And your wound. Is it better?"

"I can't walk on it. Probably need to see a doctor to have it checked out."

"No need. A doctor has already tended to it. He says you need to keep the leg immobilized for a few days."

Dave picked up the book and looked through it while trying to come up with a response. "I'd prefer to have a hospital check it out, if you don't mind."

"Of course. That would be the American thing to do."

The smile on his face and the sarcasm in his voice both made the need to beat the shit out of him that much harder to resist. "So can I go now?"

"Jordan." He spoke the name slowly, allowing both syllables to roll off his tongue. "You remind me of someone. Have you ever been in Philadelphia?"

Dave pushed the book into his jean pocket. "No."

"Hmm, this person I'm thinking of, his name is David. He went on vacation about the same time you arrived in Lahore. Strange coincidence."

"Can I go now?"

"Soon." Sayeed slid off the bed, slanted his head, and looked him over. "Excuse me for a minute. I'd like for you to meet someone."

Dave's heart slammed against his ribs and continued to do so long after Sayeed walked out of the room and shut the door behind him. Goliath, on the other hand, remained in the room, still glaring. Dave nodded at him before resting his head against the cement wall. A bead of sweat trickled down his neck as he said a silent prayer.

~

Finally showered, Sara searched through her armoire for the black, lacy lingerie Sayeed frequently requested her to wear and pulled them out. She couldn't afford to make a mistake, not even in the clothes she wore.

Meeting Eddie and realizing her family wanted to bring her home had weakened her, awakening the loneliness and ache for them that she had long put to sleep. She couldn't afford to succumb to those emotions. As the bra straps slid over shoulders, Sara locked away the thoughts and honed in on the pain and loss of the past two years. Those were the emotions that would help her achieve her goals.

She squatted, pulled off the leg of the nightstand, and took out the pouch hidden within. After slipping it under the rubber band wound around her bicep, Sara replaced the leg and finished dressing.

Eddie had no idea who he was going up against. If he thought he and his associate could take on Sayeed and win, they were both stupid. Everyone Sara cared about would die in the process. That was not an option.

After a quick glance in the mirror, she walked out of the bedroom. The eerie silence of the compound alone heightened her senses. It was usually active with people and voices this time of day. The smell of warm *naan* and spiced meat drew Sara to the kitchen. She walked in to find Reema ladling steamy chicken curry into a brass bowl, unaware of her presence. When the young woman noticed her, she jumped.

Sara closed the door and walked to her. “Is that for the boys? Here, let me. I need to talk with them anyway.”

Reema pulled the tray away before she could grab it. “Nay Didi, Nasif Uncle is already with them. He will explain everything.”

Sara turned for the door. “Those boys adore their father. What we say is very important.”

Before she could open it, Reema grabbed her wrist. “He is a smart man, Didi. Trust him.”

Trust? That was the one thing she couldn’t afford to give. As she considered what to do, Reema leaned in close and whispered in her ear. “Sayeed is here.”

Her stomach twisted at the realization time had run out.

“He’s asking for his meal. There are more important things you need to do. No?”

She nodded at Reema and walked back to the food. She stared at the bowl of chicken curry and bread already in the tray. A meal cooked by an innocent girl to feed a monster. As the steam rose, Sara’s fears evaporated. “You’re right. There are more important things I need to take care of. Go. I don’t want you to have any part in this.”

Reema wrapped her arms around her. Sara’s eyes burned when soft lips pressed against her cheek before she disappeared into the back pantry. After one last check to make sure the door to the kitchen was closed, Sara grabbed a second vessel from the stack of clean dishes on the counter. Popping the packet of poison out, she rolled the rubber band off her arm. The fine white powder dusted the bottom of the brass bowl and disappeared when she poured the steamy lentils into it. Sayeed's favorite dish. Sara poured chili sauce into the poisoned bowl of lentils and stirred. Perfect. Just the way he liked it. Once complete, she placed it on the tray alongside the serving of chicken curry and hot naan. Now to get rid of the evidence.

As soon as the knob to the stove was turned, a blue flame flashed on. She dipped the corner of the brown packet into its flame, tossed the lit paper in the sink, and watched it turn to black ash before rinsing the remnants down the drain.

"There you are."

She jumped at the sound of his voice. When she turned, it was to find Sayeed standing by the threshold, smiling. "I scared you."

Sara nodded and busied herself with his lunch tray. Swallowing a gulp of air, she tried to contain her rush of terror. "You've never come into the kitchen before. It was unexpected."

He grabbed her elbow and walked her to the door. "I am a man of many surprises. Come, I have another one for you."

She yanked her arm away and immediately wished she hadn't.

Brows raised, he glared at her defiance.

Sara lifted the tray of food. "I just finished making your lunch. Let me feed you first. Then you can surprise me."

She held her breath, waiting for his wrath.

Instead, he laughed. "Excellent. Get the food. Today, I want you to personally feed your husband."

With tray in hand, she followed him out. Instead of turning to the dining room, he veered right toward the cell that once held her prisoner. Fear crawled up Sara's spine and wrapped itself around her chest. Was he planning to kill her now?

She shook the question away and focused on Amir standing in front of the room, waiting. Too much was at stake for her to go into panic mode right now.

Even if he plans to lock me away, it will be after he eats. I will make sure of it.

The thought calmed her enough to find her voice. "Why are we here?"

Sayeed's yellow teeth flashed that smile of excitement he got whenever he was about to make someone's life miserable. "I told you I have a surprise for you."

What if Eddie works for Sayeed? The knot in her chest tightened. She squeezed the tray into her stomach and focused on the pain. "You also said you wanted me to feed you."

"And you will. In here." He waved at the door, which Amir promptly opened.

Sara hesitated at the threshold, a bead of sweat accumulating over her lip, unsure of what to do. Sayeed tugged at her elbow, making the decision for her. For the first time in two years, she was back in the prison.

Kadeen stood inside against the wall and beside the only piece of furniture in the room, the bed. Nothing had changed.

A movement in the corner caught her attention. A bearded man with the perfect mix of blue in his sea green eyes stared back. Suddenly, Sara forgot how to breathe.

~

Dave tried his best to look ambivalent while his heart raced and every muscle in his body ached to hold her. But he couldn't. Not while the asshole scrutinized his every move. Instead, he stayed frozen as she scanned the room.

When she finally laid eyes on him, Ally's chocolate browns widened slightly as recognition hit. He watched her take in his bandaged leg. As much as he hungered to know what she thought, if it bothered her to see him injured, he understood why she kept her expression emotionless. Their gazes locked again, and this time she didn't look away. Dave's chest tightened. He dug his nails into the heels of his palms as he warred with his need to run to her.

Sayeed squeezed her elbow and dragged her forward, pulling them both out of their trance. "I would like for you to meet my wife." The motherfucker walked behind her, rested his chin on her shoulder, and beamed.

An uncomfortable silence filled the room. Dave nodded his acknowledgement, but fear his voice would give him away kept his mouth shut.

"Why don't you feed our prisoner, love?" Sayeed kissed her cheek.

Acid crept its way up Dave's throat. He swallowed it and watched the bastard caress her face. Sayeed would suffer for everything he'd ever done to her.

Ally stared at the food in her hands and shuttered her eyes for a moment before opening them again. Her knuckles were white from clenching the tray. She tilted her head, eyeing the man standing beside her. "I'm confused, I thought you wanted me to feed my husband."

His smile doubled in size. "Yes, that is exactly what you will be doing. Now go, David's waiting for you."

When no one responded, Sayeed laughed and shook his head. "Sorry, I mean Jordan. Feed Jordan."

The man ran his disgusting hand up and down the side of her body. Dave palmed the cold marble floor in the hopes of reining in his anger. When the asshole's fingers lingered on the side of her breast, Dave shifted to rise with every intention of pouncing on the sack of shit, but stopped when Ally flashed her palm from under the tray. Their gazes locked, hers a silent plea for him to stay calm.

Dave adjusted his hurt leg and leaned against the wall, trying to keep his face as emotionless as hers.

She smiled. "That shouldn't be a problem, at all. There's enough food to feed you both."

"Perfect. But let's make the American feel more comfortable." He pulled off her scarf and untied her hair. Sayeed took a handful of the strands, laying the black curls over her shoulder. It was longer than he remembered, now falling below her waist.

"Much better." He ran his hand up and down the length of the hair. "Now feed him."

She placed her tray on the bed. With a bowl of food and some bread, she returned to the man's side. "I'd prefer to feed my husband first."

His face brightened and what sounded like a giggle escaped his lips. Ally tore a piece of the bread and scooped food out of the brass bowl, popping it into his mouth. He grabbed her wrist, kissing her fingers, the look of victory shining in his eyes.

While he finished his bite, she prepared another. He waved it off and grabbed the bowl, drinking its contents. After he wiped his mouth on her scarf, Sayeed pointed at Dave. "Now feed him."

Ally picked up the tray and walked to Dave's spot on the floor. She sat in front of him and busied herself filling his plate with chicken curry and naan. When he sucked in a breath, it wasn't the spices of the food that overwhelmed his senses, but the scent of jasmine that hugged every inch of her. Their eyes met briefly before she returned to the task at hand. Ally placed a piece of chicken wrapped in thick bread into his mouth. His lips brushed against her fingers and tingled from the warmth of her touch.

Her eyes slammed shut, then she pulled her hand away as Sayeed squatted between them. The man slid the plate toward Dave and patted his shoulder. "This will be your last meal with us. I suggest you enjoy it." He rose, extending his hand to Ally and pulling her up when she accepted it. The two walked to Goliath and Sayeed whispered in his ear. The monster smiled in response as Ally exited the room. She looked over at Dave one more time before she disappeared.

CHAPTER TWENTY-FOUR

ALONE

Dave didn't want her to leave him ever again, but knew he couldn't ask her to stay. Instead, he watched her walk out the door, stared as it shut behind her, and listened to the metal keys clank against the wood as the lock slid into place. When the footsteps grew distant, he exhaled the breath he'd been holding and pushed the plate of food away.

He ran a finger over his lip. Seeing her. Touching her. It made all the risks worth it. He rested his head against the wall and closed his eyes, trying to memorize everything about her. She was different. Not just the way she acted but the way she carried herself. Even seemed taller, but that wasn't it. She was stronger now. The way she'd kept her emotions locked away the entire time she was in the room and pretended not to be affected by seeing him. Dave's chest tightened at the thought of the things Sayeed must have done for her to become that way.

He shook off the thoughts. What mattered was she was alive—they all were. Dave looked over at the man standing guard inside the room. Goliath glared back. *For now.*

When the giant took a step forward, Dave rose and moved back until his shoulders hit the wall. With Eddie under the bed and Amir on the other side of the door, he wouldn't have to deal with the man alone.

The guard sneered, as if hearing his thoughts. Slowly the man unbuckled his belt and laid it across the bed, gun and all. He stretched his hands out to show he was unarmed as he popped every bone in his neck and fingers. Goliath obviously didn't think he needed weapons to kill. From the way Dave's heart thudded against his chest and brain screamed for him to run, Dave shared the same opinion.

The giant's lips stretched, displaying crooked teeth with a gaping hole in the front. Like a lion casing its next kill, he leaned forward and walked sideways, following his prey around the room.

"Now's a great time to make an appearance," Dave said as he continued to slide across the wall, but no one responded. *Shit*.

Dave moved, trying to get the man as far away from the bed and door as possible, until he found himself cornered. With nowhere to run and his death inching forward, he yelled one of the few phrases he'd managed to memorize in Urdu. "Meri maddat karain!" *I need your help!*

The man laughed and responded to Dave's plea in Urdu. Probably explaining just how he planned to help. Goliath flexed his fingers and cracked his knuckles all over again, while Dave's heart tried to leap from his chest and out of the path of imminent destruction. Stuck in a corner with his escape blocked, Dave did the only thing he could; he balled his fists and prepared to fight.

Goliath lunged at him. Dave ducked at the very last second before the man's fist connected with the cement wall instead of Dave's face. While the giant hunched over, groaning about his injured hand, Dave bent down and rammed his shoulder into the man's stomach, slamming him against the concrete.

As the man slid to the ground, adrenaline surged through Dave's veins. Aiming his fist at Goliath's nose, he pounced. The guard's large claw of a hand covered Dave's before contact was made. He pulled the arm to the ground and almost out of its socket, flipping Dave over onto his back in the process.

Stunned, Dave stared up at the guard kneeling over him and watched as the man's fist crash into his jaw. Lights exploded in his head when bone, skin, and teeth collided. Ignoring the cracking sounds resonating in his ears and currents of pain shooting through his mouth, he managed to push the heel of his hand into the man's nose until something snapped. Blood poured from his snout, making the beast fall backwards onto his ass.

Dave pulled his legs out from under the man and jumped to his feet, prepared to fight to the death when the butt of Eddie's gun slammed onto the back of the giant's head.

Goliath turned and lunged at his newest attacker. He punched Eddie's wrist, making the weapon fly out of his hand and slide across the room.

Finding the farthest corner, Dave leaned against the wall. He spit out broken bits of teeth and globs of blood as the door to the prison opened and Amir entered. The younger guard surveyed the scene and rushed to Dave's side, offering his help.

Still on his knees, Goliath attempted to wrap his oversized arms around Eddie's hips and pull him down, but Eddie leapt out of his reach, grabbing a handful of the man's hair.

"Yeah, don't worry about me. I don't need any help here," Eddie mumbled while he rammed his knee into the man's bloody head.

"You shouldn't. I already did half the job," Dave fumed. "What took you so long anyway?" He stuffed Amir's handkerchief into the wounded side of his mouth.

When Eddie's knee reconnected with Goliath's head, both fighters grunted. "Wanted to see what you were capable of. Not bad."

Dave found himself hoping the giant got one good punch to Eddie's gut before being killed. Instead, Eddie performed another straight knee strike to the face and let go of his opponent. The man fell to the floor and didn't move when Eddie kicked him in the ribs.

Out of breath, he walked over and picked up the gun from the floor.

"Why didn't you shoot him?" Dave mumbled through the stuffing in his mouth.

Eddie picked up the holster from the bed and pulled out the other weapon. He stuck his own and the new one into the band of his pants and reached for the door. "Too loud. We don't want the guards out front to know anything's going on. Now let's go find your wife and get the fuck out of here."

Dave pointed at Goliath, who was now rolling over and onto his knees. The bloodied man climbed to his feet and glared at Amir. Eddie said something in Urdu, tossing a gun into Amir's hands. The younger guard grabbed Dave's arm and pulled him out of the room, shutting Eddie and the giant inside.

Voices echoed from one of the closed doors across from the prison. Amir pressed his finger to his lips. He pointed to himself then at the door with the voices. "Sayeed." Then he handed Dave a gun and pointed down the hall. "Sara Didi."

Dave stared at the weapon then back at Amir. Although he understood what the man was trying to say, he couldn't comprehend why the guy thought he was capable of using the gun. Before he had a chance to think further, Amir pushed him down the hall and walked into the occupied room.

Alone with a gun in hand, Dave ran in the direction Amir had directed. When the passageway angled to the right, he paused, unsure of where to go. A lit room in the corner caught his eye. He leaned against the wall, listening. From inside, metal fell and clanked against the marble. His chest tightened.

Dave switched off the safety on the weapon and put both hands on the handle. He'd practiced shooting with Eddie the past few weeks, but practicing and following through were two different things.

He pushed his fears aside. This was for Ally and he'd do anything he could to protect her. After sucking in a breath, he crept inside the kitchen to find Eddie's sister standing in the room with a large butcher knife pointed at Dave while he aimed his weapon at her.

~

Alone in her room, Sara closed the door and leaned against it. She had finally done it, poisoned the man who had tormented so many. But the tears building inside her were not ones of joy or relief but sheer terror. They streamed down her cheeks, neck and disappeared under her collar.

David was here.

She slid to the floor and hugged her knees, remembering every detail of him. The bearded face. The wounded leg. They'd kill him. Those two worlds were never supposed to collide. Why hadn't Eddie told her David was the prisoner? Her chest heaved at the weight of her terror.

Sayeed knew. He'd pulled her into that room to see her reaction. If she had begged or even looked at David too long, the man would have killed him on the spot. She had no choice but to pretend, to play the game.

A quiet sob shook through her body. But it was David. And she'd left him there. Alone.

Sara pushed her head between her knees, wrapped her fingers

into her hair, and rocked. Kadeen would torture him before killing him. She had to do something. Beads of sweat dripped from her skin, yet she shivered as pictures of David's broken, lifeless body flashed on repeat in her head.

"No, that's your fear talking. He's not dead." She whispered the words, but no matter how much she said them, there was nothing she could do to stop the images from playing. Her heart pounded and body trembled. As her lungs began to freeze, she forced herself to breathe slow and steady.

A rapping at the door plunged her lungs deeper into ice. *Sayeed.*

Sara looked over as the knob turned. In her rush to be alone, she hadn't locked the door. She needed to get up. Pretend nothing was wrong. But couldn't move. It didn't matter anymore. He was probably coming to tell her David was dead. Resting her forehead against her knees, she waited.

A gentle arm wrapped around her shoulder. "Sara."

Nasif pulled her face up and rested it on his shoulder. Smoothing the hair off her face, he kissed the top of her head. Muscles and organs thawed from the warmth of his love. "It's okay. Everything will be okay, Bayti," he whispered.

Bayti? New tears flooded her. No one had held and soothed her much less called her their daughter in so long. Sara's shoulders slumped. Hungry for more, she inched closer to him. "Nothing's okay. They have David and I couldn't do anything to help him. You know what they're going to do." Her fears finally spoken made Sara's sobs return.

"Shhh. I know everything." He pressed his hands on her cheeks, forcing her to look at him. "Eddie is in the room and Amir is on the other side of the door. They will not allow anything bad to happen to David." Nasif spoke as if she were a child, and for some reason, it calmed her.

She sniffled and shook her head. "He didn't need to be here."

"There is nowhere else that man would be than here, and Sayeed *will* get what's coming to him."

Nasif's promise reminded Sara about the poisoned lunch. A bolt of excitement shot through her. She inched closer, resting her cheek against his and whispered in his ear. "I did it."

When he didn't respond, she continued. "I poisoned Sayeed's lentils and he drank it. All of it."

His body went rigid for a second before his excited voice whispered back. "When?"

"About fifteen minutes ago. So he'll be dead in about forty minutes?"

"Maybe. Each person is different. Typically the symptoms start shortly after the person takes the pill. But with his build, it may be hours before it kills him." He squeezed her arm. "But he will die."

Sara rested her cheek on his shoulder, digesting his words. *Hours?* She was hoping for something more immediate, not hours.

"What a nice surprise." Sayeed's voice echoed through the room.

Sara pulled away from Nasif and rose to her feet.

He stood by the door, arms crossed, his face darkened as he glared. "Your wife dies a few weeks ago, and it hasn't taken you long to find a replacement."

"Nasif would never..." Sayeed grabbed Sara by the throat, silencing her.

He lifted her up until only the tips of her sandals touched the ground. Pain sliced through her neck and jaw.

"Shut up," he hissed as he squeezed tighter.

When Sara pulled in air, a wheezing sound pushed through. Sayeed inched his face closer. "You have caused me enough problems."

Sara tugged at his fingers, trying to pry them open.

"Let go of her, Sayeed. She's done nothing wrong." The room became foggy, and Nasif's voice grew more and more distant. Seconds later, her toes left the ground. With his fingers still wrapped around her neck, Sayeed propelled her backward. Cold cement slammed against the back of her head before he finally released his hold on her.

Sucking in precious air, Sara stared into the eyes of the man about to end her life. His lips curled into a sneer. He clenched the sides of her head, slamming it into the wall, but Sara felt nothing. Heard nothing. All she could see was his face inching closer then moving farther away, and the smile stretched across his lips when impact was made a second time.

Behind Sayeed stood Nasif, with her steel chair raised over his head. When he rammed it into Sayeed's head, the smile on the evil man's face faded, and he finally released his grip on her.

Sara slid to the floor. She watched as his shoes turned away from her and approached Nasif's sandaled feet.

Seconds later, the man whose love helped her survive the past two years crumbled to the floor. Black patent dress shoes kicked into his thin frame over and over as Nasif tried to block off the assault with his frail arms and legs. His body lifted inches off the floor each time Sayeed's foot slammed into it and fell with a thud. She watched as he tipped his leg back and prepared for another hit.

Hatred filled Sara's soul, leaving no room for fear or pain. He had hurt enough people. No more. Pulling herself from the floor, she ignored the pain shooting from her head into every inch of her body and crawled to the metal chair Nasif used. She wrapped her fingers around the sides, pulling it and herself to her feet.

Sayeed's back was to her as he unleashed his venom on Nasif's body. She raised the weapon over her shoulders and slammed it into the rear of his head.

He froze.

She rammed him again. And again. For every person he stole away from her. Every humiliation they'd suffered at his hands. She pounded the steel into his skull until Sayeed fell to his knees before collapsing to the floor.

Sara stared down at the crumpled man who had terrorized her for the past two years. A slow trickle of blood oozed from his hair, forming a dark puddle on the marble. A laugh escaped her lips until Nasif's labored breathing pulled her away from the heavenly sight.

Her head throbbed and the room spun, but she focused on her friend's broken body and made her way to his side.

Eyes closed, he wheezed.

Kneeling beside him, Sara took in the sight. His leg was twisted in an awkward position at his side. The jagged tips of white bones from his arm poked out of his thin skin.

Her heart pounded with fear. "Nasif, can you hear me?"

When he didn't answer, she caressed his face and pressed her lips against his cheek and sobbed. "Please, Nasif. Please."

Fingertips brushed against her arm. She looked up to find Nasif staring back. A bluish tinge colored his skin, and his wheezing became more pronounced.

"You're going to be okay," she lied and gritted her teeth to keep from wailing.

His eyes filled as he shook his head in disagreement. His fingers moved to her face, wiping her tear as Sara struggled to find the words.

"None of this was your fault, do you hear me?"

His cheek twitched.

"I forgive you for everything. *Everything*."

Tears welled in his eyes and spilled down his face.

Sara shuddered. The sobs made it hard to speak, but for him she continued, "You are a good man, Nasif. I owe you my life."

The blue hue on his face began to turn purple and she spoke faster. "You have loved and protected me from the beginning. I'm okay now. You don't need to keep me safe anymore."

A moan escaped his lips.

"Allah," she whispered and pressed her fingers against his lips, only to shake when he kissed her hand. "Allah sees everything. Not just the bad but the good. Your kindness, your support, your love. He knows all and will bless you for it."

When he turned his head, he coughed out a mix of blood and spit. Sara put her hand under his cheek and nudged him to face her. Her throat tightened at the prospect of saying goodbye. She choked out the words. "Your Hasna waits for you, my friend. Go to her and find your peace."

A faint smile tugged at his mouth before all spark left his eyes and a gush of blood streamed from his lips. After one full rise, his chest stilled. Sara searched his face and body for a sign she was wrong, but none arrived.

She rested her head on his chest, and the sobs she'd pushed away finally escaped. Trying to absorb his warmth one last time, Sara lost herself in her grief. Before she had a chance to pour out all of her pain, a hand grabbed her hair and pulled her to her feet, away from Nasif's warmth.

Sayeed.

CHAPTER TWENTY-FIVE

GRATITUDE

"Ungrateful whore." Sayeed dragged her across the room by her hair. When the scalp lifted from her skull, it felt like tiny razors were being shoved from the top of her head into her spine. Sara pushed his hand down into her hair to ease the pressure while she continued to stare at Nasif's lifeless eyes, still open as if watching her.

Soon my friend, I'll be with you soon. The idea soothed her.

Pain exploded down her arm when she slammed onto the metal cabinet. Sayeed jerked her forward only to shove her against the full-sized mirror secured to the armoire. Breaking glass sliced into her back, sending fiery pain through her.

Sayeed's body shook and his pupils grew in size and shifted from side to side. "No one touches me. Do you understand?" His fist slammed into her cheek.

Sara's vision blurred, lights flashed. When he punched her a second time, her legs buckled. Sayeed tugged on the clump of her hair still wrapped around his hand, stopping her fall. He sandwiched her body between him and the armoire, grinding his thickening arousal into her stomach and whispered in her ear. "Especially not a whore like you."

She swallowed the metallic taste in her mouth, leaned against the metal surface, and tried to catch her breath. Sara's back, head, mouth, every part of her burned with pain.

In one day, he had thrown away the lives of people she loved as if they were meaningless scraps. Although exhaustion and grief immobilized her limbs, her brain fixated on the only hope she could find. “You will die for everything you’ve done,” she whispered, praying for the poison to work and make her words reality.

His mouth curled into a smile, and he pressed his fingers into her cheek. The pressure made the injured area explode with another surge of pain. A moan escaped her lips.

“By whose hands?” He laughed, hitching her skirt up. “Yours? Who’s going to protect you?”

Sara turned her head and waited for the inevitable. Instead Sayeed stepped away, releasing his grip on her skirt.

He wrapped his arms around his waist, took a sharp gulp of air, and let out a moan.

She slid away, watching him fall to his knees and howl like a wounded dog. Her heart pounded. No longer the victim but the predator, power surged through her veins. Sara closed her eyes and savored every note. Not even the greatest tenors in the world could surpass the beauty of the music she currently heard.

All pains forgotten, she walked around him to the door. Sayeed’s eyes rolled up and fixed on her as she moved. He rose to his feet but, after a few steps, fell to his knees a second time. “No matter where you go, I’ll find you,” he hissed through gritted teeth.

The red flush of his face, the bead of sweat across his forehead, all of it made her smile. Instead of opening the door, she locked it. No one would save him today. “Why would I leave? A good wife stays by her husband’s side during his times of troubles. Until his last breath.”

She stumbled to Nasif and stared longingly at his body. He’d stayed with Hasna until her death, and died trying to protect Sara. Until today, she never grasped the old man’s love or loyalty. A tear slipped out and she brushed it away.

His trademark glasses lay shattered a few inches away. She bent over and closed his eyes before returning the frames to their rightful home.

Then she turned her attention to the man who had destroyed all their lives. “Ungrateful whore. Is that what I am?” Sara sat across from Sayeed on the floor and smirked as he moaned and rocked. His every wince strengthened her confidence.

"What part should I be grateful for? The kidnapping? Forcing me to marry you? Or the hundreds of times you raped me? Thank you, husband, I am the woman I am because of you." The bile of hate rose up her throat as the words she'd wanted to say finally spewed. "Thank you for taking everything away from me, and teaching me that even then I am strong enough to defeat the mighty Sayeed."

His teeth clenched, he glared at Sara before squeezing his eyes shut and throwing up.

~

She refused to turn away as liquid and clumps of food tinged in pink swooshed out of his mouth onto the floor. Nor did she cover her face when the stench of sour cottage cheese overwhelmed her senses. No, she would watch every part of his death.

His body heaved while the endless amount of liquid continued to flow. Finally, Sayeed leaned his head back and wiped the trickle of blood and fluid from the corner of his mouth. And as he stared at the red stains on his hand, for the first time in two years, she saw fear in his face.

"What did you do?"

Sara shrugged. "Poisoned your lunch." She pulled the hem of her dress away from his mess, and leaned against the wall. "To show you just how grateful I am for all the things you've done. When mixed with your bile, the poison turns into an acid and will burn holes in your stomach. It's the acid and the pain that are making you nauseous. When you throw up, you're spreading the mixture up along your throat where it will continue to burn until death."

His breathing grew more erratic, and he pulled out his cell phone. When he attempted to dial, it slipped from his fingers into the wet mess. He stretched to retrieve it, but the movement sent him howling and doubling over onto his side.

"Don't bother. No one can help you. You will die alone."

"You think you can kill me and live in peace?"

The truth in his threat forced a tear out of Sara's eye. She wiped it away and shook her head. "No. I will never be able to live in peace because of the things you've done."

He hurled more of the contents of his stomach onto the floor. This time instead of pink, the liquid was blood red. His body twisted into a ball as he moaned.

The pained sounds stirred no pity inside of Sara. The empathetic part of her died the first night he raped her. As the years progressed, it turned to pure hate. Now that he'd taken advantage of Umber's love and killed both him and Nasif, all she wanted was vengeance.

"There might be one way for me to find peace, and that's by making sure every second you have left in this world is spent experiencing some of the pain you inflicted on others."

Sara grinned as she shifted the conversation from English to Urdu. "Let's start with Wassim. It seems you and your trusted guard have similar tastes in women."

Sayeed raised his head and stared at her in shock. She wasn't sure if it was the fact that she was speaking fluent Urdu or what she said that stunned him.

She smirked. "Don't worry, it wasn't me he was after."

He sat on his knees, his gaze rooted on her. Sara could see his mind working, slowly putting the pieces together, and decided to help it along.

She leaned in, raising her brows. "When you sent them off together, I'm sure Alyah didn't even argue, did she?"

"Shut up!" he whispered, shaking his head.

"And that baby she carries, did you really think it was..."

His wet hand slammed over her mouth and nose before she finished. Purple-faced, he trembled as he pulled her onto her back and put all of his weight onto his palm. "I said shut your filthy mouth."

Too consumed in watching his agony, it never occurred to her that he was strong enough to still hurt her. Sara's lungs squeezed out what little air they had and contracted in search for more. But there was none. Her muscles clenched and fingers wrapped around his hands in an attempt to pry them away. Instead, he pushed down harder.

"She carries *my* son. Do you understand?"

Her legs thrashed and hands clawed at his face. She tried to knee his stomach, each time missing the target until the room darkened. A loud thump in the distance was the last sound she heard before everything went silent.

Like a slideshow, images of her past flashed.

Mommy and Pappa playing with a little girl in dinosaur pajamas and pigtails.

Reya and Nikhil drunk and singing karaoke during one of their many family vacations.

Reema resting her head against Sara's shoulder after waking up from a bad dream.

Umber sitting next to Sara under the shade of the banyan tree.

Nasif kissing her head and holding her close on the floor of her room.

And then.

Finally.

David.

In the prison.

Alone.

Reema. David. Who'd protect them?

"*They will be safe.*" A soothing voice filled her head, making the pictures fade and allowing the sweetest of images to come into view. His hand outstretched, a young boy stood over her body with a toothy smile and big ears.

Peace, complete and unabated, filled Sara's soul.

Umber.

~

Dave kicked the door for the hundredth time, and it partially broke free from the hinges. Backing up to the other side of the hall, he slammed his shoulder against its cracked wood. The stench of vomit hit his sinuses as soon as the door gave way. He crashed onto the floor, his gun flying out of his hand in the process.

He climbed onto his good knee, searching for his weapon and finding it on the middle of the floor, inches from Nasif's broken body. The old man's trademark glasses were shattered but rested on his face.

Was he too late?

Jumping to his feet, he surveyed the space. Sayeed, with his back to Dave, knelt over Ally, screaming for her to shut up. The man's hand was pressed against her mouth and nose. Her arms stretched out on the floor, she didn't move while he grunted and pushed every ounce of life out of her.

Rage burned through Dave. He slammed into the bastard and the two men slid across the room until Sayeed's head rammed into the wall.

Fists drawn, Dave scrambled to his knees and pounded his knuckles into Sayeed's pathetic face over and over until a garbled sound came from the man. Another fist to Sayeed's eye and thick, bloody foam poured from his mouth. Dave leaned back in shock. *What the fuck?* Sayeed's eyes rolled. His body seized.

Dave jumped off him and focused on Ally.

Her cheek was pressed against the floor. His world stopped moving and his brain shut down as he took in her slightly parted lips that were pale with a tinge of blue. "Ally, can you hear me?"

Silence.

He repeated the words but they sounded distant, as if spoken from a faraway source, not him. When he moved her face up, one side was perfect while the other was bruised and swollen. Purpled fingerprints formed a C around her mouth.

Dave rested his cheek next to her nose, praying for the warmth of her breath to moisten his skin.

But it didn't. Stunned, he stayed there with his face pressed to hers, willing her to cough, push him away, something, as the same words whispered on repeat inside his brain: *It's too late.*

He pressed his fingers to her wrist and searched for the rhythmic thumps of her heart, but his hands shook too hard to get a good read. It didn't matter. He knew the answer.

Tilting her head back, Dave pinched her nose. He covered her mouth with his and pushed air into her lungs. Her chest rose and fell with each puff. When he stopped blowing, her lungs stopped moving. The voice in his head was becoming louder, making it hard for him to think of anything else.

He slammed his eyes shut, silently screaming to the voice in his head. No, it wasn't over. There was no way in hell he was giving up.

Straddling her, Dave pushed into her chest.

"Ally. Open your eyes!" he screamed. But she didn't. Instead her eyelids stayed closed and mouth open, while her head moved forward as if nodding with each compression.

This is not supposed to happen. It can't end like this.

It took every ounce of self-control he possessed not to pound full force on her chest to wake up her dormant heart. As frail as she was, it would probably break her bones. Instead, Dave maintained a steady rhythm and pushed on her ribs.

"You can't die. Do you hear me? I just found you. I can't lose you again." Tears streamed his face. "Baby, wake up. Please."

He circulated between chest compressions and rescue breaths while the "if I had only's" played in his head.

If I had only gotten here a few minutes earlier...

If I had killed him in the prison when he showed up...

...she would still be alive.

The whispered voice inside, saying it was too late, got louder. Again, he shook the thought away.

She's not dead. She can't die.

Not like this. Not after everything she's gone through.

Dave leaned forward, wrapped his lips around hers, and blew.

Her face jerked away, and his heart about jumped out of his still open mouth.

Frozen, Dave watched. The way her thick eyelashes pulled open. How she stared around the room. How she turned her sweet, beautiful, injured head to look at him, and the way her eyes widened when they met his.

A sob tried to push its way out his throat, but he swallowed it and rested his forehead against hers, steadying himself while his hand caressed her cheek. How long had it been since he'd touched her?

A tear slipped from the corner of her eye. "Thank you," she mouthed, and he couldn't help but laugh because that was exactly what he was about to say to her.

"I love you," he whispered. *There's nothing in this world I wouldn't do for you.*

Another tear fell from her eye. The mixture of salt and the softness of her skin when he kissed it away overwhelmed him. She leaned her face deeper into his lips.

Hungry for more, Dave kissed her forehead, her chin, any part of her face that wasn't bruised, savoring her until a loud series of popping noises forced him back to reality.

He looked over to find Reema standing a few feet away with his gun. Pointed at Sayeed's still seizing body, she emptied the magazine into him.

CHAPTER TWENTY-SIX

FAMILY

She had never been in Alyah's bedroom before. The woman would never have allowed it. But with her in another country, and dead people in Sara's, it was the best option. With its coffee-colored walls and teakwood furniture, the space was much nicer anyway. The orange sofa and rich-toned fabrics exuded regal importance, in line with Alyah's perception of herself. Aside from the two corpses currently in her own, there wasn't anything attention grabbing about Sara's room. Like her, it was plain and empty.

Her fingers caressed the silk thread of delicately embroidered roses on the quilt while she did her best to ignore David. He sat beside her, quietly pulling tiny shards of glass from her back. She bit her lip as pain radiated from the cuts he tended.

Even though every part of her burned or pulsed from her wounds, none of it compared to the crippling panic coursing through her body. At one time, being dressed in only black lacy panties with David hovering over her would have been exciting. But not now. Each time his fingers brushed against her skin, which in this case was often, the urge to push them away overwhelmed her. Instead, she focused on her breathing and talked herself through it. *David is not Sayeed. He will never hurt me.*

But her body and brain seemed to be disconnected because the only thing keeping her on the bed currently was sheer willpower.

"How's your leg?" she asked in an attempt to fill the silence.

"It's fine. Nasif's stitches held up. The shot he gave me numbed the area. And...I think I got the last piece of glass." He ran his fingers down the length of her spine.

A shiver followed the path he traced and a fresh set of goose bumps erupted.

Focus on something soothing. Her vision of Umber from an hour ago popped into her head. Dressed in clean, pressed navy shorts and a white, short-sleeved shirt, he was happy, alive. He didn't touch her. His mouth didn't even move. But she heard his thoughts. "*You don't need to worry about me anymore, Sara Mommy*." Peace and calm overcame her then, and it seeped into her now. The idea of staying in that world with the child, forever, felt heavenly.

Heaven? Sara's face heated and eyes watered. After what she'd done to Sayeed, heaven was not exactly the place she figured she'd end up. Was that a dream or the afterlife? Whatever it was, it was where she wanted to be.

"Ally, I need to clean the wounds." David's voice interrupted her thoughts.

Her muscles tensed for the hundredth time in the past half hour. *Ally?* Was that who she was? So many questions. None of which she had answers to.

"Ally?"

"Okay."

Cold gauze swept across the cuts. When the alcohol ignited into her skin, she clenched the quilt. Finally, an emotion that overpowered her fear. His fingers moved into her hair, pressing against the scalp. He touched the tender part of her head. The pressure sent fiery currents of pain through her skull, making her wince. His hands left the source immediately and rested on her shoulders.

David let out a long breath and cleared his throat before finally breaking the silence. "There's a bad bump over here. It's bruised and might be bleeding. Do you remember how you got that?"

She ignored the edge in his voice and lied. "No." As tense as he was now, telling him about having her head slammed into a wall repeatedly didn't seem wise. There was so much she wasn't ready to share.

His *I know you're lying* silence that followed made her shift uncomfortably.

After another long pause, he let go of her shoulder.

Sara covered her naked chest with a pillow and sat up, waiting for the room to stop spinning. "Can I get dressed?"

David returned the medical supplies to Nasif's brown leather bag. "Yeah. Do you feel any different? Dizzy? Trouble walking? Anything?"

"No, besides the headache, I'm fine," she lied.

His cheeks reddened, the way they did when he was angry and trying to keep it under control. "We need to get you out of here now and into a hospital for more tests."

She climbed off Alyah's bed to get her abaya from off the floor. As soon as her feet hit the marble, the walls moved. The pillow dropped when she reached for the bed. Before Sara had a chance to grab the mattress, David's arms wrapped around her waist, pulling her against his chest. Too unsteady to resist, she rested her face on his shoulder, clinging to him until everything stopped turning. When Sara's breasts brushed against his shirt, vivid images of a clothed Sayeed violating her streamed into her consciousness, making her heart pound and stomach churn. Turning her back to him, she grabbed the bra and gown from the floor and hugged it to her chest.

"Ally." He stood so close his breath warmed her neck. "It's me."

The bra snapped and she pulled on the straps. The heat of him behind her, his mouth inches from her skin stirred the hunger she'd worked so hard to kill. A part of her craved for him to hold her. To love her and show her that she could be happy again. But the other part, the louder one, screamed to move away. It reminded her of how broken and dirty she had become. That her fantasy of a life with him was unrealistic and impossible.

Sara pulled the abaya over her head and kept her back to him. "I'm not that person you remember anymore."

"Maybe." He inched closer until his cheek grazed her temple. "But I still love you and would never do anything to hurt you."

Without her permission, her head leaned into his, allowing more of his skin to rest against hers. She closed her eyes, filling her lungs with the faint scent of his soap. How easy it would be to get lost in him. To forget about Sayeed and the woman from the pictures...

Sara's lids popped open at the thought of the blonde with the curly hair. The one who waited at home for him. It pulled her out of her fantasy.

She shook the effect off and walked to Alyah's armoire in search of distance and a scarf. "It's not about you. It's me. I'm different. Trust doesn't come easy anymore."

He followed and stood behind her. David pulled her hair out of the collar of the dress and smoothed it down. When his fingers grazed her neck, her body warmed. She pretended to be unaffected while he played with the strands.

"Think about us. The way we were before all of this."

In the mirror, she inspected the injuries on her face and neck for the first time. The Ally he loved never endured pain like this. The Sara staring back had no clue what a life without it would look like. The memories he held onto were with someone who no longer existed.

She grabbed the first scarf she found and twisted it around her head, tucking the strands he held into her collar. "I will never be that person again. You have to let go of the past."

"Maybe not, and I will. But I'll never let go of you."

Like a magnet, she was drawn to his eyes in the reflection. The love she saw in them tugged at her soul.

"And if part of moving forward for me is letting go of you?" she whispered.

Pain flashed on his face, and as unbearable as it was to see, she knew it was necessary.

~

Dave had fought to rein in his anger for Sayeed the whole time he dug through Ally's flesh and pulled out the tiny glass fragments shoved into her skin. He was still pretending that her face and neck looked just fine, when all he wanted to do was bring the bastard back to life so he could force sharp objects up every inch of the man's fucking body. Hell, he even pretended to believe her lie about the mountain of a bump on the back of her head. They both knew who'd done that to her. But none of that was as hard to digest as the words she just uttered. It felt like someone punched him in the gut and then ran him over with a tank.

Twice.

He fixed his gaze on her, waiting for her to continue. Was she really trying to tell him they were over?

Ally turned away and fiddled with her scarf, avoiding his stare, the way she used to do when she didn't want him to know something. His muscles eased as realization hit. She was lying. After everything that had happened to her, did he really think she'd just run into his arms? Although he knew better, the sad answer to that question was yes. A small part of him had hoped for the impossible. The reality was she needed time to heal.

Dave wrapped his hand around one of hers, and although she stiffened, she didn't pull it away. "This emotionless, not-needing-anyone kind of person you're trying to be is probably how you survived and I get that. But I know you, and no matter what you say, you're not getting rid of me."

Eddie opened the door and entered before anything more could be said. To Dave's disappointment, Ally tugged her fingers away, leaving his skin cold without her warmth. He glared at the unwelcome guest.

"Sorry, man, but I need to borrow your wife." Eddie waved at the empty hallway behind him. "The kids are all worked up, and I hear you're good at calming them down."

"I'm coming."

Ally only got a couple of steps before Dave stepped into her path. "No, the only place you're going is to a hospital."

She maneuvered around him and continued to the door.

He followed her, aiming his frustrations at Eddie. "I thought you were working on getting her out of here? Her heart stopped and she might have some internal injuries. We need to get her medical attention *now*."

Ally answered before Eddie had a chance. "Might. Which means I might not have any either. I'm not leaving without Reema and the boys."

Ignoring her, he looked at Eddie, begging for the man to back him up.

Instead, he rubbed his neck and shrugged. "I'm afraid we can't do that. Ayoub has about twenty minions that we're aware of wandering outside the compound, looking for anything suspicious. If they see us sneaking anyone out, things could get explosive. We're staying in the compound until they tell us we can leave."

"Ayoub," Ally gasped and lowered herself onto the sofa. "I

forgot about him. Sayeed has a meeting with him..."

"Tonight," Eddie finished and sat on the couch's armrest, inches from her.

"He needs to be stopped," she whispered.

Eddie nodded. "And if you're healthy enough, we really need your help with the kids."

Dave shook his head in disbelief. "What are you talking about, healthy? If she has a head bleed, she *will* drop dead. We need to get her out of here now."

Ally ignored Dave and focused on Eddie. "And how exactly do you plan on capturing Ayoub?"

What the fuck?

The agent kept his gaze locked on Dave, while responding to her. "I have friends in the area."

More of a growl than a yell, Dave pointed at the door and glared at Eddie. "Your *friends* need to get her ass out of here and to a hospital now. Do you hear me?"

Instead of complying, the man shook his head. "It's too dangerous. Everybody's suspicious after the gunfire from earlier. Anyway, she may not have anything wrong with her. We're stuck here until Ayoub shows up and is taken down."

"All you fucking care about is the damn mission." Dave stopped mid-sentence when Ally raised her palm at him.

"Eddie, can you give us a minute, please?" she asked.

The agent stood, cleared his throat, and disappeared, leaving the two of them alone in the room.

"Do you understand that you died today? Your heart stopped, Ally. I had to bring you back." Dave shut the still-open door and ran his hand through his hair. "They don't give a shit about whether you live or die. I do." His body shook as he spoke. "*This* is not your problem. It's theirs. Let *them* do their fucking job. You've done enough."

She rose from the couch, her dark brown eyes drilling into his soul. "I'm not dead. Thanks to you, I'm fine."

"You don't know that. There could be—" Before he could list all the internal injuries she may have, she cut him off.

"Even if you're right about me, we're stuck right now. And you're wrong. This *is* my problem. The boys and Reema are my family and they need me."

The words stung him as soon as she spoke them. "What about your family back home? They need you too. Alive." Dave knew better than to ask her to stay for him, but for her parents and siblings, there was a chance. She went rigid, as if considering his question. For a second or two, he believed he was getting through to her until she shook her head and walked to the door. "This is where I'm needed."

His feet stayed rooted to the floor as he tried to find the words to convince her to change her mind.

When she grabbed the doorknob, he swallowed down the ball of emotion in his throat and spoke the words in his heart. "I need you, too. I...I can't lose you again. Please."

She turned to face him.

His breath caught in his lungs as she walked to him. When she wrapped her arms around him, the way she used to do, emotion burned his eyes.

Dave pressed her against him, savored the feel of her cheek on his shoulder. Resting his chin on the top of her head, he closed his eyes and memorized every part of her. Her skin. The way her body molded perfectly into his. Her lips against his neck. *God, it had been too long.*

All anger dissipated and the murk of sadness moved in. He knew what she was doing. She was saying goodbye. He held her tight and prayed he was wrong.

"David. I have to help them. I'm sorry."

"I can't stop you, can I?"

Ally didn't respond. Didn't need to. When she stepped back, his body ached to pull her back. To carry her away from this hell. But he knew better. She was having a hard time trusting him as it was. If he took her away, it would only prove he was no different from Sayeed. And if those people were her family, she would never forgive him for forcing her to leave them behind.

Dave shook his head. "Promise me something."

Her brows rose as she waited for him to finish.

"When this is done, you'll come home with me."

She searched his face for a moment before answering. "Okay."

Dave leaned in and kissed the corner of her mouth that wasn't bruised. Now he just needed to make sure she stayed alive to make her promise a reality. "You go take care of your family and know that I'm planning on taking care of mine."

Ally hesitated for a second before turning and walking out the door. He grabbed Nasif's bag and followed just in time to watch as the door closed behind her, reaching it seconds after the lock slid into place on the other side.

"What the...?" Dave tried to pull it open but couldn't.

She'd locked him in.

CHAPTER TWENTY-SEVEN

BANYAN TREES

Sara slid the metal bolt and locked David in. A spasm of guilt rippled through her and tugged at her chest.

"What the?" The door thudded. "Ally, open the door!"

Her fingers hovered over the brass lock when the banging intensified but she pulled back.

No.

David should have never come to the compound. He was making it hard to think. She'd already promised him things she never intended. Voices from down the hall grabbed her attention. Sara walked away from him and the door he currently was slamming into, in search of the source.

The pulsating ache in her head had spread to her face and neck. It felt like someone's giant hands were wrapped around her brain. When she touched the most tender spot in the back, a current of electricity shot through it, making her wince. What if David was right about the internal injuries? She pushed the worry away and listened to the conversation up ahead.

"That's not going to happen," Eddie snapped.

"Bhai, he's already on the grounds," Amir's gentle voice responded.

He who? Sara leaned against the wall, out of view, and listened. *Who was on the grounds that had them this upset?*

"First of all, I am not your fucking brother," Eddie growled. "Stop calling me Bhai. And second, my team is already out there looking for him..."

Amir interrupted him. "Sayeed has a secret passage somewhere on the property. I've looked for it for months and still haven't found it. Ayoub is hiding in there and your team will not find it or him."

A chill crept up her body. Ayoubhad arrived. The same Ayoub who bought Umber and sent him into that mall. Not only was the man responsible for the murder of thousands, he was in their yard, dangerously close to Reema, the boys, and David.

"If there's a passage, my men will find it. We don't even know he's still here. As soon as the shots fired, his guys probably got him out."

Amir's voice rose. "Then why are his two most-trusted guards still out there? They would never leave his side."

Fingernails scraped against nylon as a zipper was pulled. "Look at this," Amir continued. "Dollars. American dollars. He has already paid Sayeed for the weapons and the children. Do you think someone like Ayoub will just give away this much?"

The room began to spin. Sara rested her head against the wall and tried to stay focused on Amir. "Ayoub is a proud man. He will not leave us alone until he gets what he paid for. Let me go. I will tell him Sayeed is ready for him, and when he comes out then your team can take over."

"He's the second-most-wanted terrorist in the fucking world. If it doesn't work, you and everyone in here will die. I can't risk that. We will wait until it's dark to move."

Amir let out a laugh. "Dark? That's not for another four hours, enough time for Ayoub to sneak out of here and disappear. If he gets away, he *will* come back for what's his."

"This is the plan and we will stick with it. Understood?"

Sara's mind raced. Amir was right. Ayoub needed to be stopped now. When she tried to sneak past the room, the walls slanted and she lost her balance, stumbling onto her palms and knees.

Strong hands grabbed her shoulders, lifting her to her feet.

"Are you okay?" Eddie asked.

She nodded and tried to hide the terror consuming her.

"Sorry, I'm just exhausted."

"How's your head?"

"Fine."

He frowned as if not believing her lie. Amir stood nearby with his hands on his hips, worry lines creasing his forehead.

"Really. I'm fine. It's been a long day." She stepped out of Eddie's grasp. "The door to Alyah's room is locked, and I think it's best if it stays that way."

Eddie fought a smile, obviously understanding exactly what she meant. He cleared his throat and nodded. "If that's what you want. I need you to talk to the kids and tell them Ayoub killed their father."

Sara's gaze floated between the two men, and ideas flowed through her throbbing skull. "Ayoub?"

He jutted his chin toward her open bedroom door where Sayeed and Nasif's bodies rested. "It's either that or the truth."

She cringed at the thought. "Okay, I'll tell them."

"They're in the living room. How about I walk you?" Eddie cupped her elbow.

She pulled her arm out of his hand. "If you treat me like an invalid, I'll lock you up too." With her shoulders back and head up, she walked past them before he could argue.

Sara could feel their eyes drilling into her back. With each step, pain coursed through her spine and hips. Her nails dug into the heel of her palms while she kept her gait normal. If they thought she was in pain, they'd want to come with her. Which was the last thing she needed. What she was about to do needed to be done alone.

The hallway curved left and led to the room where the boys and Reema were holed up. She checked to make sure the door was closed and walked past it. At the back entrance, Sara turned to assess the hall for witnesses—empty.

She wrapped her fingers around the knob as her stomach twisted. Sara closed her eyes and tried to focus. She had no clue how she was going to do this. But it had to be done and soon. At any moment, Eddie or Amir could walk up. If they figured out what she was up to, they'd stop her. With a shaky breath, she opened her eyes and the door, exiting into the courtyard.

The late afternoon sun blinded her as soon as she stepped out.

She made sure the door closed securely and squinted to adjust to the light. Car horns blared. The voices of people from the street outside made everything seem like a normal day. But it wasn't.

She scanned the courtyard. Ayoub and his men were lurking somewhere among the trees. He would need to be drawn out and stopped before this nightmare could end.

Sara turned toward the back of the compound and walked into the little forest. The thick-trunked banyan trees that had provided her comfort these past two years suddenly looked like giant monsters ready to swoop down and crush her with their spiny branches. She shuddered and shook the image away.

No birds sang. No insects chirped. It was as if they were holding their breaths. Green foliage blocked the compound from view and darkened the path. The hair on her arms stood. Her feet dragged with every step. The voice in her head screamed to turn and run, but instead, she hoisted her skirt and stepped around the roots poking out of the ground as she continued forward. Even the crunching sound when she treaded on dry leaves made her heart flip.

Sweat dripped from Sara's hair to her face. With the corner of the scarf, she wiped it away. The beige fabric turned dark red when she swiped the area of her neck under her ear. Before she had a chance to consider why there was blood, large hands grabbed her arms, pulling her deeper into the forest.

A muscular frame pressed against Sara's back and soon she was sandwiched between the man and a large, thick tree. She tried to fight him off but he was stronger, bigger. The attacker wrapped her arms around the trunk, grasped her wrists, and used them to keep her restrained against the bark.

Hips pressed against her rear, and his legs were planted between hers. Hugging the tree, she was immobilized. Her body shook as the reality of what was happening sunk in.

A stubbly cheek pushed into hers. From the corner of her eye, she watched his yellowed teeth and blackened gums flash when he spoke. "Apka nam kya hai?" his deep voice hissed.

The smell of his unwashed body and rancid breath was nauseating.

She swallowed her terror. "I don't understand."

He twisted her arms tighter. Pain shot from her shoulders down her back. "What is your name?" he asked in a heavy accent.

The more she tried to twist free, the tighter he pulled on her arms and crushed his face harder into her. A large nose pressed into her cheek. Unable to move, she stared at the branches beside her as a plan finally formed.

"My name is Sara Irfani."

"Sayeed's second wife?" another, deeper voice asked.

"Yes," she spit out as the wooden surface scraped against her already-bruised cheek. "Yes, I am."

A taller, leaner man walked into her line of sight. He looked her over. His light-colored shirt was loose and fell to his ankles, matching his baggy pants. A large, brown shawl was wrapped around his head and shoulders. With his hazel eyes, high cheekbones and light brown beard, he could have been considered handsome if it wasn't for his frigid stare and the way his lips curled up at the sides. He crossed his arms behind him and moved closer to her. The man reached for her face, stroking her cheek. "You're not as beautiful as I've heard."

The man restraining Sara laughed, blowing more of his breath into her nose.

"Why are you doing this?" Her voice came out strained.

Instead of answering, he waved at the other man. Immediately her hands were released. Before she could move, she was flipped around, her back slammed against the trunk's bark, and the already swollen wounds along her spine burned upon impact.

She kicked at the attacker in front, but he stepped out of reach. A third stranger's hands grabbed her wrists, pulled her arms behind her, and tugged, making Sara's hijab fall from her head.

"What happened to your face?" The scarfed man pointed to her bruised cheek.

"First tell me who you are," she choked out through the icy panic building within.

His smile stretched and brows rose. "A guest of your husband's."

"If you're a guest, why are you hiding in the woods?"

"I heard gunshots and decided to wait before visiting." He jutted his chin in the direction of the compound. "What happened in there?"

She took a breath and whispered her confession. "I killed my husband."

His smile dropped. "*You* killed Sayeed Irfani?"

"Yes."

The man wiped a trickle of wetness from her ear. It stained his thumb red. "Why?"

She stared at the blood on his finger. "For doing that to me."

The stranger stepped closer, cleaning his finger on her sleeve. "In Islamic law, there are severe consequences for murder. You are supposed to be killed the same way you killed your husband."

Sara's pulse continued to climb as she watched the other man rub his gun. Around her, everything began to spin. She focused on the rifle, waiting for the vertigo to stop. After a few seconds, the forest stilled and she looked at the man in charge. "That's why I'm here. I want to talk to Ayoub. To make a deal with him."

The man leaned in, amusement sparkling in his eyes. "A deal? What kind of deal?"

"I have things he wants. Things he paid for. I will give them to him in return for my freedom."

She scanned the trees for Eddie's team but saw no one.

What if they weren't there?

When he laughed, it was as if he heard her thoughts and confirmed her doubts. "Freedom? What do you mean freedom?"

Sara pushed the fear away. "I want the As-Sirat to take credit for Sayeed's death."

His brows rose and head tilted. After an agonizing moment, he nodded his understanding. "So you can live a free and happy life."

When she didn't answer, he waved his hand. "But those things are already paid for, so why would we help you?"

The man behind her pulled her arms back tighter making her yelp out in pain. "The children and the weapons aren't here. Only I know where they are."

His smile turned to a scowl. The stranger nodded at the gunman seated on the ground. The man rose, pointed his rifle at her, and peered through the eyepiece.

"I need to talk to Ayoub first. Please!" she screamed, praying the mysterious team was real and would arrive.

The man removed his shawl from his head, revealing brown, shoulder-length hair, and whispered in her ear. "You have." He ran the back of his hand across her cheek. "And I don't make deals with women who murder their husbands and steal my property." Ayoub turned and walked away.

Sara stared down the gun. Lungs heavy, a moan escaped her lips. She had failed. He'd kill them all.

David flashed in her thoughts. The realization that he was still locked in the house and would die there stabbed at her chest. "No!" she cried to no one, anyone.

Red spots flashed over the gunman's forehead, and she worried she was having another panic attack. She closed her eyes and braced herself for the shot that would kill her.

Popping sounds broke the silence of the forest. Bursts of air whizzed past her skin, followed by a thud. She opened her eyes to see the gunman dead on the ground and Ayoub running away. He zigzagged around the trees as the same red lights scattered spots on the back of his head and body. Again, popping noises exploded through the air. The sounds continued until he fell to the ground.

Her arms still restrained, lights flashed in all directions. Puffs of smoke and a burning smell surrounded her.

Everything was happening too fast. The man behind her released his grip on her hands, screaming. The black barrel of his rifle popped over her shoulder. Its blasts deafened her. The sound so piercing, it was as if someone had stabbed her ears with a knife.

Something slammed into her, throwing her to the ground. Sara's head connected with the rock-hard surface of a banyan tree's root in the process.

"Alisha!" Eddie's distant voice echoed through her brain.

His team had come. Her family would be okay, she thought as darkness took her.

CHAPTER TWENTY-EIGHT

DELTA

After what seemed like an eternity of banging his fist against the bedroom door, it finally unlocked. Dave rushed out before the person that opened it had a chance to change their mind. He scanned the hall for Ally but she wasn't there. Instead, a lanky boy stared up at him from behind the door, the kid's red-rimmed eyes the size of hockey pucks.

"Where is she?" When he didn't answer, Dave moved in close and softened his tone. "My name is David and I am here to help Sara. Can you take me to her?"

The boy nodded and grabbed Dave's sleeve. "I am Razaa. Come with me." He dragged him down the hall until they got to a closed door. He pointed at it, encouraging Dave to enter. Dave poked his head in to find about a dozen more lanky boys and Farah. Some sat wide-eyed on the sofas, staring back at him. They were all dressed the same in navy shorts and crisp white shirts. Farah was too busy trying to calm down a couple of them who sobbed on her shoulders and lap to notice him at the door.

Ally was supposed to take care of the boys so then why wasn't she with them? When one of them waved for him to join them, Dave shook his head, shut the door, and focused on the kid beside him. "No, where is Sara?"

Razaa pointed down the hall. "Outside."

Eddie said no one was allowed out of the compound until it

was safe. They must have gotten Ayoub. Which meant he could now get Ally to a hospital.

Dave headed in the direction the kid pointed. "Take me to her. She needs a doctor."

He led him down the hall and stopped at another closed door. This time when Dave opened it, he stared out into the compound's yard. Before Dave had a chance to ask why, the boy pushed him out of the building and pointed at the brush of trees. "Sara Mommy is there." He slammed the door shut in Dave's face, locking it.

Dave turned to face the direction the kid pointed. Somewhere among those trees was Ally. He resisted the urge to run through the overgrowth and call for her. Instead, he treaded lightly and submerged himself into the vegetation.

Thick foliage blocked the sunlight, dimming the space. The dents and deep veins in the ashy trunks added to the forest's eerie vibe. Heat and the smell of dust filled his overactive lungs. Surrounded by hues of brown and green, everything looked the same.

The place was quiet. The only sounds were from the busy street outside the concrete wall and his own heart pounding. The snap of twigs under his feet made him jump. He hid behind a tree for a brief second to catch his breath and steady his thoughts. It didn't help that the meds Nasif gave him earlier were wearing off. The dull throb around his wound was starting to burn. Ally wasn't the only one who needed to get her injuries checked and soon. He swallowed his fear and pushed on.

A blanket of unease weighed heavy on him. Something didn't feel right. He tried to ignore the gnawing feeling in his stomach. Eddie and his men had to be nearby. Dave stepped over the roots, poking out of the ground and walked deeper. Sweat beaded down his neck, clinging to his clothes. They wouldn't have let Ally out here unless it was safe. Would they?

Before he could think further on the question, two pairs of hands grabbed him. One set held his legs and lifted, while the other covered his mouth and pushed him on the ground. Terror turned to excitement when Dave saw his reflection glaring back from their face shields. Dressed in dark combat fatigues, they squatted on either side of him. Each man carried a machine gun, and belts stuffed with ammo hugged their waists and legs.

A soldier put his gloved finger in front of his armored mouth.

After Dave nodded his agreement, they helped him to his feet.

"I'm a U.S. citizen. My wife is somewhere out there. I need to find her," he whispered.

The soldier nodded and pointed to the house.

When he opened his mouth to ask if she was inside, her frightened voice silenced him. "I need to talk to Ayoub first. Please!" The terror in her tone chilled him, making him forget the soldier's order and sending him running in her direction. When someone tried to grab his arm, he shoved it away and pushed forward.

In the distance, he caught sight of her with her back pressed against a tree and arms wrapped around its trunk. A man restrained her hands behind her while another stood beside her. Rage shot through Dave, making his legs push harder to reach her. Nobody would *ever* hurt her again.

An arm stretched out from nowhere and grabbed hold of him. Before his ass hit the ground, he was caught and his back shoved against a hard surface. Soldiers grabbed him, immobilizing his limbs. Again his mouth was covered. One got in his face, jabbing a curved finger into the dip above his sternum. Pain ripped through his body instantly.

The man flipped his shield up, moved in close until his mouth was next to Dave's ear. "If you so much as cough, they'll kill her. You understand?" It wasn't until after Dave nodded his consent that the soldier slid his face shield back in place, pushed off Dave, and signaled two others on his team before vanishing.

The two pointed to a tree seconds before pushing Dave behind it. One glued himself to Dave's back, while the other vanished like the first.

Dave swallowed his fear and kept his focus on Ally a few yards away.

A man, his face hooded under a brown shawl, stood beside her. As soon as he pulled the fabric from his head, Dave's organs turned to ice.

Ayoub.

Goose bumps spread across his body. Ayoub inched his face so close to hers, it was as if he were about to kiss Ally.

Dave's fists clenched and body shuddered as he fought the urge to run to her.

They're here. She'll be okay.

When she tried to pull free of the one restraining her, a third man rose, facing her, but with his back to Dave. The man aimed the laser of his rifle between her brows.

And when she shook her head and cried out the most painful sound he'd ever heard, terror shuddered the length of his spine. His chest tightened with a painful ache to go to her and kill the son of a bitch threatening her.

As if reading his mind, the soldier's grip on him tightened. "We won't let anything happen to her," he whispered.

Tears and sweat drenched Dave's face as he watched Ally, praying the man was right.

Knowing this might be the last time he'd see her alive, Dave memorized every detail. Her golden skin purpled with bruises. How her thick black hair fell to her waist. The way her teeth clenched through her sobs.

Gunshots and smoke exploded through the area.

Dave's knees weakened. He dug his nails into the tree waiting for her to fall. But she didn't. Instead, the gunman collapsed.

A soldier appeared nearby, crouched by a tree just as another series of shots detonated through the forest. Somewhere, a man screamed out in pain.

Through it all, Dave's focus stayed fixed on Ally. Her body trembled like his. Tears streamed her face, as they did his own.

But she was alive.

The man behind Ally raised the black barrel of his rifle, resting it on top of her shoulder. Everything was silent except for a soft hiss of air. Seconds later, the gunman fell to the ground.

Dave let out the air he'd held since everything started. The crouched soldier ran across the expanse, tackling her to the ground. The soldier leaned over her and turned her face up. Her head fell back, lifeless as bullets fired around them.

"Romeo EKIA," the soldier behind Dave said into his microphone, "I repeat, Enemy Killed In Attack."

In the distance, rounds of machine guns went off, followed by screams. None of it fazed Dave. Getting to Ally was the only thing that mattered, and as soon as the soldier released him, he ran. The couple of yards between them seemed like miles. The soldier squatting next to Ally pulled up his shield. The concern etched on

Eddie's face validated his own fears. Dave slid to his knees, pushing Eddie aside and began to check vitals. The pulsing of her wrist was normal. Her breath warmed his cheek. He searched her body for signs of new injuries but there were none.

Dave's heart turned to ice when he scanned her face and head. A few drops of blood pooled in the curve of her earlobe.

The head bleed.

The world stopped moving and fell silent.

He had warned her.

Warned them all.

With shaky fingers, Dave lifted each eyelid.

Shit.

One pupil was larger than the other. The area under her unbruised eye had purpled.

"Listen to me, we need to get her out now. The pressure is too much on her brain," he screamed to anyone who would listen.

Eddie nodded and waved. Another soldier rushed to their side, standing over Dave. With weapon in hand, the man scanned the forest as a second appeared.

"We have five minutes," the first said.

Eddie jumped to his feet and pointed to Ally. "We need a stretcher. Get everybody out now." He then focused his attention on Dave. "There's a doctor in the chopper. I'll send some of my men over. They'll keep you safe and take her to the medivac. Do whatever they tell you," he said seconds before disappearing into the trees.

Out of the woods, more soldiers arrived. With their backs turned and weapons pointed into the forest, the men formed a ring around Dave and Ally as an explosion erupted in the distance.

Dave wiped away the dirt and leaves from Ally's cheeks and stared at her. She was dying and he didn't have the tools to save her. Crazy thoughts of breaking her skull with a rock to relieve the pressure ran through his mind. He pushed them out, held her hand, and prayed. It was all he was capable of doing.

Eddie reappeared, leading his sister and the boys through the forest. More of his men followed, forming a human fence on either side of the kids. The children kept their hands clasped behind their backs, silently following Farah. She stopped when Ally's body came into view. The girl's lip quivered and soon tears spilled on her face. After sucking in a big gulp of air, she averted her gaze, continuing on. One by one, the kids wordlessly glanced over when they passed by, as if saying their own goodbye.

Dave's eyes burned as his heart broke watching them. Were they right?

The boy who led him into the courtyard lingered a bit longer than the rest, staring longingly. A tear trickled down the kid's cheek before he was urged forward.

Fear gripped Dave's throat, trying to crush the life out of him. There was a good chance they were right. The impact her head bleed could have was terrifying. Paralysis. Death.

No.

He gritted his teeth and squeezed her hand. "Ally, listen to me. You have to live. You can't die. Do you hear me?"

Two soldiers rushed over, carrying a stretcher. Dave helped them shift her onto the fabric and kept her hand in his grip the entire time. There was no way in hell he planned on ever letting her go again. Surrounded by the armed men, they moved quickly out of the forest. No one spoke. There was nothing to say. None of this would have happened if he'd kept her safe and not let her out of his sight. He had failed.

At the edge of the compound, there was a gaping hole in an otherwise solid concrete fence. When Dave tried to follow Ally's stretcher and the men through it, a soldier grabbed his arm, pulling him aside. "They need to take your wife out first."

Dave yanked himself out of the man's grasp, only to be restrained by two more soldiers. "It's the only way we can keep her safe."

He knew they were right. But how many times was he supposed to let her go? Her hand slipped from his fingers as the rest of the men ran through the hole with her. Out of breath and defeated, Dave watched while two guards kept a tight grip on him.

A Black Hawk sat a few yards away, peeking out from behind the trees. Any other time in his life, seeing the helicopter would have been exciting. Something he'd want pictures of. Today, all he cared about was the woman they slid into it.

The soldiers returned for him and rushed him down the field. Dave froze when he noticed the handful of what looked like Pakistani men with machine guns, standing along the perimeter of the field with their backs to the copter. One turned, locking eyes with him. The man flashed him a peace sign before waving him along.

When Dave tried to continue to the Black Hawk, soldiers dragged him to a bus idling a few yards away. "Sorry, you're coming with us."

This time when he yanked his arm away and ran off, they didn't stop him. Eddie stood by the entrance of the helicopter blocking him. "Between your wife and Ayoub's body, the medivac copter's already at capacity. It can't hold you too." He pointed to the two uniformed men inside checking Ally's vitals. "That's our med sergeant and nurse. They're the best there is and will take care of her. You need to get on that bus."

Dave hesitated, staring at the black body bag positioned beside her just as new gunshots erupted in the distance.

"Now." Eddie grabbed his arm, pulling him to the bus, and then shoved him up the stairs. Inside, Farah and the boys sat silent along the aisle seats of the bus. All of them looked the way Dave felt. Stunned and robotic. Amir held Farah's hand, whispering to her while she stared out blankly.

Soldiers climbed in after him, stripping off their fatigues as soon as they were inside. Under the uniforms, they wore traditional Pakistani attire. The Army fatigues were quickly deposited into a compartment beneath the floorboard and some even pulled out hats, shawls, and accessories. In a matter of seconds, the men in the bus transformed from Delta Force Operatives into Pakistani natives. They climbed across the kids, positioning themselves by the windows, their guns discreetly hoisted in their laps.

Eddie pushed him into an aisle seat. He stripped off his own fatigues like the other men, climbed around Dave's legs and sat.

Dave looked out the window, watching the helicopter. As its rotors began to turn, four Delta Force Ops paired off. Each pair sat on the floorboard of the Black Hawk at the two openings. With guns propped, they hung their legs out of the chopper and buckled themselves in.

All this protection, and there was no guarantee she'd even make it to the hospital.

"That bird is equipped with top-of-the-line medical technology. There's even pints of blood on there. If she needs surgery, they can do it in flight. Trust me," Eddie said.

The silence in the bus was broken when someone whispered. "Ten."

"Nine."

"Eight."

"Seven."

The Black Hawk rose a few inches, hovering off the ground.

"Six."

"Five."

The bus began to move out from the cover of the trees.

"Four."

"Three."

The pair of Deltas on the copter pointed their weapons at the road below while the bird floated into the air.

"Two"

The bus pulled into the street.

"One."

A loud explosion rocked the vehicle. Dave turned to see flames erupt from Sayeed's compound. When he looked back into the sky, the Black Hawk was gone. Ally was gone. Some of the kids on the bus were crying. Others covered their ears, and a couple were doing both.

People on the sidewalk screamed and ran up and down the street, seeking shelter next to cars and in stores, unaware of the bus driving away. Another explosion shook the vehicle.

"There goes the armory," Eddie whispered.

Emotionless, Dave watched a man run after the bus, his machine gun pointed directly at him. An armed man materialized on the sidewalk, shooting at the one whose gun was aimed at them. The first man flew backward, falling onto the road. Dave looked up, staring at the man who'd just saved their lives. The man gave him a nod as the bus moved on, undeterred.

Eddie shook his head. "That guy who just saved our asses? Unit 777. Egyptian Special Forces. Today, Ayoub bombed their mall and killed a dozen Egyptians. Wrong group of people to piss off. They called us and said they wanted in on whatever plans we might have for the As-Sirat. Long story short, they've probably killed about fifteen of those roaches by now but we got Romeo."

He recognized the name from earlier. "Romeo?"

"Ayoub. I bet they started celebrations right after they hung up with us," Eddie said.

Celebrations? Dave stared ahead. Was Ayoub's death worth it? Especially if the price was Ally.

They pulled onto an empty airstrip. A large Army cargo plane sat alone on the runway, its huge nose flipped open. The bus moved into the hole at the head of the plane, stopping once inside. The head closed behind them and the lights dimmed. Minutes later, the plane lifted them off the ground.

Men high-fived and cheered while the rest of them sat silently, still staring ahead.

CHAPTER TWENTY-NINE

THERAPIZING

4 WEEKS LATER, KAISERSLAUTERN, GERMANY

A large oak tree provided the perfect shaded spot to sit and have a clear view of the lake. Ally lowered herself to its base, rested against the trunk's hard surface, and opened her bag of pistachios. Cracking a shell, she popped its crunchy seed into her mouth, savoring the saltiness as a family of ducks swam underneath a wooden bridge that stretched across the water. She watched the birds while a cool breeze played with her hair. Ally filled her lungs with the fresh German air and worked on releasing her stress.

The past four weeks had been hard. She'd never fought so hard for anything as she had since arriving in Germany. Every presentation, letter, and tear-filled plea to the powers that be had one objective: To let her live with her family. Each time, their answer had pulled her heart out and torn it to pieces while she helplessly looked on.

"The decision is final. For their safety and yours, you can never see them again."

No one cared that Reema and the boys were her family, that they belonged together. The bitterness left a constant acidic taste in her mouth and an undercurrent of anger she couldn't shake.

They kept telling her to let go. Move on. And she was trying. The fact that she no longer saw herself as Sara was indication of that. It took her weeks of intensive therapy to realize that she was a free woman and no longer someone's possession. But some of the things the agency was asking, like walking away from Reema and the boys, were impossible. How did they expect her to let go of her soul? Move forward when a huge part of her had been ripped away?

Ally wiped a tear and stared into the pond at the ducks.

The tiniest of ducklings chased something in the water, and in the process, he moved farther and farther away from his family. As she admired the baby, a hawk swept down, grabbing it, and disappeared into a clump of trees. Except for Ally's gasp, not a sound was made and the rest of the ducks continued on, oblivious to their loss.

She couldn't help but wonder if the family would ever notice the baby was gone. As she contemplated the value of life, she heard footsteps behind her crunching on leaves and gravel. Ally popped another pistachio into her mouth as Eddie sat down beside her.

Her muscles tensed. She placed her bag of nuts between them and stared into the water. From the corner of her eye, she assessed him. Dressed in jeans, a pale, button-down short-sleeved shirt, and dark aviator sunglasses, he smiled and stared ahead as well.

They hadn't spoken since the compound. He'd attended every one of her meetings with the CIA and sat quietly while she pled her case, never saying a word or lifting a hand to help.

He pulled out some of the shelled treats from her bag and cracked them, popping out the seeds. "How's the hole in your head?"

Ally cringed and fought the urge to scratch around the stitches. "Still there, but it won't kill me."

"Good." He shucked another handful of her afternoon snack, tossing the shells into the water one by one.

Annoyed by his intrusion on her food and her time, she glanced over at him. "What do you want, Eddie?"

He shot a nut into his mouth and shrugged. "I hear you got the all clear to go home."

Maybe it was the chilly air, or her fear of what awaited her in Philadelphia. Whatever the reason, Ally shuddered. She bent her legs and wrapped her arms around them. Resting her chin on her knees, she looked ahead.

"It wasn't anything personal," he said, before tossing and

catching another pistachio into his mouth. "You were unconscious and in the middle of brain surgery, and we needed to make a decision."

He stretched his handful of shelled nuts out to her. "Pistachio?"

Ally shook her head and noticed how the movement no longer hurt.

The feathered family climbed to land, pecking at Eddie's discards. He chuckled at their antics. "The smartest thing is for those kids to spend the rest of their lives thinking their father was a good man. Not someone who kidnapped his wife and tried to create mini-terrorists. Even if we told them the truth, they wouldn't have believed it. This way, they get to blame the As-Sirat for Sayeed and Sara's deaths, and see the West as the hero. Things worked out the way they needed to."

She rolled her eyes. There was no reason for Reema and the kids to be told *she* was dead. But Ally was tired of arguing the point. "Are you going to see them?"

"Yeah. I'm leaving in a few hours."

The ache grew. Ally blinked away the tears. "How is she?"

He stared out at the mountains. "Hanging in there. She's taking your death pretty hard, but she's tough. Tougher than I realized."

"I kept your sister safe for two years." Getting pulled away from David and her family in America had been painful, but somehow she'd survived and created a whole other family to love. For it to happen a second time felt worse than the first.

"She told me about that. Thank you for doing that."

Although she could tell his words were sincere, it didn't ease her anger. "There's no reason for any of them to have to go through all of this without me."

He shrugged. "The decision to keep you apart was made by the committee, and we can't change it."

"I didn't get to say goodbye," she whispered and grabbed a twig from the ground, ignoring the tears that escaped.

"It's better this way."

The same words she'd heard daily for the past four weeks. Ally broke the branch into splinters. "I'm supposed to go *home* and pretend they never existed. How is that better?"

"You've survived worse. You can handle this."

The heat of anger moved up her chest to her face. "Why do I have to handle this?"

He kept his gaze fixed ahead, avoiding her glare. "They're starting to move on. You need to do the same."

Ally considered responding but changed her mind. It was a waste of time talking to someone like Eddie or any of the other people on the base. Trying to explain how emotions weren't connected to a switch she could flip when they told her to was like speaking a foreign language. So she changed the subject. "Did you give them the jewelry?"

His face relaxed. "Sold it. Between the money from the sales and the duffel bag of cash, they have more than enough to live comfortably."

"What happens to them now?"

He shrugged. "They have new names, a new address, and a new life. I told my sister she needs to go to school and then to college. I'm not going to agree to her marrying anyone, much less Mustache Man, until she's independent. And I told him if he touches her before then, I'll kill him."

Ally shook her head. "Amir's not scared of you."

He smiled, returning the uneaten pistachios to the bag. "No, but I'm the only family she's got, and he wants my blessing."

Eddie's words were a slap to her already bruised soul. Up until a month ago, *she* had been Reema's family, and it had been Ally's opinion that mattered. So much had changed, all without her permission.

She grabbed another branch and ripped it apart, trying to ignore the jealousy bubbling within, when she noticed a figure on the other side of the pond.

Dressed in a white linen shirt and jeans, David sat on the bench and leaned against the backrest. Ally wondered if the breeze that currently chilled her also rustled his thick brown locks. He ran his fingers through his hair, answering her question.

"How long are you planning on staying mad at him?"

She picked at imaginary pieces of grass from her jeans and didn't respond.

"None of what's happened is his fault. If you want to be mad at someone, be mad at Sayeed. He did all of this."

As much as Ally hated Eddie telling her what she was and was not allowed to feel, he was right. None of this was David's fault, but every time he showed up, which was often, her ability to think rationally shut down. Instead, she turned a cold shoulder to him and treated him like a monster. She just didn't understand why and how to stop.

"He got his ass on a plane, saved your life, and was nearly killed twice in one day. All for you. And even more dangerous than all that, he had to live with me for two weeks. Poor bastard."

She chuckled at the image of the two of them.

"Well, what do you know, the Ice Queen laughs."

Ally cringed. "Is that what they call me?"

"Are you kidding?" he grinned. "You killed Sayeed Irfani and helped us find and assassinate the second-most-wanted terrorist in the world. You're kind of a bad ass. Ice Queen's just my term of endearment for you."

"Thanks."

Eddie laughed at her obvious sarcasm. "You know, Ice, we're a lot alike."

Ally rested her head against the trunk. "I don't see it."

"Well, we are. I could tell you a long story of how, but I'm not up to being therapized right now."

She shot Eddie a questioning glance. "Therapized?"

"Yup. Today, I get to play the role of therapist and you're going to listen."

Ally rolled her eyes. "You've told me enough of what's wrong with me. I don't need any more therapy. Thank you." She shifted her weight to get up, but before she could, he grabbed her hand. "Give me five minutes and I promise I'll disappear forever after that."

She pulled her arm away and inched farther away from him. "Forever?"

He grinned. "Forever."

She looked down at her watch. "Clock starts now."

Eddie sucked in some air and began. "You're scared that once he figures out how fucked up you are, he won't want you anymore. You'd rather be with the kids and my sister because they love you, in spite of the fact you're all sorts of messed-up."

Ally's mouth dropped and her face heated.

"Give him a chance. He deserves that much. If it doesn't work, even if it hurts like hell, he'll know it was the right thing and get over it. You push him away without giving it a chance, and he'll never be able to move on."

She considered arguing but couldn't think of a response. Instead, she shut her mouth and fought back the tears threatening to escape.

He paused, flashing her a smile. "I hit a nerve, didn't I?"

When she didn't answer, he patted her shoulder. "Told you we were alike."

When Ally looked across the water, her gaze locked with David's. Her throat tightened. Why had she pushed him away? Her therapist at the base asked her the same question every time she went to a session and still they had no answers.

"Don't treat him like shit because *you* feel like shit. None of this was his fault."

His words stung and she had reached her limit. "Are you done? Or is there any other part of my life that needs fixing?"

"That's all I got for now." He laughed, pulling himself to his feet, and brushed the grass from his jeans.

"Eddie?"

"Ice?"

"Give her a hug from me," she choked out.

"Will do. You take care of yourself." He turned to leave but hesitated. "I know I was hard on you just now, but it's because you can handle it."

For fear he'd keep talking, she didn't move until he walked away. He had said a lot in a short amount of time, all of which hit her hard. When Ally reached for another pistachio, trying to process the things he'd said, her fingers hit grass instead. She didn't even have to look.

Eddie took the bag.

~

Across the park, Ally sat under a large tree. Dave tried to ignore Eddie's presence beside her, but the jealousy twisting in his gut made it hard. She looked comfortable around the guy. Even laughed at something he said. When he grabbed her hand, Dave's muscles tightened.

He understood it would take time for her to trust him. What stung was that she seemed to trust every man on the planet *except* him. She only spoke to him when necessary and stiffened every time he got close, much less touched her. There had been a couple of times in the past few weeks where he had to force himself to walk away before he did something stupid—like punch some guy in the face who could make her smile when he couldn't.

What if she never felt safe with him again?

Dave watched Eddie rise from the coveted spot beside her and walk across the bridge.

Punch Eddie?

He wasn't as tall as Dave, but way more muscular. From his aviators, the buzz cut...everything about the man screamed intimidation. Even the way he strutted across the park, he knew he was a bad ass.

Dave chuckled. Eddie would kick his ass.

With both hands tied behind his back.

Blindfolded.

He let out a breath and gazed at the only woman he'd ever loved. The last four weeks had already been good for her. Her face was fuller, her skin glowed, and the shine had finally returned to her chocolate brown eyes. A soft breeze swept across her, pressing the curls across her face while she stared into space. She looked lost, and none of his efforts was helping her find her way home. After the two years of hell she'd gone through, she needed time to work through all that. The fear that it might be better for her if he wasn't around while she did that work kept crawling into his thoughts. Was he being a selfish prick by sticking around and not wanting to leave her?

Dave kept his attention fixed on her and tried to ignore the man approaching, but Eddie made that next to impossible by sitting down beside him.

"Pistachio?" When Dave didn't answer, Eddie cleared his throat. "I'm heading out today to take care of some stuff. You guys will be home by the time I get back."

Dave shook his head. "She won't come."

"She'll come. Sayeed fucked her up. But you're not him. You're going to have to help her figure that out." Eddie got up and tossed a crumbled brown bag in Dave's lap. "Can you give that to your wife for me?"

It took a while after Eddie left before Dave gathered the courage to head over the bridge to Ally.

She hugged her knees and fiddled with her sandals when he stepped in front of her.

"Hey. Can I sit down?"

Ally didn't look up but nodded. Dave lowered himself beside her. He cleared the tension in his throat and handed her the wadded paper bag. "Pistachios?"

When she didn't respond, he tossed it to the ground and tried again. "I know you're mad at me, but we're going home in a week and we need to talk."

Pain flashed across her face. "I know," she said, biting her lip.

The desire to pull her into his arms, kiss that lip, and promise to protect her overwhelmed him. Instead, he picked up splintered pieces of wood and tried to piece them together. "How do I fix this?"

"You can't. It's not yours to fix."

Dave tossed the pieces of bark and rubbed the dirt off his hands. "I've been reading a lot of books lately."

"About?"

"How to be there for you. What you need."

Her gaze locked with his, and for a moment, he let himself get lost in her eyes.

"And?" she whispered.

He cleared the lump that seemed to constantly find its place in his throat whenever Ally was around. "They all say the same things. I need to be patient. Do what it takes to help you feel safe."

Dave reached over and played with the buckle of her sandal, relishing the feel of her skin when his hand brushed against her foot. "And I will, but you have to know this is hard for me."

Ally inched her feet away from his fingers, sending another jolt of hurt through him.

"The way you ignore me and don't let me touch you. I get it's normal. But you're only like that with me." His voice cracked. "Sometimes I wonder if it would be better for you if I weren't around."

"Da—"

He cut her off and rushed through the words before he

chickened out. "I want you to be happy, and if I need to disappear for that to happen..."

Her hand wrapped around his arm. "Stop."

Her grip on his wrist made Dave forget how to breathe, much less think.

"I haven't been fair to you, and you're right, we need to talk. I just need some time. Please?"

He stared at their connection, savoring the feel of her. How long had it been since she'd touched him?

"How long?"

She rubbed her thumb against his skin, sending jolts of electricity shooting through him.

"I need to take care of something. Come by my place in two hours and we'll talk."

"Okay."

When Ally took her hand away, he ached to grab it back and beg her to come back to the States with him. From the way she'd been treating him, he doubted that would ever happen. He fixed his gaze on the family of ducks in the pond. "We need to do what's best for you. Whatever that is, I'll do it. Just be honest with yourself and me."

Dave rose to his feet and walked away from her.

The hardest part was not looking back.

CHAPTER THIRTY

NEED

Ally squeezed into the empty elevator before its doors closed. She hunched over, holding on to her knees, gasping for air, probably because of the half-mile sprint across the base she had just run to get home.

"Come on," Ally whispered to the number plate above the doors. Considering she was already thirty minutes late, David might have given up and left by now. Not that anyone would blame him if he did. But if he wasn't there, how would she find him? She didn't know where he was staying. So caught up in her own anger and pity party, she never asked. Not that she needed to. For the past four weeks, David had just shown up. Every doctor's appointment, CT scan, debriefing, he was always there. Even though she'd ignored him, he stood by her side, asking the questions Ally had been too upset to ask or think about.

The heat of shame rose from her stomach to her face at the thought of how she'd treated him.

As soon as the doors opened, Ally rushed out of the elevator and slammed into a firm body. Arms wrapped around her waist and a familiar musky cologne filled her lungs.

David.

He pressed his face into her hair, and her ear warmed from his breath. Dave ran his fingers up and down her spine, the way he used to. Instead of soothing her as it once did, goose bumps followed the path he traced.

Before her head had a chance to tell her body it was safe, her arms reacted, pushing him away.

He took a huge step back and leaned against the wall. They both pretended not to notice the flash of hurt across his face.

Ally stared at the floor, his shoes, everywhere else but him. “I'm sorry.” *You don't deserve any of this.* “I was in a rush to get here. I wasn't paying attention to where I was going.”

He ran his fingers through his hair and nodded. A brown curl dangled over his forehead. Ally's mind flashed back to happier times. A time when she felt safe enough to brush the strand away for him, even tug at it and kiss the spot.

Her therapist's words from a few minutes ago echoed through her head. “*Because of the trauma, your brain's wiring has changed. Its instincts are to run away. To protect you from harm at all costs. You need to work on re-teaching your body, rewiring your brain. Challenge its reactions and prove to yourself that you are safe.*”

Ignoring the screaming cells in her body ordering otherwise, she stepped toward him and forced her hands to unclench. Dave was watching her, his gaze burning through her skin. Ally wasn't breathing, and from the rigidness of his body, he wasn't either. She grazed her fingertips across his forehead and touched the softness of the fallen strand. When his eyes closed, a surge of energy flowed through her. Finally, she was doing something right.

When she started to pull her hand away, he grabbed her wrist. The war of wills continued within her. One side shrieked to pull away and run as fast as her legs could propel her. Then another much smaller part, deep within her chest, whispered to her. *Don't move. Risk everything. Remember.*

Ally honed into that tiny voice and focused on the goodness of David.

He pressed her fingers against his lips. “It's okay. I'm just glad you came.”

The warmth of his breath flowed down her fingers and into her chest, thawing a lifetime of pain. It continued lower, awakening a part of her she believed died a long time ago. The heat so unexpected and intense, Ally yanked her hand away and took a huge step back.

David cleared his throat and tucked his hands into his jean

pockets.

Her heart clenched at the look of defeat that flashed across his face. She'd done it again.

Her need for him mixed with her urge to run was overwhelming. But Ally knew she couldn't do that to him. Not anymore. "Let's talk inside."

His beautiful sea-green eyes fastened on her and warmed her core, again. Tearing away from his heat, she headed to her apartment and let him in.

With its wood flooring, a kitchenette, and an outdated but comfortable beige sofa set, the room was small but quaint. A short hallway led to a bathroom and bedroom. In the weeks she'd lived here, no one had visited—until today. "I'm sorry I kept you waiting. My session with Dr. Harmon ran over."

"Dr. Harmon?" He sat on the apartment's only couch.

Ally turned on every light in the space before lowering herself into the armchair across from him.

"If you'd like, you could sit at the kitchen table."

She looked behind her at the oak table and back at him, confused. "Why?"

He flashed a smile and shrugged. "Other than the bedroom, it might be the seat farthest away from me."

Ignoring the sting, she laughed. "Don't give me ideas."

"It's nice to see you smile," he whispered.

The hunger in his eyes was so powerful, Ally lowered her gaze. How did he do that? Look at her as if she was the epitome of perfection, especially when there was nothing further from the truth? She cleared her throat. "What were we talking about?"

David leaned forward, planting his elbows on his thighs. "You were going to tell me about Dr. Harmon."

"Right. She's the Army psychologist I've been seeing twice a week since I got here. She was able to squeeze me in today last minute. At the park earlier, Eddie said some things and I realized I needed to process them with her."

"Eddie?"

She laughed nervously. "Yes. He's an insensitive ass but he's perceptive. He told me that he and I are a lot alike."

"Are you?"

"Maybe, he pointed out what my issues were and Dr. Harmon helped me make sense of it all."

She left out the part about how for the first time in a long while, she felt hopeful about her future, one she hoped included David. One step at a time.

Ally pulled out the pillow from behind her and hugged it. "My life with Sayeed was hell. But no matter what he did, no matter how hard he beat me or tore me down, I always got back up. Do you know why?"

His stare was so intense, she avoided it and fiddled with the pillow's fringe. "There was a picture. It was of you sitting on a park bench. I looked at it every day and chose to believe you were waiting for me. It became all I thought about. Somewhere out there, my David waits for me."

The room was quiet. Ally wasn't even sure he was breathing. She sucked in a gulp of air. "So when I saw the picture of you and that other woman, it devastated me." Her voice cracked, but she ignored it and tried to push forward. "The idea that you weren't waiting for me to come home anymore was hard."

"Ally, I never stopped..."

"David, you didn't do anything wrong. Just...let me finish. Please?"

He nodded and laid his head against the back of the couch. Ally's heart ached for him. "I couldn't cling to you anymore. I had to accept it was over and find another purpose. A reason to wake up and keep moving. And I did."

David's eyes closed, his fists clenched, turning the knuckles white.

"Reema and then the kids became that for me. I chose to believe my survival was essential for theirs. What Eddie helped me realize today is, I was wrong. I was never that for them. Nasif and Amir were the ones who protected them. But I couldn't see it at the time and I'm glad I couldn't. If I had, I'm not sure I would have made it through. The reality is they don't need me. They didn't then and don't now. As much as it hurts, Reema and the boys have moved on, and it's time I do the same."

Ally glanced over at him. Did he understand what she was trying to say?

Lines around his eyes deepened. His lips stretched the way they used to when he was trying to rein in his emotions.

David sat up, pulled out his cell phone, and fiddled with it. "So how do you move on?"

"I need to figure that out," Ally said and prepared for the next part of her speech. She owed David her life and after everything he'd done for her, she had treated him badly. Now she needed to work up the nerve to ask him to wait and to apologize for all she'd done. A hard task considering he was obviously upset.

David tucked his phone in his shirt pocket. "I think it's best if I go back to Philly tomorrow morning so you can have time to do that."

Ally's mouth dropped open. "I...I'm not ready to go. I finally made a breakthrough today. There are other things I need to work on with Dr. Harmon." *Like us.*

"I didn't mean you. *I* am going back. Alone."

She sat in silence, blinking back the tears as the weight of his words slapped her. "Why?"

He shrugged. "Like you said, your work here isn't finished, but there are responsibilities, things I need to take care of back at home." The coldness of his voice, how he kept his attention everywhere but on her, made it hard for Ally to breathe.

He was going back to the woman. "Oh."

The silence in the room became overwhelming. The thought of David not being with her terrified Ally. But she understood. She'd hurt him repeatedly. Pushed him away every time he reached out, and she'd probably do it a hundred times more. There was still a long road ahead and no guarantee they'd even be together at the end of it.

Having to choose between someone like her, crippled with flashbacks, nightmares and fear, or the woman waiting for him who was able to give him what he deserved... Of course he'd pick the other woman. Who wouldn't?

Ally's stomach twisted. Crushing the pillow for strength, she searched for the words to let him go. "I'll never forget what you did. You didn't have to do any of this, and it means a lot that you came for me. Thank you."

"Of course I did. How could I not?" He flashed her a look she couldn't quite read before pulling out his phone and fiddling with it again.

Ally's fingers went numb because of how tight she had them clamped onto the pillow. Everything he did was out of a sense of obligation.

If that was true then obviously, there was no reason to tell him the rest. "Just know it means a lot."

It was becoming harder and harder to push her tears away. She rose and walked to the bathroom. "I'm going to take a shower, could you let yourself out?"

"Ally?"

She froze with her back to him.

"Will you call me when you get into town?"

Her tears broke free, streaming down her cheeks. She cleared her throat, trying to sound calm. "Yes," she lied and walked into the bathroom, locking the door behind her.

~

Dave laid his head against the backrest, hating himself. This had been their first real conversation, and he'd fucked it up and made an ass of himself. Why the hell did he tell her he was leaving?

Because you wanted her to tell you to stay, dumb shit, that's why. Instead, she thanked you for your time.

Her mention of *the other woman* just about killed him. By allowing Kate in at one of the lowest points in his life, he'd let Ally down. Yeah, he fucked up, but she was wrong. He hadn't moved on. How could he explain to her that he used Kate? How did that explain anything except that he was a piece of shit? What difference did it make anyway?

The bigger question was could he really leave her? Yeah, she'd pushed him away every time he'd tried to step in, but after everything she'd gone through, she obviously didn't know who she was or what she wanted anymore. She pretty much said that, didn't she? The reality was if he left her there alone to figure things out, she would, but he wouldn't have a chance in hell with her. And when she did get through this, someone would be there to swoop in and take his place.

Dave tried to breathe through the tightness in his chest as he considered his options. He pulled out his cell and scrolled through his reservation when the shower turned off.

He ran a hand through his hair. She wouldn't be expecting him to still be there. It would probably scare the shit out of her. Maybe he should wait outside and knock?

Before he could think further, the door opened and Ally stepped out.

Her naked back, scarred from Sayeed's attack, faced him. Hair in tight, wet spirals clung to her skin. Ally's perfectly shaped ass flexed when she bent over and twisted her hair into a white towel.

Dave's jaw tensed and his pulse quickened as he watched the way her body moved and hips stretched. His fingers twitched to touch. To explore. Another part of him twitched, as well, at the hunger to be inside her.

When she turned around, he sucked in a breath. Legs longer than he remembered led to a mound of curly black. He swelled at the prospect of connecting with the piece of heaven hidden below the curls. Her stomach, lean and smooth, drew him higher, every one of his organs on alert.

Two full, perfect breasts with velvet peaks pointed at him. His mouth watered. When her chest rose, the fabric around his crotch tightened. Rising from the chair, Dave's gaze moved further up until they locked with hers. Her beautiful chocolate brown eyes stared back, void of emotion. Frozen.

When he stepped forward, she stepped back.

Son of a bitch.

Realization screeched through him, chilling him to the bone. "Ally. It's me. I'd never do anything to hurt you." Dave's words came out hoarse, full of the sadness for the pain he saw in her.

Long, thick lashes sealed her lids shut seconds before a tear spilled onto her cheek. Everything in his being wanted to go to her and hold her, but he knew better. That wasn't what she needed from him right now.

Ally nodded, as if hearing his thoughts, and walked into her bedroom. When the door closed, Dave remained rooted to the spot, staring at the door. There was no way in hell he was leaving.

CHAPTER THIRTY-ONE

SAFETY

A soft knock on the bedroom door made Ally jump. She ignored it, hoping he'd go away, and scanned the space. A queen bed with a perfectly good mattress sat in the middle of Ally's room. Beside it was a desk and vanity. A television hung on the wall over the desk. On the other side, sat a large and very comfortable armchair. With all this furniture around her, why did she always end up sitting in a corner on the floor? Another one of the crazy things she found herself doing.

She and her therapist had spent weeks analyzing it. Of course it was PTSD related. Safety was the explanation they could come up with. The spot gave her a clear view of the bedroom and balcony doors. Yes, rationally she knew no one was going to hurt her. But every night, Sayeed visited her dreams, taunting her. By the end of it all, she'd wake up covered in sweat and, seconds later, find herself huddled right there in the same corner. She wouldn't move from the spot either. Instead, she'd stay on guard, watching and waiting until sunlight broke through the darkness, allowing her the ability to leave the emptiness of the room.

Right now, it wasn't safety Ally needed but comfort. David was going home, leaving her alone to face a world she didn't know anymore. One that had moved on while she lived in an alternative universe. Now she had to figure out where she fit.

Piece of cake.

The heat of anger spread across her face. Closing her eyes,

Ally tried unsuccessfully to ease the pressure of building tears. She was tired of crying. The back of her head thudded against the wall as she thought of all she'd lost.

Umber. Nasif. Reema. The boys. Now David. And none of them was by her choice. If she had died that day in the compound with Ayoub...

Ally forced the thought out. She wouldn't let herself go there. What were the things she had to look forward to? Her parents, brother, and sister. There had been numerous phone calls between them once she'd arrived in Germany, mostly them initiating and her avoiding the calls. The few times they had talked, it was obvious they wanted her back. They'd all try to put their lives on hold to babysit her, but for how long? Nik Bhai had a busy practice and a family of his own. And her parents and Reya would be absorbed in wedding plans.

The knock on the door became louder, pulling her out of her thoughts. The suffocating panic that rocked her when David saw her naked was a good reminder of how messed up she was, both emotionally and physically. If she couldn't trust him, she definitely couldn't give him the kind of life he deserved. It made sense he'd decided to leave.

"Ally, I hope you're dressed because I'm coming in."

The door opened and fluorescent lighting filled the dim space. With nowhere to hide, she hugged her knees to her chest and played with the hem of her white cotton summer dress. When his shadow fell over her, Ally's hand trembled. "I told you to leave."

He squatted in front of her, leveling his gaze with hers. She pretended not to notice.

"I couldn't."

"Couldn't or wouldn't?" Ally worked on keeping her voice void of emotion as she continued to pleat the cotton hem.

David's index finger traced over the hills and valleys of her knuckles while his thumb caressed her wrist. His touch had always been her weakness, and now was no different. Ally's limbs froze as waves of electricity shot in different directions, some down to her fingertips and others into her chest.

"Couldn't. It physically hurts to be away from you," he whispered.

The words she'd ached to hear, brimmed with a promise she knew he couldn't keep. She moved her hand out of his, planting both palms on her knees and rested her chin on them. "That'll go away as soon as you leave."

He laughed, shaking his head. "No, it won't."

His touch, his words, the fluttering in her chest, all of it made pushing him away that much harder. Ally closed her eyes and tried to stay focused because none of it mattered. He was leaving in the morning.

"You know what scares me the most about leaving you?" Something about the way he asked it forced her to meet his gaze, and the sadness she saw there tugged at her. "That if I walk away from you, someone else will step in. Because you are so easy to fall in love with. The way things are right now, I don't know that you'd fight for me." His voice cracked. He cleared it. "I can't risk that. It'll kill me to let you go."

As messed up as she was, Ally knew she'd never let anyone else get close to her, but it wasn't a point worth arguing.

He reached over and tucked a loose strand of her hair behind her ear and twisted the end of the lock around his finger.

So gentle, soothing. It made it hard for her to think.

"Say something," he whispered.

What was there to say? She was messed up beyond repair, sitting on the floor in a corner and waiting for the man she murdered to come back and kill her. Sadness warmed her face. "You need to go home," she whispered.

David brushed a stray tear off her cheek. "I am home, and I haven't been here in a long time."

When his hand grazed her neck, something tugged from deep within. A hunger for him, screaming to let him in. Ally fought the urge to rest her cheek on his hand. He was a good man and deserved so much better.

She moved his palm away and fiddled with her dress. "Go home. You'll be fine. You've already adapted."

He rested his hand on her shoulder and, after a quick squeeze, sat beside her with his back against the wall. "That's a good way of putting it. Yes, I kind of did adapt. But adapting doesn't mean I was happy. It just means I tried to move on."

David's leg pressed against hers, and even though she knew she should move it, she didn't.

"Since you left, every thought I've had has been of you. I can't sleep at night without you showing up in my dreams." He grabbed her hand, sandwiching it between his two. "No matter how hard I pretended, I couldn't make you go away. I tried everything humanly possible, none of it worked."

David pressed his lips against her fingers, melting another layer of ice. "You know how I am. I've always had a plan, a goal. When you disappeared, none of those things mattered. I've never felt so helpless in my life. I couldn't breathe and I didn't want to. I don't want to feel that way anymore. Ever."

She kept her gaze fixed on the sliding patio door for fear of what she'd see in his face.

Ally pinched the bridge of her nose as the damn broke and tears fell. "Dave, I'm really messed up."

"I'm listening." His stubble grazed her knuckles, and she found herself imagining it scraping against her cheek.

When Ally inhaled to steady herself, his musky scent filled her lungs, soothing her. "I'm scared that I'm broken, unfixable. That if somehow I do figure out how to put the pieces together, they won't fit like before. I won't be the same."

Silence filled their space and her anxiety grew. She had shared more than she'd ever planned. Ally tugged at her hand, but he tightened his grip, refusing to let go.

"Baby, I don't expect you to be the same person. Hell, I'm not either, but I know when we're together there's nothing we can't handle."

"What if this is too much? What if this time is different?"

"Then we'll figure it out. Together." His lips stretched into a mischievous smile while he kissed her fingers for the hundredth time, leaving her breathless.

Ally pulled her hand away and swatted at him when he reached for it. "Why do you keep doing that?"

He grinned. "It's what I used to do when you were mad or had a bad day. Remember? I figured I'd give it a try."

She sat on her palms, trying not to laugh. "Stop it. I can't think straight when you do that."

"In other words, it still works," he chuckled.

"David, please."

"Sorry." He rested his arms on his knees and stared at her.

~

Dave grinned as he watched Ally. It was nice to see her relaxed. Well, she wasn't really relaxed, but at least the dull look in her eyes was gone. The way her lips pressed together to keep from laughing, and knowing he did that, made his chest swell.

One of the straps of her white sundress had slipped off her shoulder while they played tug of war with her hand. His fingers brushed against her soft skin when he grabbed the thin strip of fabric. It had been an innocent gesture. One he used to do all the time before the kidnapping. But this was different. They were different.

His hand lingered on her arm, craving to kiss the spot. He leaned close, shifting the strap back into place. She smelled exotic, like a rare flower he couldn't quite place. Whatever it was, his mouth watered at the thought of tasting it. The smooth line of her collarbone led to the hollow spot below her throat. He moved his thumb from her shoulder, tracing a path to the dip. A single kiss right there was all it used to take...

When Ally jerked away from his touch, Dave froze as realization hit. "Sorry." He raised his palms in surrender, moved back to his spot, and tried to shake off the effect of her. "What were you saying?"

"What if it's too much?" She rested her cheek on her knee, staring at him.

One glance at her fear-filled eyes and everything finally made sense. "Is that why you want to be with Reema and the boys? Because you think being with you might be too much for me?"

She turned her head, but he saw the look that flashed across her face before she did. *Bingo.*

Ally shrugged her shoulders. "They love me for who I am now, not who I was before. They'd never leave me." She messed with the bottom of her dress.

Dave tried to keep his emotions at bay as the final piece of the puzzle fit snugly into place. "But I could?"

"When you realize how messed up I am. How much work this might take."

He swallowed his anger and the hurt that her lack of faith in him stirred up. "In the years we've known each other, have I ever given up on you? Or on anything for that matter?"

A tear fell down her cheek. "A lot of things happened to me. I killed someone. Those things are going to have a lasting impact."

Dave broke the rules in the books he'd read and put his arm around her, pulling her close. Surprisingly, she didn't resist and even rested her head on his shoulder. "Sayeed was a bastard. He hurt you and was killing the people you loved one by one. You had no choice but to stop him." He slid his hand down, resting it over her heart. "And no matter what's happened, you're still the same Ally in here."

She closed her eyes and stiffened but didn't move away.

"It's why so many people risked their lives to protect you. It's why I love you."

Dave's chest tightened. When she had needed him most, he hadn't been able to keep her safe. He pressed his lips against her hair. "You know what kills me the most?"

"What?" The warmth of her breath brushed against his neck.

"Every time I close my eyes, I see you, swollen and bleeding." His throat tightened but he choked out the words. "I didn't protect you." He gritted his teeth and squeezed his eyes shut as moisture leaked out. "It's something I'll never forgive myself for."

Ally pulled away. Her eyes wet with tears of her own; she gazed up at him. Embarrassed and unable to stop, Dave leaned his head against the wall and stared at the ceiling. He could count on one hand the number of times he'd cried since becoming an adult, and most of them had been in the past twenty-seven months.

Gentle fingers brushed the wetness off his cheeks. He leaned his face into her hand, savoring the feel of her.

"Is that what you think happened? That you didn't protect me?"

He didn't answer. Couldn't even if he tried. The giant bottle of sorrow he'd kept tightly corked since the day she disappeared had finally popped open. His body shook as the intensity of it hit him, and he cried for what he'd failed to do, for the deep void her disappearance had left in him for those two years, and for finally getting the second chance he thought would never come.

"Dave," she finally whispered. "This wasn't your fault. There was nothing anyone could have done, and in the end you did something. You showed up. *You* saved my life."

He shook his head, unable to respond. Ally crept onto his lap and ran her fingers through his hair, soothing him. When she wrapped her arms around him, he pulled her close, burying his face in her neck.

Even after the tears had stopped, they sat tangled in each other. Having her in his arms, feeling her heart thud against his chest, he felt whole for the first time in a long time. Dave filled his lungs with Ally. He savored the feel of her chest rising and falling against his, the heat of her breath against his skin.

When she pressed her lips against his cheek, it sent currents of energy rushing through him, lengthening an already growing problem. Before he realized what he'd done, he nipped at her throat. A small gasp escaped her lips.

Dave pulled back, worried he'd ruined their moment. She sat rigid on his lap, her thick lashes hooded.

"I'm sorry. I shouldn't have done that," he said.

When he tried to move away, she grabbed his shoulders, resting her forehead against his. "Don't."

Her breathing came out ragged, puffing the scent of peppermint in his face. "I want this. You. I need to know I can still feel things."

When she traced his cheek with the back of her hand, his jeans tightened. The more she caressed his face, the tighter they got. Ally leaned in and pressed her lips onto the corner of his parted mouth.

His pulse raced and he fought the urge to kiss the hell out of her and rip every article of clothing off her body. She needed to trust him. Which meant she needed to take the lead and do what she wanted, not what he wanted.

"Ally, are you...?"

"Shhh." She silenced him by covering his mouth with hers.

Hot. Sweet. Slow.

The war between lust and logic waged inside him, with the latter losing ground each second her tongue connected with his. She pulled back sooner than he would have liked. The voice in his head screamed for her to come back. Instead she sat in his lap, close to his crotch, staring at his mouth while her chest heaved.

He rested his forehead against hers and traced a path along the side of her neck with his hand. "Can I kiss you here?" She bit her lip and nodded.

He smiled. There was so much he wanted to do to her and for

her. As his mouth explored the sweet, tender skin, she leaned her head back, granting him better access. This was his Ally. The woman he remembered. Somehow, he needed to help her remember how good their love was and could be again.

The top of her dress bunched up, revealing a clear view of two of his favorite Ally parts. Heat pulsed straight to his crotch. He lowered his head, kissing the spot where her breasts formed a perfect V.

She shoved him away, her hand covering her chest. "Just kissing. I'm not ready for more."

He nodded his understanding and then silenced her with a kiss.

CHAPTER THIRTY-TWO

DESENSITIZATION

Out of breath from their kiss, Ally curled as deep into his embrace as possible. His love, patience, willingness to give, all of it enveloped her in a layer of peace she hadn't experienced in a painfully long time.

Today, David took her to a place she thought she'd never be able to reach again. For the first time in two years, she was made a priority. He and Sayeed were two different people, and the message David sent was clear. Unlike Sayeed, he would never try to dominate or hurt her, and she believed him. The thick walls that took two years to build crumbled under his touch.

A tear spilled from her closed eyelids. Soft lips brushed it away before it hit her cheek. The kiss was so sweet, so him.

David moved loose strands of hair off her face. His sea-green eyes speckled with blue and gold stared into her soul. "You okay?"

Ally got lost in his gaze. What would have happened if he had given up and left like she'd wanted? The thought made more tears flow.

"Ally?"

She rested her face in the crook of his neck and inhaled his musky scent. She kissed the side of his neck. "Thank you."

"Anytime," he said while his fingers worked to loosen neck muscles she never realized were stiff.

After all the things she'd done and said, he still stayed.

"Why?"

"Hmm?"

She pulled away just enough to face him but kept herself wrapped in his arms. "Why'd you stay? After the way I've treated you, why didn't you leave?"

He pecked the tip of her nose and stroked her cheek. "Because you're worth fighting for."

She opened her mouth to argue, but David silenced her by pressing his lips onto hers. When they finally broke free, she glanced down at the bulge in his jeans. A twinge of fear crept up her spine. As much as she wanted to have sex with him one day, she was scared she couldn't. How long would he wait, especially when there was someone else offering to replace her?

Her stomach twisted. "David, can I ask you something?"

"Mmm hmm," he mumbled as he moved her hair and planted kisses along the side of her neck. Each time his lips connected with her skin, heat fluttered through her, leaving her breathless.

"Tell me about her."

He froze mid-kiss, the warmth of his breath tickling her when he sighed. After a peck at the base of her neck, he rested the back of his head against the wall behind him and shut his eyes. "Do we need to have this discussion now?"

Ally leaned into him, listening to the steady, rhythmic beats of his heart. The one thing she realized from the hell she went through was there were no guarantees. So many people had come and left her life. If he asked to leave as well, would she be strong enough to let him go? "No, we don't."

When she shifted to get up, he tightened his legs and arms, squeezing her close. "Stay. I like you there."

She didn't move away but didn't get any closer either. Instead, she stared at her hands as the images of him kissing the blonde flashed on repeat in her head. "I've seen pictures of the two of you, but I don't even know her name."

After an eternity of silence, he twined his large fingers into hers, kissing each one. "Her name's Kate."

Kate. She's real. She's Kate.

"What do you want to know?"

Ally choked back the tears and fiddled with the buttons on his shirt. "How'd you meet her?"

He pressed his lips against her hair. "She's a nurse. I met her a year after you disappeared." When she pulled away a second time, he tugged her back to his chest and kissed her head. "Let me finish. I had to give an early-morning lecture at the hospital. She came up after the presentation and asked me out."

"And you said yes."

"I did. She was fun and helped me forget...about things for a little bit. I needed that."

Things? She swallowed the rising jealousy. *Me. She helped him forget me.*

"Do you love her?" Ally held her breath.

He sighed. "Yes."

Amazing how deep one single word could cut. She wasn't sure if it was how tight he was holding her or the weight of reality slamming into her chest. Whatever it was, all the air in her lungs had just been squeezed out.

"But you need to hear it all."

She shook her head. What he'd said was enough. He loved someone else. Everything in her screamed to run as fast as she could, but she couldn't move, it hurt too much to leave.

"Yes, I love her. But"—he cupped her chin and tilted her head, looking straight into her soul—"not like I love you. There's no comparison. I always felt guilty with her. She loved me more and all I ever wanted was you."

His words flowed through her, relieving some of the pressure that had settled on her chest. "And now?"

"And now, I'm going to tell her it's over."

Ally lowered her gaze. "Is that what you want?"

"Yeah, it is. It's always been you. That's never going to change."

When she started to ask how he could be so sure, he pinched her lips shut. "Shhh, no more talking."

His free hand moved down to her hips, pushing her core against his erection.

An image of Sayeed grinding himself into her crept into her mind, sending icy currents of fear soaring through her. She tried to ignore the flashback and stay focused on the moment, but Dave sensed the change. He put his hands on her face and stared into her eyes. "You okay?"

She shook her head. “We’re moving too fast.”

He planted a chaste kiss on her nose. “I know.” Eyes closed, he returned his forehead to hers. “We’ll take it slow and work on desensitization.”

“On what?”

He crinkled his nose and twirled an imaginary mustache. “You see, desensitization is where you expose the person to their fears with the intent of extinguishing them.”

His awful German accent and the way his brows rose and fell made her laugh. “Yes, Dr. Freud, I know what it means. Wow, you really have been reading.”

David traced her bottom lip with his thumb. “It’s nice when you laugh, and yes, I did my research. I even have a plan.”

Her cheeks heated. “A what?”

He beamed. “A plan and kissing is involved in the first five parts.”

“Oh God.” She covered her face in embarrassment.

David kissed the backs of her fingers before pulling them away, his eyes hooded. “And I’m loving every minute of it.”

Her shame turned into molten lava when he kissed her, showing her just how much she enjoyed the experience. Ally wrapped her fingers into his hair. She drank in all he offered and tried to give him the same. When she finally came up for air, she was sweating and panting but managed to wheeze out her opinion of his desensitization idea. “Good plan.”

“I.” He planted a kiss on her left lid. “Sooo.” Then on her right lid. “Agree.” He put his mouth on hers and delved in again. She had forgotten how much she loved his lips on her.

“What comes after the kissing, Dr. Freud?” she panted while he assaulted her neck.

Full lips nipped at her shoulder.

“For now just stay where you are, and let’s make out. And when you’re ready, the next step is oral.”

CHAPTER THIRTY-THREE

HOMECOMING

The taxi stopped at a red light a few blocks from their Philadelphia condo. Dressed in a pair of dark jeans and a cream-colored shirt, both of which hugged her curves, Ally sat beside Dave, looking like she'd just returned from vacation instead of two years of a fucked-up life. With her fingers tucked under his, she craned her neck and stared at the high-rises.

"Come here." He tugged at her hand. The hesitation she once had for him was gone. She moved into his arms and rested her face against his neck. He pressed his lips against her hair. "We could always turn around and go back to Germany."

"Mmm, another week at least would have been nice."

Her breath blew warm spurts of air on his skin, heating him in all the right places. Up until a few months ago, Dave hadn't even known if she was alive, now he was taking her home.

He squeezed her tight, absorbing the warmth and scent of her. "Agreed."

The past fourteen days had been amazing. Rediscovering the Ally he'd missed, and falling in love with the new parts of her...heaven.

Having her back made everything seem like before, even though so much was different.

Dave reached for a fistful of the thick ringlets that covered her face but stopped short. Her neck and hair were danger zones.

Sometimes she was fine with him touching her there, but other times she'd freeze and forget how to breathe. Understandable, considering the piece of shit dragged and choked her more times than Dave ever wanted to know.

His attention drifted down to the plump, light caramel-colored skin peeking out from under her V-neck. As usual, his mouth watered at the thought of tasting her there. But he hadn't and probably wouldn't any time soon. That was a *don't even think about it* zone.

Dave ached to sink himself deep inside her and become one hot, solid mass of energy. Another hurdle they hadn't crossed yet. Key word being yet, he reminded himself. They would...

Eventually.

One day.

Hopefully soon.

He reminded himself to be patient. Hell, up until a couple weeks ago, he wasn't sure they'd make it so fast to the kissing stage. A smile tugged at his lips. Thank God they'd moved on to more, much more.

Dave tore his gaze away from her cleavage and pressed his lips against the top of her head.

One day soon, we'll get there.

His mind drifted back to their first night together in Germany. After spending the day talking and kissing, he fell asleep holding her in his arms. When he woke up, she wasn't in the bed but asleep, huddled on the floor in a corner.

He stood over her for a long time, watching and aching to somehow heal her. Since he had no clue how to do that, he ended up lying beside her on the carpet. When he brushed her hair off her cheek, Ally's eyes popped open. She jumped to her feet, crouched and ready to run, like a deer staring into the face of a hungry lion. It wasn't until that moment that Dave realized what she meant when she said she was broken.

No amount of time spent reading books and planning, prepared him for the way she stared at him. How many years would she be fighting the demons that bastard had created? Swallowing the anger that one man was solely responsible for doing this to the woman he loved was hard. It took everything Dave had to not let the rage boiling within seep to the surface. Not when she needed him to be strong.

When she finally calmed down and allowed him to hold her, it was first with an apology. Dave made a silent promise that night to do whatever it took to wipe every ounce of fear out of her.

Sayeed did things to her most people would have never survived. Not only did she make it to the other side, she brought survivors along with her. And now, she was finally going home. Dave stared down into the eyes of the toughest person he'd ever met, and his chest filled with awe. "You know what I liked about Germany?"

She played with the buttons of his shirt, one of her new habits that he loved. "I can guess."

The heat from her gaze, filled with a promise of things to come, shot directly through him, straight into the area below his belt. And the bastard he was wanted more. To touch and savor every part of her body, no clothes, no restrictions.

He pushed the thoughts away. Ally was worth waiting for.

As hard as it was to hurt Kate, it was exciting to know that finally there were no more people standing in their way. He just hoped Kate understood what Ally meant to him. The conversation they had over the phone last week didn't go so well. Hurting her was hard, but he was honest, as honest as he could be under the circumstances.

"David?" Ally stared up at him.

He kissed her smiling lips and savored their sweetness. "Hmm?"

"I was asking you what you'd miss most about Germany."

"Oh yeah, sorry. Not the sex," he said absentmindedly.

Guilt flashed across her eyes.

Shit.

He kissed her mouth shut before she could apologize. "The reason I'm not going to miss the sex is because of our ten-step process, remember? We have a lot of work and practice to do, too. I can't miss something I plan on getting lots of."

Ally's smile was contagious. He saw more of them now, but they were still few and far between. "No, what I liked about Germany was that I didn't share you with anyone. Now that we're home, everybody's going to want a piece of you."

She leaned in close and pressed her lips to his ear. "True, but some of my pieces are only yours, and maybe tonight after they leave we can explore *those* pieces a little bit deeper?"

Dave leaned over to the driver, fully intent on paying the man double if he'd drive faster.

~

Philly seemed to have leapt forward in a time machine while she'd stayed behind. Although it all looked the same, there was something different, almost foreign about this world. When the taxi stopped in front of the brick high-rise, Ally's stomach flipped.

Dressed in jeans, David's striped, button-down shirt was untucked and sleeves rolled above his elbows. He opened the door, tugging her out before she had a chance to tell the cabbie to keep driving. Once on the sidewalk, Ally leaned back and counted up eight floors to the window she once considered her own. The glare of the sun reflected off the glass. It was hard to see in, but she was sure there were heads peering down at her from up there.

My family.

Her heart thudded inside her chest and stomach fluttered.

Can I do this?

For some reason, the idea of being back in the compound, locked away, sounded a lot more appealing than going upstairs. At least, that world she understood. This one was full of unknowns. People she considered family but hadn't seen in years. They'd ask questions she didn't have answers to, and have hopes she'd probably never be able to fulfill. The thought of it all overwhelmed her.

Ally turned around to do...she didn't know what and ran into a wall of strength.

David's arm moved around her waist, steadying her. "Ready?"

She considered her answer. The crazy thing was if she said no, he'd get them back in that car faster than she could blink. Ally noticed the way he smiled and looked at her as if she was the most valuable thing in the world, and it stilled the nervous fluttering.

Ally rose up on her toes and kissed his cheek. "I am."

His fingers twined with hers and together, they entered the building she once called home. The elevator took a painfully long time to reach the eighth floor.

"Inhale," David ordered. She nodded, filling her lungs with air while crushing his fingers.

When the doors slid open, a man with short black hair and glasses leaned against the wall across from the elevator, staring at her. Ally's mouth went dry, while her heart raced.

Nik Bhai.

David gave her hand a reassuring pump, reminding her she wasn't alone. Ally rounded her shoulders, exited into the hall, and finally returned her brother's gaze.

Dressed in gray slacks and a blue shirt, he looked good. Perfect. Her face heated. She wanted to go to him. To put her head on his shoulder the way she used to when she was younger, but instead Ally remained rooted to the floor as tears spilled down her cheeks.

"Hey." Her brother's voice came out choked and his eyes turned glossy.

The rush of emotions tightened her throat, leaving her speechless.

Nik Bhai pointed to his chin. "You know how you used to bug me about the scar?"

She scanned his face, honing in on the small mark below his lower lip. Decades ago, it had been a gaping bloody mess that required stitches. Mommy and Pappa yelled and threatened for him to tell them what happened. Ally had bugged him about it for years, but he never told any of them how he got the gash.

"I got it fighting Chad Lassiter and his big brother."

Ally's eyes welled as soon as he whispered the explanation. The blond-haired giant of a boy whose favorite pastime had been to torment her when they were in the fifth grade together. Scared they'd make the situation worse, she kept his taunts and ugliness a secret from her family. One day, it magically stopped—around the same time Bhai came home bruised and bloodied.

Letting go of David's hand, she stepped closer. "You did that for me?"

He nodded.

Ally took another step. "But how? I never told anyone."

"Reya saw him push you."

Her lip quivered as the tears continued to flow. "Why?"

He shrugged, his face wet with emotion of his own. "It was my job to treat you like shit, not his."

Before he could finish his explanation, she was in his arms.

Ally kissed the scar on her brother's chin. "I missed you, Bhai."

"Did you miss me too?" The feminine voice from behind made her smile and cry even harder.

Reya.

Wet-faced and snotty-nosed, her little sister had her arms wrapped around David. Reya's black hair was cut in a bob, and she looked stunning in her blue summer dress.

Not ready to let go of Nik Bhai, Ally grabbed his hand and walked to her sister.

Reya pointed at Nik. "His story was better than mine and with the *GQ* model pose he was flaunting, I figured I didn't stand a chance. So I'm here." Her voice rose several octaves before finally cracking. "Not so patiently waiting for my turn."

In seconds, the three of them were wrapped in each other, their love all-consuming and healing. For the first time, she truly believed she'd be okay. No matter what demons she would have to fight, she'd never have to fight them alone.

Her brother jutted his chin toward her door. "Mom, Dad, Sonya, and the kids are inside waiting for you."

Ally glanced at David, Reya, and Nik Bhai and smiled. There was no more fear or hesitation.

EPILOGUE

Eddie sat in a parked car across the street, watching Ally and Dave exit their taxi.

What the fuck am I doing here?

The same stupid question he'd asked himself since he followed them from the airport. He kept telling himself he was doing it for Farah, omitting the whole issue of how he couldn't think straight whenever he was around Ally.

The woman in question leaned back and stared up at the apartment building. He grinned at the way she clenched and unclenched her fists—obviously scared. But fear wouldn't stop her from going inside. It wasn't how she was built.

That's not how she's built? Eddie narrowed his brows. *How the hell would I know how she's built?* He shook his head and mumbled, "I'm losing my fucking mind."

His thoughts drifted to the day before when he was packing for his trip back to the States. Farah sat on his bed watching Eddie in silence as he shot out directions on what to do and who to call if she needed him.

"Bhai?"

He paused at the sadness in her voice. "Yeah?"

"Keep her safe."

Eddie rolled his eyes, closed his carryon, and zipped the bag shut. "I've told you already, she's dead."

She stared at the wall as if lost in thought. "I saw them slide her into the helicopter, still alive."

When he began to repeat the same story he'd told her a hundred times, her small hand wrapped around his wrist, silencing him.

Her eyes glistened with emotion. "If I am right and she is alive, you will keep her safe, if for no other reason than because you love me."

Eddie's cell rang, pulling him out of memories of his sister's conversation and returning him to the present. He looked across the street at David and Ally before pressing the button on the Bluetooth. "Yeah?"

"Wassim. Does the name ring a bell?" Chris's deep, familiar voice filled the silent car.

Eddie nodded. "The guard I told you about. He's the one who took Sayeed's wife out of Pakistan before everything went down."

"Well, he ain't the guard anymore. He's her husband now."

The statement made him stare down at the phone in his console. "What did you say?"

"Sayeed's wife was pregnant when he died, right? Well, Wassim has sworn to raise the baby as his own and carry on where Sayeed left off."

Eddie smiled. Wassim was going to carry the secret of his affair with the boss's wife to his grave. "That could be very helpful. Does anyone suspect Sayeed's not the baby's daddy?"

"Not as far as we can tell."

He glanced back at the couple across the street. "Does he believe everyone's dead?"

"Not sure, we haven't gotten close enough to him to find out. Where the hell are you, by the way? You owe me lunch."

"Needed to make a quick stop. On my way." If Wassim ever found out who Sara really was and that she was still alive, he'd kill her. "Any luck finding her kidnapper from two years ago?"

"Not yet. We have leads but nothing solid."

Ally embraced her husband. Her eyes closed, she rested her chin on his shoulder and flashed one of her rare but beautiful smiles.

Eddie's chest tightened."We need to track him down. He's the only one who can lead them back to Philly and to her."

"Intel indicates he might be in Florida..." Chris's voice became background noise as Eddie watched her. He didn't know how or why, but she'd gotten under his skin.

Dave picked up a suitcase and grabbed her hand before they entered the building.

Long after she'd disappeared, her smile stayed etched in his brain.

"You there?"

Eddie shook off the vision. "Yeah, I'm on my way. We'll talk more when I see you." He hung up on Chris and merged into oncoming traffic.

Farah was right, he'd keep her Didi safe.

~

Keep reading to find an excerpt from The Widows Keeper

(Book 2 of The Second Wife)

THE WIDOW'S KEEPER

BOOK 2 OF THE SECOND WIFE SERIES

PROLOGUE

TWO YEARS AND TEN MONTHS POST-SAYEED

Razaa ran a hand through his thick, black hair and knocked on the hotel room door. He scanned the hall of the five-star building as questions flooded his brain. What if he had the wrong address? Or for that matter, what if he had the right one and the man turned him away? He answered each question the same: Those were risks he had no choice but to take.

Over two and a half years ago, the life he considered blessed vanished. His father was murdered, and he and his fourteen brothers were ripped apart, scattered across the globe. Forced to live with strangers and take on new identities, he had no contact with the rest. But if their situation had turned out even half as bad as his, he could only imagine the brutality they endured. Marks of his one year with his foster family were forever imprinted not only on his body but seared into his mind.

A few yards down, a door slammed shut, making the nervous young man jump. He sucked in a breath and knocked a second time. If he could survive the past two and a half years, he could survive the next few minutes. Somehow, he managed to escape his hell only to enter another. He traveled the world as a migrant worker searching for the familiar faces of his family. Food and money were scarce and the beatings plentiful. The memories of pain flooded him, making his eyes prickle and burn with emotion. He blinked to cool the heat and kept his gaze fixed on the hardwood surface in front of him.

When the deadbolt slid, his heart tried to leap out of his throat. Razaa swallowed it down and rolled his shoulders back. Very soon, he'd come face to face with his only hope.

A man well over six feet tall opened the door, naked, except for a towel wrapped around his waist. His deep black curls hung to his light brown shoulder. Drops from the damp hair spilled onto his muscular, bare chest.

"Can I help you?" His words were spoken with an English accent.

Razaa's hopes fell, as did his face. "I am sorry, I must be at the wrong place," he stammered and walked away.

"*Aap kaon hain*?" The question made him stop in his tracks. He asked the same question as before, but this time in Urdu. The sound of it sent a jolt of calm through Razaa's anxious soul. It felt like home. He turned to face the stranger. "I have lost my family, and I need your help finding them."

The man leaned against the doorjamb, his arms crossed. A smile tugged at his mouth. "And why would I help you?"

He fisted his hands to hide the way they shook and said the words he'd practiced. "Because I am Razaa Irfani. Your brother was my father."

The man's smile dropped but he didn't move.

The young boy crossed his arms, matching his uncle's stance, trying hard to be the man his father raised. Inside however, fear squeezed his throat, making it difficult to breathe much less speak. He didn't know if he was doing the right thing by showing up at the man's hotel room, but he was desperate. This wasn't just about saving himself, it was about saving his family.

As if reading his mind, the man nodded and pushed away from the wall. "Come in, Razaa Irfani."

He gulped down his excitement and followed. Razaa learned long ago to never get his hopes up. Like the sun, they were fleeting.

The hotel room was enormous. A sofa bigger than the cots he'd slept on most of his life sat in the middle of the space, along with two matching armchairs. At the far corner was an open door. Razaa caught a glimpse of a woman asleep on the bed inside.

"Excuse me for a moment while I change," the man said before entering the dark backroom and shutting the door behind him, leaving Razaa alone.

He stayed glued to the floor until his uncle returned a few minutes later. Thankfully, he now wore pants and a shirt. The man sat on the chair and rested his bare feet on the coffee table in front of him. "We both know my brother did not have a son your age, and I don't have a lot of time for this nonsense. So tell me quickly what you want and be off."

"I may not be his blood, but he will always be my father." Razaa stuffed his fists in his pant pockets and cleared his throat. "Sayeed *Babba* adopted me and fourteen other boys from an orphanage in Islamabad a few years before he died. He loved us as his own." The man rested his elbows on his chair and pressed his chin on the tips of his fingers. "I am aware of the boys my brother adopted. I am also aware they died two and a half years ago with him."

"Nay, *Chacha*. We did not die." Razaa noticed the way the man's brows lifted as soon as he called him uncle. He ignored it and continued, "We were separated, given new names, and sent to live with different strangers." His face warmed with emotion. "I have searched for the others, but I don't know where they are. If their lives are as hard as mine, I must find them."

"And what makes you think I'd believe you, much less help you?"

Emotion filled Razaa's eyes. "When my brothers and I would fight, Babba would tell us about you two and your lives together in Karachi. He told us you never fought with him but that you admired him. He wanted us to be like you and him." The young boy's throat tightened. He cleared it and forced out the words. "And we were. We may have been adopted, but we were as close as brothers could be. Chacha, I need your help finding my family."

"Don't call me that," the man snapped.

The tone startled Razaa, but he tried not to show it.

"Call me Shariff." He waved at the sofa. "And sit down."

He slid on to the edge of the couch, keeping his focus on the man.

"So tell me, Razaa, if you and all your brothers are alive, what happened to your Sayeed Babba? Did the As-Sirat not kill him?"

Heat prickled at the back of his neck. Memories of that day, and of his father's bullet ridden body, tortured him. "He is dead but not by the As-Sirat."

Shariff sat motionless for a long while, making Razaa wonder if he should repeat what he said.

"If the As-Sirat did not kill him, then who?"

Razaa cleared his throat. "His wife."

Shariff laughed. "My brother was killed by his wife?"

The disbelieving smirk on his face made the young man shift

in his seat. "Yes, Cha...Shariff."

"What was her name?"

Muscles in his body tightened at the prospect of uttering the name of the woman he'd tried to block from his mind since the murder. "Sara."

Shariff's brows. "Sayeed Irfani was murdered by his second wife?"

Buy now: The Widow's Keeper: Book 2 of The Second Wife Series

Information About Human Trafficking and How You Can Help:

The sad and unfortunate truth is that slavery is alive and well in our world. According to the Polaris Project, an estimated 20.9* million humans are trafficked globally. It is believed that 5.5 million of them are children and 55% are female*.In the United States alone, it is believed that an estimated 100,000 children are involved in the sex trade. There is no country untouched by this evil. *

* (http://www.polarisproject.org/human-trafficking/overview)

If you would like more information on human trafficking and how you can help, check out the following websites.

The Polaris Project: www.polarisproject.org

Human Trafficking. Org: http://www.humantrafficking.org/

Freedom Fund: http://freedomfund.org/

IJM: International Justice Mission: http://bit.ly/1EWbo7K

ARE YOU PART OF KISH'S COLLECTIVE YET?

To stay in touch with Kishan Paul, be in the know about upcoming releases, have exclusive access to ARC's, giveaways, and sneak peaks on the stories she is working on, be a part of a fun interactive group of book lovers.

https://www.facebook.com/groups/KishsCollective/

KEEP IN TOUCH!

If you have not already, subscribe to Kish's Connection. Sign up to be a part of Kishan Paul's exclusive mailing list. You will be in the know about exclusive chapters, release dates, and giveaways.

https://app.mailerlite.com/webforms/landing/q0d2q0

ALSO BY KISHAN PAUL

The Second Wife Series
***The Second Wife*: Book 1**
***The Widows Keeper*: Book 2**

Blind Love

Taking the Plunge
Stolen Hearts

ABOUT THE AUTHOR

From daring escapes by tough women to chivalrous men swooping in to save the day, the creativity switch to Kishan Paul's brain is always in the 'on' position. If daydreaming stories were a college course, Kish would graduate with honors.

Mother of two beautiful children, she has been married to her best friend for over 20 years. With the help of supportive family and friends, she balances her family, a thriving counseling practice, and writing without sinking into insanity.

TO KEEP IN TOUCH WITH KISH:

http://kishanpaul.net
https://www.facebook.com/KishanPaulAuthor
https://twitter.com/@kishan_paul
https://www.facebook.com/groups/KishsCollective/
http://www.pinterest.com/kishanpaul